Brian O'Connor
Threaten to Win

POOLBEG

Published 2012
by Poolbeg Press Ltd.
123 Grange Hill, Baldoyle,
Dublin 13, Ireland
Email: poolbeg@poolbeg.com

A catalogue record for this book is available from the British Library.

ISBN 978-1-84223-497-6

Typeset by Patricia Hope in Sabon 11/14.5

Printed and bound by CPI Group (UK) Ltd, Croydon, CR0 4YY

www.poolbeg.com

About the author

Brian O'Connor is the award-winning racing correspondent of the *Irish Times*. He is author of the novel *Bloodline* as well as a number of non-fiction books. He lives in Wicklow.

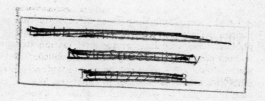

Acknowledgements

Thanks to everyone at Poolbeg, especially Gaye Shortland and Paula Campbell. Thanks also to "Virgil" for coming up trumps again. There are many close to home that sparked too. Thank you all.

To Niamh and the Heartbreakers –
Peter, Johnny and Jessica.

1

After a couple of hours he emerged. The stocky figure briefly stood outside his red-brick house on the expensive South Dublin road and inhaled deeply. Despite it being close to summer he was heavily wrapped up in a coat and scarf. Long grey hair swept untidily out from underneath a tweed cap. One more appreciative breath and he skipped down the steps and walked towards where I was sitting in my car.

There were barely fifty metres between us but it felt like an age as he approached. I got out and stood on the footpath. I still wasn't sure what I was going to do, or what I wanted to do. It was a new experience. How are you supposed to behave with someone who has torn your life apart?

His stride shortened when he saw me but he didn't stop. Pulling iPlayer leads out of his ears, he pulled the strap of his laptop case higher over his shoulder and thrust his hands into his coat pockets. But that deeply tanned face that had plagued my sleep looked anxious. I stood there, still trying to decide what to do.

Logically, I found it hard to be outraged. It was a male thing after all, making the most of an opportunity. What man hadn't at some stage been at least tempted? Logic, though, doesn't apply when that opportunity is your wife.

Other gender generalisations had been swirling in my head too, like how sex is always the woman's choice. No doubt there were any number of exceptions to that rule but Cammie was not the sort to be cajoled or intimidated into anything she didn't want to do.

There had certainly been nothing indecisive about the way she had run to Thorpe outside the city-centre hotel just a week earlier. The pair of them had kissed intensely in full view before going inside. I'd stayed in the car then.

They actually made sense as a couple: both musicians, both artistic, both much more in thrall to the cerebral than a broken-up ex-steeplechase jockey. Camilla's passion for music was rivalled only by her passion for our child: Max, a tiny two-year-old bundle of energy that had transformed everything. But there wasn't a time Cammie could remember when her musical love didn't exist and even motherhood couldn't shake it.

The biggest regret of her life was not being able to play it well enough. I looked in awe at her hands sweeping over the piano keys, but she dismissed her playing as merely competent. There was regret in her voice when she said that, but not pain. Years of practice had got her so far, but no further. She likened it to being able to ride a horse but not being good enough to compete. Since I'd spent much of my adult life competing, she'd often said she envied me the proficiency I'd developed.

It was that open-hearted enthusiasm that had first attracted me to the terribly well-bred daughter of an old and still tolerably rich Anglo-Irish family. That, and a smile saved from perfection by a little gap between her front teeth, which could drive me insane with desire when combined with a look from dark eyes that never attempted to hide their owner's open and hearty attitude to love. The fact Cammie also possessed tawny skin, long almost jet-black hair and a leanly magnificent body only deepened my despair at the idea of this man enjoying it.

Thorpe had slowed almost to a standstill. He was forty-nine, a decade older than me, Australian, and a piano virtuoso married to an Irishwoman. An internet search had revealed the details. The idea of contacting his wife and telling her how our respective partners had been having an affair had briefly flashed across my mind and then disappeared. It wouldn't achieve anything and nothing would change. Better to spare the woman that.

He was shorter than my six feet but heavier. A never-ending battle with weight when I was riding hadn't resulted in any ballooning when I stopped: still tall, still thin. But with ten years on my side and still reasonable fitness, there was little doubt in my mind I would be able to hurt this man.

It had been an afterthought to come here. The spirit-sapping domestic dramatics had consumed the last week. What did it matter who Cammie had gone off with? She'd gone, that was all that mattered. She'd risked everything we had to furtively meet this older guy who probably couldn't believe his luck to be pursued by her. She really was too old for hero-worship, too classy and stylish to be some groupie. And yet she'd still gone with him.

I wanted very much to hate this guy, and hurt him, indulge in a violent physical release that would make this abstract pain disappear, however briefly. Who cared how stupidly macho it might seem? Some things needed to be done. Parse it down any which way and he was still fucking my wife.

There was a tic under Thorpe's eye. It flickered again and he touched it with a finger to make it stop. I could see him glancing sideways, maybe wondering if there was anybody to shout to for help. But if he was worried it didn't stop him walking straight towards me.

He was close enough for me to smell his aftershave, just a couple of metres away and aiming to walk straight past me. Our eyes were locked on each other. I balled my fists and willed myself to hit him, to smash that stubbled, ruddy face into a pulp, to make him and her suffer.

But I didn't. He walked past, and I did nothing. Just let him by. My arms felt like they belonged to someone else. I could hear Thorpe striding away quickly. Then I heard him shout "Taxi!"

He smiled at me as the car pulled away.

2

The sound of a bomb exploding in Iraq woke me up. Halfway between sleep and wakefulness came that split second where everything was unfamiliar and wrong and disconnected. But then the television news voiceover reminded me that explosions happened far away, thousands of miles from a bland hotel room on the outskirts of Dublin.

I stiffly got up and went to the bathroom. The blemishes of more than fifteen years riding racehorses were pock-marked all over me. Lumpy collarbones, fading stitchmarks and scars from a couple of inserted bits of metal testified to a physical toll that never came close to diluting the thrill that race-riding had provided. I'd never been a real top-notcher, but had still won nearly five hundred races, made a decent living, and competed at something I loved. For many years that was enough to make anything else seem just a diversion. How straightforward it seemed now.

It was five years since I'd chucked in race-riding: five years of being a normal citizen, eating three squares a day, getting married, weaning myself away from the self-absorbed pursuit of beating everyone else. I no longer felt the dull ache of missing competition and speed. I was too old now anyway, too comfortable, though maddeningly the sudden freedom to eat anything I wanted hadn't made me put weight on my bones in the way my hungry, dehydrated dreams had fantasised about for all those years. One of those quirks of fate, I guess.

Drying off in front of the TV, my mobile phone beeped into life with a text message. The screen filled with a tiny, smiling face, all blond curls and massive blue eyes. Max, my son – our son. Just the sight of that little face renewed all those familiar emotions of despair, love, guilt. It had been three days since I'd seen him, buried my face in that lovely blond thatch and felt the best part of me remaining with him. Thinking too much about Max, and what was happening with his mother, produced an intolerable ache. Best, then, to try not to focus on it, especially not on a day like today. I could ring later when it was all done.

I briefly answered the text-message enquiry, then finished togging out in one of the good suits, managed to knot a tie that didn't look like a piece of twine and swiped an apple from the breakfast buffet on the way out. Traffic was light on the M50 and I made the airport in good time. It was only eight thirty but the phone rang as I entered the terminal building. An English journalist's name appeared on the screen. The past week had been one media enquiry after another, but this was early enough in the day to knot my gut. Why would anyone need me this early?

"David, how can I help you?"

"Relax, Lorcan. There's nothing wrong with Kentish Town – at least not that I know of. It's about that French filly who won the Group 3 last week. Are you going to send her over here for York next week?"

Talking to reporters was part of a job that my former colleagues in the jockeys' room reckoned might just be the best in racing. It was certainly good enough not to have me arguing with the consensus that I was the jammiest git on the planet. It might have meant having to get into quotable-quote mode at strange times of the day, but being Jacob Weinberger's racing manager really was a gig to savour.

The old man's blue and yellow colours were famous throughout the racing world, the most visible expression of a multi-million-dollar bloodstock empire that over the years had produced one top-class horse after another. What we were about to find out in Newmarket later in the day was if a tall bay colt by the name of Kentish Town could turn out to be damn near the best of the lot.

"Yes, we're considering Margural for York, but no final decision is made. Marc-Pierre has to work her first and see how she comes out of that."

"Okay, thanks, Lorcan. Sorry for bugging you again. Good luck today."

"Thanks, Dave. That's no sweat."

The demands of twenty-four hour news, even in something as comparatively frivolous as racing, meant the pressure was always on for a line about some horse or other. Since Jake usually owned a bunch of newsworthy animals at any one time, and since a billionaire industrialist in upstate New York couldn't be expected to answer every query about them, it fell to his manager to inform the great betting public.

My primary role though was keeping Jake informed. That meant being in constant contact with his trainers –

two in Britain and one each in Ireland and France – and presenting a picture of what was happening on this side of the pond in lengthy phone or video-phone conversations every couple of nights.

There were other functions too, like being in charge of an administrative set-up at Annagrove Stud twenty miles south of Dublin, spotting future talent for racing or breeding, and generally being the eyes and ears for someone whose passion for horses competed with the duties of being one of the wealthiest business people in America. In effect, it meant playing at racing's top table with someone else's money. I was indeed a jammy git.

As I walked towards the departure gate for the flight to Stansted, there were a few more calls – one from Marc-Pierre Dutroit at his stables near Paris.

"Good luck today, my Irish friend. I hope he wins by a hundred metres. And from what I hear of his last gallop on the Curragh, he might just do that," he chuckled.

It was almost possible to hear Marc-Pierre's bushy eyebrows rising as he laughed. The Frenchman was the youngest of Jake's trainers, just a couple of years older than myself, and as urbane and charming a Frenchman as only Chantilly could produce. That smoothness didn't extend to a dress sense that changed from jeans and boots only when racecourse duty made it strictly necessary. But that just added to a cocktail of diligence, ease and devotion to the job that made him very easy to like.

"Jake is coming to watch, isn't he?" he asked.

"Yeah. He'll stay with Bartie, look over the horses tomorrow morning and be over with you in the evening."

"Excellent. I'm sure Sir Jocelyn is thrilled about the overnight arrangements." Marc-Pierre chuckled again.

Jake's two trainers in Britain, Bartholomew Montgomery and Sir Jocelyn De Beaufort, were long established at the top of their profession, both with outstanding records at moulding embryonic talent into winners and famously detesting the very sight of each other. Jake kept twenty horses with each of them and the other's twenty held almost as much fascination as their own. Every movement by a Weinberger horse was analysed intently, no opportunity was lost to curry favour with Jake, nor was there a chance missed to denigrate the other. It seemed to me Jake knew this all too well and used their competition to his advantage.

"Margural is looking very good – I think she will be ready for York," Marc-Pierre added.

"Great. I'm not going with Jake tomorrow so be nice and don't go mad on the wine trying to get him to send you more yearlings."

"As if I would," he sighed. "By the way, did Kentish Town work very well?"

"It was almost too good to be true."

"Fingers crossed, eh?"

"Here's hoping."

A lot of people were hoping Kentish Town would do in the 2,000 Guineas what he had promised for almost all his career to date. But probably no one more than the man waving to me at the coffee stand, who was quietly and unobtrusively dissolving with anxiety.

Public displays of emotion weren't Gerald Gunning's thing at all. But I'd found out that the deliberately neutral front he presented to the rest of the world hid any amount of stress and tension about how the most powerful string of racehorses on the Curragh performed. It didn't matter if it was a bad handicap in Ballinrobe or the Derby, Gerald Gunning liked to win.

It was that desire, coated as it was in a veneer of wry detachment, that had helped make him Ireland's top trainer for the last decade and which made him an automatic pick for a billionaire American owner with thirty bluebloods on his hands. Together they had a success rate that made their horses feared wherever they went. But ever since a barely two-year-old colt had taken his first tentative steps on a wind-blasted Curragh the previous spring, even Gerry Gunning couldn't disguise his enthusiasm.

"Lorcan, this is the finest prospect I've ever had, and by some way," he'd said one morning on the Curragh before Kentish Town had even run. "You can tell Jake this is the one he's been waiting for. And well done."

The 'well done' was because I'd bought the colt at the Newmarket yearling sales the year before. He hadn't even been expensive, at least not by the standards that Weinberger prospects usually sold for. There were only a limited number of candidates at the top end of the equine gene pool and an even more limited number of people able to afford them. Buying them was comparatively straight-forward: just identify their physical and genetic perfection and spend Jake's millions.

But impetuosity took over at that sale and a gawky colt with a slightly parrot mouth and parentage that was more yeoman than gentry kept catching my eye as he skittered around the parade ring. There was an ease to his movement that had little to do with the comparative plainness of his pedigree page, along with a kind eye that took everything in without appearing fazed by it.

That was all there was to go on. None of the yearlings

had even had a saddle on its back. Even the best-bred and most expensive often turned out not able to run worth a damn. But there was something about this fella that made me take the plunge.

He ended up costing a hundred thousand – peanuts for a top-class prospect – and both Bartie and the knight immediately turned their noses up at the idea of taking such a comparatively nondescript animal. But Gerry liked the look of him too, agreed to take him, and didn't forget who'd picked him when the gamble turned spectacular. It was hard, then, not to warm to the man.

"Regular or large coffee, Lorcan?" he asked.

"Make it large, Gerry, and black."

"Bloody uncivilised drinking tar like that," he muttered, shaking a packet of sugar into his own frothy confection, and nodding towards a pair of empty seats near the departure gates. Gerry confessed to despairing sometimes about my uneducated palate. As someone who quietly appreciated quality, almost as much in food as in horses, he regarded my tastes as woefully proletarian.

"I'm just getting the coffee in its purest form," I replied, indulging him. "All you're doing is hiding the fundamental under layers of different tastes. If you want coffee, drink coffee."

"Jesus, it's like trying to talk Shakespeare to a monkey."

We settled down to wait for the flight. Gerry was one of those people for whom silence wasn't an embarrassment. I was the same. More than once it had been remarked that our silences were monastic enough to make us appear uneasy with each other. In fact, the opposite was the case. Even after just a few years working with each other, our relationship had developed a sort of shorthand. If I thought about it, there was quite a lot that Gerry didn't need to say any more. As a man who relished precision, my guess was that he appreciated that. But who knew? Even the idea of a conversation about such a thing would have embarrassed both of us.

"Thanks for having us over to dinner the other night," Gerry said. "Russian food! Honestly, Cammie never fails to surprise me. Sturgeon kebab, I couldn't believe it. Absolutely gorgeous – and she has to tell Lynn what she pickled those mushrooms with."

"I'll pass it on."

"I always thought Russian food was inedible grey lumps. Cammie is an incredible girl. You landed better there than you ever did when you were riding."

He was rambling like I'd never heard before, almost giddy: a sure sign of nerves. With his legs crossed, it was impossible not to notice how his foot appeared to be conducting the airline personnel, urging them to move faster. When the call came, he sprang out of his seat.

"Anything you'd have done different, Gerry? Any little glitch you're worried about?"

"Not really, no. Why?"

"Then we'll see what happens. For what it's worth, I think you've done a fabulous job."

"I guess that's why you were such a good jockey. Cool as a cucumber. Nothing much fazes you, does it?"

If only he knew.

3

The centre of everyone's attention plodded around Newmarket's parade ring, happily oblivious to any anxiety. Kentish Town had matured from that gawky yearling into a gleamingly powerful three-year-old. Unbeaten in four starts the previous autumn, Kentish Town's first public appearance since then had added an extra layer of anticipation to the first classic of the season in the 2,000 Guineas.

Crowds pressed around to get a closer look at him. It was impossible not to be impressed. The colt radiated health. His coat shone in the early May sunshine, muscles rippling underneath with months of carefully cultivated power timed to explode for just a minute and a half up Newmarket's famous straight Rowley Mile. Horses had been attempting to win the Guineas for over two hundred years. Some of them were legends of the sport. I reckoned none of them had looked better.

"Your horse doesn't look too shabby, Jake," I said.

"Enough of that European understatement. He's magnificent."

My boss's eyes never left Kentish Town as he continued to be led around by two of Gerry's best men. One was the colt's lad. The other was the travelling head man whose physical bulk might have made a riding career unfeasible but came in handy as an extra layer of security for perhaps the most valuable racehorse in the world. Not that anyone was likely to fly-leap into the parade ring and try to nobble the favourite there and then. However, it never hurt to try and cater for every eventuality. Prepare for everything and then pray was Jacob Weinberger's philosophy.

He finished his inspection and smiled at Gerry and me. That familiar tanned face with its deep wrinkles and perfect teeth could exude remarkable warmth. I'd never seen him angry, and apparently not many ever had. Instead, Jake's ability to make people feel worse with a simple resigned look of disappointment was famously much more effective than any bollocking. The man had the priceless gift of making other people want to please him. I'd felt it myself right from the start.

Original contact had come through a trainer I used to ride for. She rang and asked if I knew Jacob Weinberger. Even ex-jump jockeys who'd suffered more than a few bangs to the head knew one of the world's top flat owners. Then she said he wanted to talk to me. At the time I was just starting a degree course in History as a mature student at university in Dublin, just married and finding no problem in filling my time away from racing. But still there was no denying that if Weinberger wanted to talk it wouldn't do any harm to listen. Even if I'd no idea what he wanted.

Within a couple of days I'd landed in JFK to be picked up by an extremely officious woman who accompanied me in a limo to a massive property in upstate New York. Over the years I'd ridden for some wealthy owners and got a sense of the privilege that their money brought them. But this was on another level again.

An internet search before flying had revealed generations of financial success that saw the latest patriarch in the Weinberger family born into remarkable privilege. American East Coast royalty, it said. Estimates that ran into umpteen billions made the Weinberger conglomerate apparently worth more than many small countries dotted around the globe. Far from his being described as the pampered curator of a massive inheritance, newspaper profiles talked about an unusually shrewd business mind that managed to co-exist quite happily with a taste for art, family and bacon cheese-burgers. I wasn't sure what to expect, but least of all the ease with which all this money and prestige was carried.

Jake met me at the door of his mansion and it needed a second to connect the face so well known from television with the blocky guy walking towards me, hand outstretched.

"Welcome to this part of the world, young man," he said. "Tell you what, seeing as it's such a nice day, why don't we clear the pipes before dinner with a little walk. How was the flight?"

We walked down a well-worn path into a wood of sycamore and elm, him firing casual questions that after no time at all appeared to have provoked me into revealing more of myself than I'd realised. Family, schooling, my racing career, likes and dislikes, whatever vague ideas I might have had politically, what I wanted to do with the rest of my life, what I valued. In the forty minutes it took to get back to the house, it felt like being turned inside out, examined intently and then folded back.

"Mind if I ask you something, Jake?"

We were in his study, sipping glasses of whiskey that must have been at least a couple of decades old. The walls around us were covered in works of art that even a philistine like me could recognise as masterpieces. An enormous piece of glass dominated a fourth side to the room and allowed a spectacular view over a deep gorge into which spilled a waterfall that began a few metres above our heads. We stood side by side at the window, gazing at the water as it fell.

"What do I want?" he said in reply to my question.

"Not wanting to be blunt, but yeah."

"Don't worry. I like to get to the point. George Fitzroy is my racing manager in Europe. You know him?"

"Of him. I was a National Hunt jockey, not flat."

"Don't worry, I know that. But do you know what George's job entails?"

"Vaguely, I guess. He's your link to everyone else. He buys and sells your horses, subject to your approval. He has some input with the trainers about running plans and there's the media stuff as well. Basically he has to be a Jack-of-all-trades. But most of all he has to have your confidence."

"How much of a Jack are you?"

"Not much."

"Why?"

"I don't have a huge knowledge of pedigrees for one thing."

"Trainers don't train pedigrees. They train horses. You know horses, right?"

"Yes, but . . . ."

"But what?"

"I'm not indulging in false modesty but I've been out of the game for a while and flat racing is different from what I know."

"I realise that."

"So why are you asking me all this?"

He pressed a button and suddenly the noise of water rushing past and crashing to earth beneath was all around us. He flicked the button again and it was as if a mute button had been pressed on the world.

"I'm a very fortunate man, Lorcan. I've been blessed, especially with my family. Three kids and a wife that I love dearly. You'll meet Judith later by the way. All the money in the world can't compare with such a blessing. And I know it's a sin for someone in my position to be envious, but I envy you. You've been able to spend your life with horses, feeling all that power and grace underneath you, probably taking it for granted, right?

"Well, not me. I look at a thoroughbred and I see what I see in that water there, something beautiful. I swear I go to the track and see my horses gallop past and my heart just soars. Even the slow ones do that for me. Of course, I realise there's nothing much natural about a thoroughbred. There's three hundred years of human influence there for starters. But all that history still comes down to one horse running faster than another. I love that. Always have."

He turned back to an enormous desk and sat on the edge of it, motioning me to sit in a chair opposite him.

"George is not well. Cancer. Hasn't got long. It's a bastard. He's only sixty-one, just a couple of years younger than me. George is a decent man and showing a lot more class in the circumstances than I could manage. He's been in charge of things in Europe for me for almost twenty years so he wants to make sure the set-up is in good hands. He mentioned you."

I was stunned. This man who I'd never met was putting me up for a job that almost anyone in racing would kill for. Being a jockey meant the randomness of life was not unfamiliar. But this was something else again.

"Well," Jake said, "do you want the job?"

It was mad that such an offer could be made so casually. The job was completely different from anything I'd ever done. Riding horses was straightforward. Just beat the other guy. This job required being in charge of people, of budgets, of the dreams that this man was willing to fork out millions for. It meant actual responsibility, where getting it wrong didn't cost only a broken bone or a lost race. Suddenly the limits of my abilities became all too obvious. I was a guy struggling to get to grips with the Cromwellian Settlement of 1640's Ireland. Content in my own company a lot of the time, the prospect of leadership was daunting. And yet . . .

Suddenly the door opened and a tiny, elfin figure with blonde hair and a smile that took up most of her face marched towards us. She took Jake's face in both her hands and kissed him on the lips.

"Is this him?" she asked.

"It sure is. Lorcan, this is my wife, Judith."

"Pleased to meet you, Mrs Weinberger."

"Call me Judith," she replied. "He looks kind of thin, Jake. Should we trust him?"

"Now, Judith . . ."

"My husband is much too genteel to mention this, Mr Donovan, but I'm not. The reason George Fitzroy is such a darling is because he has never stiffed us. It doesn't really matter about knowledge, qualifications or anything else. Jake has so much to contend with in his life and racing is his great pleasure. What he cannot afford is constantly second-guessing what those working for him might be doing. What he needs is straight-shooting. Are you a straight-shooter?"

"Now, Judith, Lorcan has only just arrived. It's a bit soon to be reaching for the third degree. What do you say to dinner, Lorcan?"

Not surprisingly for a friend of Gerry Gunning, dinner turned out to be a lot more elaborate than bacon cheeseburgers, although Jake washed everything down with cola rather than the wine that Judith frugally sipped. It was noticeable too that she slipped out of the dining area to bring in the various courses herself.

Passing by his chair, she always touched Jake, either on the shoulder or hair. Such displays always made me suspicious. Usually only those trying to prove something made a point of being all over each other. I was no expert but the Weinbergers looked the real deal. There was obvious warmth in the familiar re-telling of how they met on a ranch in Montana thirty years previously. Contrary to appearances, Judith was the one with experience of the outdoors while Jake could hardly have been a more out-of-place New Yorker if he'd shown up in a yellow cab, desperate for an anonymous western vacation.

"I'll never forget how we were branding cattle one day and the smell of burning flesh had the big, tough guy running for the bushes to heave," she laughed. "But he came back – eventually."

"I had to. She'd have been after me with the iron if I hadn't," Jake shrugged.

Judith was from Oregon and hadn't a clue about the Weinbergers or their money. That was intriguing enough for the heir to the empire to ask her out. Their first date was in a cheap diner in the middle of nowhere. A fortnight later she was heading for the East Coast.

"He doesn't say much, does he, Jake?" Mrs Weinberger said towards the end of the meal. "But he's been taking everything in alright. What are you thinking there, Cool Hand Lorcan?"

"I'm thinking you're not half as tough as you like to think. And that Jake's a lucky bloke."

"Ass-kisser!" she scoffed, although there was a smile there that robbed the words of offence.

Jake said nothing, just kept his eyes on me. Whether he meant it or not, there was a challenge in his stare. Or at least that's what I took from it. And it was enough. There's a saying in racing that when it comes to jumping fences, you throw your heart over the fence and hope the horse will follow. It was time to throw.

"Okay, if you're offering the job I'll take it. But just to the end of the year. That way I get an idea if it's doable and you don't get stuck with an incompetent. Agreed?"

"Agreed," Jake said, extending his hand again. "Welcome aboard."

"I don't know if I'm up to this but I will be straight with you about it."

"That's all I want."

And it had mostly worked out. Most women might have baulked at their new husband coming home and telling them they were moving into a new house on someone else's property because he had accepted a new job on the spot.

But Cammie had taken one look at Annagrove and described it as a piece of heaven – which it was.

Inevitably there were teething problems and mistakes made, but Jake mostly left me to make them and never interfered. Both English trainers had at various times warned him that his new manager was too inexperienced for the job. Having Montgomery and De Beaufort against you was an intimidating challenge for a rookie and keeping the peace required a diplomacy and tact I hadn't presumed of myself. But weeks turned into months without outright war being declared and by the end of the first year there was a presumption that I would continue. Since Jake said nothing to the contrary, I played along.

Much more surprising was waking up one morning to discover that the American billionaire and his pixie wife were among our best friends. And real friends, not the sort mentioned at the ritzy industry shindigs where the greater the wealth the deeper the friendship. It helped that Judith and Cammie got on like a house on fire. They shared a mischievous wit that was often best not heard even by those closest to them.

As for me, it wasn't long before those midnight phone calls to New York got longer and longer despite a decrease in actual information being relayed. It took even less time to realise the short man with the endless pockets was a pretty remarkable individual. He never seemed rushed which, considering his workload was immense, never ceased to amaze me. As if running the Weinberger empire wasn't enough, he was patron of any number of charities and foundations and took those responsibilities seriously. My own tenuous link through racing gave me some inkling of the pressure on Jake to provide, listen, almost perform, for any number of worthy causes.

Yet he carried it off with a grace it was impossible not to admire. Best of all, there was the man behind the public face. There was nothing false about that face presented to the world but it wasn't the full one. It couldn't be. Certainly some of his earthy gags wouldn't have sat well in polite society. A love for the arts competed with a devotion to baseball that he zealously but futilely tried to inculcate in his racing manager. Best of all there was an interest in others. Sometimes I noticed that could turn into a slightly overbearing desire to get things fixed. However, that was just part of a genuine desire to be involved.

When Max was born, the first person I spoke to after my parents and siblings was Jake. And it was his words that struck home most – "Your life is going to be so much more straightforward now, kid. Now you know what your function is: to rear this son of yours. Nothing else matters. You're not the most important person in the world any more."

He was right, too. While he was telling me, Judith was talking to a drained Cammie on her mobile. Whatever she said made an exhausted but ecstatic new mother cry with happiness. I was indeed a jammy git.

"What are you thinking there, Cool Hand?"

Judith slipped her hand into my arm and shivered theatrically against the strong breeze blowing across Cambridgeshire from the North Sea into Newmarket's parade ring.

"I'm hoping this horse wins for you."

"So am I. Look at Jake. He hasn't taken his eyes off that

damn horse since we got here. He hasn't looked at me like that since Montana!"

Gerry was standing with Jake, trying to avoid the eye of a TV reporter who wanted a quick word before the horses left to go to the start. A quick word was what every journalist wanted and since such words were part of my gig, and provided Gerry with an exit, I stepped into the breach. By the time I rejoined the circle, Mike Clancy was standing in the group, getting his final instructions.

That famously craggy forty-year-old face sat incongruously on top of the schoolboy body which was covered in garish blue and yellow silks. One of the most successful classic jockeys of his generation, Clancy was dwarfed physically and yet possessed the biggest personality of any of us. I'd noticed before how the short, eight-and-a-half-stone figure could dominate most rooms he walked into. It was the same out on the track. The unconscious pecking order in any field of endeavour is established by achievement and there was hardly a race worth mentioning that the little man from Belfast hadn't won. But there was also an intimidating assurance about Mike Clancy that meant many were beaten against him even before any whips started flailing.

"How's the gumshoe jockey today?" he enquired breezily. "Come here to see how proper jockeys ride?"

It was astonishing how cool he remained no matter what the circumstances. There wasn't an occasion invented that had yet phased him. Instead of wilting under pressure, he thrived. It was why he had ridden for Jake for nearly a decade and had been retained to ride the pick of the string for the last four years. It had been one of George Fitzroy's tasks, signing up the British champion jockey for a six-figure annual fee.

Our own paths had crossed in various weigh-rooms over the years, mainly when Clancy came over to Ireland, where there were more race meetings mixed between flat and jumps. There had always been a slight wariness between us. His inclination was to stand in the middle of any room and invite attention; I was more comfortable observing. Civilities were always maintained but I'd heard he felt I was stand-offish and for my part there was sometimes a hint of cruelty in Clancy's banter that overstepped the mark.

What was in no doubt was that he was one of the best jockeys in the world and was now at his peak. If forty was prehistoric for a jump jockey, for flat riders it represented an optimum time when experience and dash merged to make a complete package. Clancy's days of chasing championships were over. Cramming in two meetings a day for seven days a week, while maintaining a gruelling regime to control his weight, was no longer sustainable. However, years of riding hundreds of races a season meant both his eye and his nerve were perfectly in synch for the big days. And they didn't come any bigger than this.

"Right, we've gone through the race and opposition until we're blue in the face," Gerry said, leaning conspiratorially towards his jockey. "You know the horse and how he likes to be ridden. He's in brilliant form and you know what I think of him. Just ride him with confidence."

I guessed Clancy wasn't Gerry's cup of tea personally. He only rode Jake's horses on the big days and Gerry rarely showed an inclination towards engaging the jockey for any other horses he trained. But when it really counted, the little man from the back streets of Ardoyne was unquestionably a rider to have on your side. That was

Jake's logic. If Clancy was on his horse, he didn't have to worry about beating him.

The bell for riders to mount up rang out and Jake walked alongside his jockey, arm around his shoulders, escorting him to Kentish Town who didn't miss a beat. Gerry legged Clancy into the saddle and walked towards me, binoculars banging off his knee.

"There's no more we can do," he said. "Let's go see him win."

4

When the stalls opened, Kentish Town's head went up in the air and he reared. Clancy's balance was skewed slightly and for a split second horse and jockey threatened to go in opposite directions. Back in the stands at the other end of the straight mile, my knuckles whitened on the binoculars. Kentish Town skittered out of the gate, jinked right and looked lost before being straightened up to begin his pursuit of the nineteen other runners.

The field had been drawn in the middle of the wide track but quickly drifted left towards the stands-side rail and bunched together under the bright early summer sunshine. It made for a mad collage of colour even from a mile away. But it was the blue and yellow silks that momentarily disappeared and had me frantically scanning the outside of the tightly-grouped pack. Except Kentish Town wasn't there. Instead a flash went diagonally across my vision, the jockey urgently pushing and shoving at the colt in order to make up the lost ground. They made the rail at the same time as nearly running into the heels of the second-last runner. Clancy snatched at the reins and hauled his mount back to avoid coming down. Kentish Town dropped back a couple of lengths and the race was already a couple of furlongs old: just six more to go.

"Clancy is having a nightmare on the favourite," announced a man squeezed in next to me to nobody in particular. "Bloody horse isn't helping him at all."

The pace at the front was typically frantic. I could see the black and red colours of the second favourite in fourth or fifth place, poised to pounce. Kentish Town had ten lengths to make up on him and Clancy was working even harder to try to bridge the gap.

"Mike's got to stick to that rail now," announced my commentating neighbour. "He's lost too much ground already."

If anything the pace increased again as they passed halfway and made their way to the famous dip, which had to be negotiated before the final climb to the post. Running downhill at speed often found out those not completely at home on quick ground. Any physical kink could be ruthlessly exposed. Remarkably Kentish Town was now travelling well enough but was stuck in a pocket on the rail. The horses on his outside might have been hard-driven but were responding well enough to maintain their position. In front of him, though, the early pacesetters were dropping back right into his lap. Clancy had to snatch up again, forcing the colt into a sideways two-step that unbalanced him at a crucial stage of the downhill run.

At the front two colts started to pull away and settled down for a scrap. That final pull to the line was steeper and more severe than it could look at first sight and while optically it looked like they were quickening up, it was in fact stamina in the final couple of hundred yards that usually won out. The crowd screamed their encouragement at the pair fighting out the finish but my eyes remained glued to Kentish Town.

They were close enough now to drop the glasses. Finally our horse had room to stretch and he attacked the uphill climb with relish. Clancy sank deeper into him, toes coiled in the irons, balancing his tiny body on the withers to make himself as unobtrusive as possible. I could feel myself nodding with the memory of that final, desperate surge to the line. At the end of a mile there was no obvious huge physical effort from the jockey like there was over jumps. Instead it was all subtlety and balance and a mental cajoling to an inexperienced colt to go through the pain barrier.

Kentish Town had won all his races before this on the bridle. Never before had he felt real pressure, a whip cracking on his backside with venom. But there was nothing wrong with his courage. That elegant head stretched out in pursuit of the two horses in front of him, the genetic impulse to get to the head of the pack living true to hundreds of years of careful cultivation and nurture. His stride lengthened and the gap to the front two narrowed.

"Look at the favourite!" shouted my neighbour. "He's flying!"

He was too. In the final hundred yards he must have made up nearly four lengths which was remarkable considering how much energy he'd expended. Except the line came too soon.

"Bad luck, old boy!" the man shouted, suddenly recognising me and slapping my shoulder. "Very unlucky. Got no run. It happens. Better luck next time."

I nodded and attempted a smile – it must have looked grim. Nobody else came near me. I was grateful. Anything but a straightforward route back to the parade ring would have required an impossible level of civility right then. My mind was a blur. Defeat hurt enough anyway. But this was different. Unlucky, got no run, better luck next time: the usual gamut of excuses that didn't apply to this. As I entered the parade ring there was no getting away from the reality that Kentish Town had been stopped.

Only the pea-green innocent believed it didn't happen. Hell, I'd been approached myself over the years: 'Get this one beat and there's a few grand in readies, no questions asked.' The temptation was always there for a jockey, especially one short of money. That hadn't been a consideration in my case, which was lucky for me. Winning was the thing, and I always figured money would take care of itself on the back of that – which it had. But who knew what I'd have done in more straitened circumstances.

Did I know guys who stopped horses? Of course I did. And did I shop them? Of course I didn't. Was that unethical? Probably. Would I have done anything differently given the chance again? Probably not. Was it as endemic in racing as people liked to believe? Definitely not.

Roguery might have been as ancient a part of racing as betting, but those who objected to roguery were usually those who would have relished it most had they been in on it. However, real sinister stuff was rare. The difference between deliberately stopping a horse and giving one an easy ride was subtle but real. And it happening in a top-class race was mind-boggling.

But there was no getting away from what had happened. Clancy had made as many mistakes in one race as he normally would in a year. And they were preventable mistakes for anyone trying not to make them.

Jake and Judith walked to the No. 3 sign and shrugged their shoulders.

"Bad luck," he said, patting me on the arm.

Gerry I noticed hanging back, hands firmly in coat pockets, peering intently at Kentish Town as he pranced sweatily back to us. There were blood spatters on one of his white-haired back socks. A closer inspection revealed a cut on his ankle, probably from knocking himself while being hauled off some of the other runners. He looked sound but we wouldn't know for sure until he'd cooled off. Gerry stood to the side, staring at those powerful legs skittering around.

"Well, isn't that a bastard," he said to me. "Damn near everything went wrong and he still came third."

Gerry didn't suspect. Instead he wore the stoical face he reserved for when he was beaten, the one that said anything else but defeat would have been a pleasant surprise. The possibility that the Guineas favourite mightn't have been trying probably couldn't occur to him. It was too far off his radar. That quiet determination to win that permeated his life was what he presumed the rest of the world worked off too. Deliberately not winning as a concept was alien to Gerry Gunning.

He went towards Kentish Town, patting him on the neck, telling him he was great and letting him know he was still the King. Most horses knew when they were beaten. The good ones didn't like it. Some of them even got depressed. This one didn't deserve that. Clancy was talking to the owner.

"Sorry about that! He made a bags of the start and

we were always fighting a losing battle after that," he practically shouted. "But he's still some horse. Once we got a run he really ran on. Based on that I'd say he has every chance of getting a mile and a half in the Derby. It's still all ahead of him."

It was a word-perfect debrief for a disappointed owner: praise the horse and give encouragement for the future. Even the apology was calculated to generate hope. Next time would be different, it said. Having had to return to disappointed connections many times myself, a little part of me could admire the performance.

The jockey took a step towards me. "It was desperate," he said, peering up at me. "What can I say? Everywhere I went we ran into trouble. We'll put it right at Epsom. No question."

I looked him in the eye. It was all I could do not to punch his smug face in. Not the time or place though. Or was that just another excuse?

He took his cue to weigh in.

"Better luck next time, Gerry," Jake said. "As Mike says, we'll make up for it at Epsom. That's when it really counts."

I looked around at the faces staring over the parade-ring rail. There was no outrage there, no seething resentment at the big favourite not winning. That rail could provide a crucial illusion of distance to irate punters determined to mouth off their frustration, an insignificant piece of cast-iron which encouraged resentment from outside against those supposedly in the know inside. But there were no shouts, no knowing grins.

Maybe I'd got it wrong. Gerry was no betting-ring shrewdie but he knew racing. No set of glasses would have been held more resolutely on Kentish Town than his and he was simply deflated by defeat, not outraged by it. Jake had watched enough racing too. He was busy being upbeat and trying to lift everyone's morale. I could see Judith making a fuss of the stable staff taking the colt away to be washed down and maybe stitched up. There was nothing but disappointment. No affront.

It was the same with the reporters that surrounded Gerry and me: no sniggering innuendo, no conspiratorial smiles. As always the trainer presented an utterly rational and sane face to the world. We would have to see how Kentish Town came out of the race, he said, but if he was okay, the Derby would definitely be considered. You certainly couldn't say stamina over the extra half mile would be an issue judged on the way he'd run on in the closing stages just now. The journos scribbled these thoughts and didn't notice how the supposedly media-savvy racing manager said practically nothing.

It took a while to disentangle myself but eventually Jake and Judith went back to their box in the stands where they were entertaining guests. Gerry decided to try and get an earlier flight home. I walked quickly into one of the cavernous halls under the grandstand and found a TV showing race replays. Thousands of punters interested only in the most important race of all – the next one – were concentrating on other screens, which provided a tiny oasis of calm under mine. The Guineas was shown twice. After both viewings I was convinced even more that Clancy had stopped the horse. The thing was what to do about it.

There hadn't even been a steward's enquiry after the race. Nothing official called against the jockey at all. If I marched in and accused Clancy, it would ultimately come down to his word against mine, all played out against a backdrop of the millions of other words that would be written and spoken on the back of such a newsworthy story. Clancy could sue for slander, and he'd win. There was no proving anything in a case like this. No one could present a logical, water-tight one about a jockey stopping a horse. It all came down to opinion. Even the most blatant stop-job came down to opinion, and this was anything but blatant. But it had happened, and he would get away with it too, if I didn't do something.

The next race had started and I watched as Clancy powered up the windswept track to win a twenty-runner sprint handicap by a short head. There was nothing iffy about this, just a remorseless crescendo of momentum crashing over the line at just the right time. It seemed absurd to equate this jockey with the one who'd ridden Kentish Town.

I waited for him in the weigh-room, caught his eye as he weighed in after his victory and motioned to meet him outside. He emerged a minute later, strut intact.

"Pity about the Guineas – things just didn't go our way," he said, winding thick elastic bands over the sleeves of the silks he was putting on for the next race.

He'd just poured over a minute's worth of intense energy and focus into controlling and encouraging half a ton of keyed-up sprinter and yet there wasn't a hair out of place, nor a bead of sweat on his face. Small as he was, I knew all too well the struggle Clancy faced to keep his weight under control. There was no sweat because there was little or no fluid inside him. Most flat jockeys lived on a diet of fresh air and dehydration. Clancy was no exception.

"You're sticking to that, are you?"

"What do you mean?" he said, paying me only the slightest attention.

"What do you think I mean?"

"I haven't the foggiest idea, chief," he said, that famous Belfast accent hardening a little now at even a suggestion of confrontation.

"You know, when I was riding, one of the lads in the jockeys' room told me about you. He said Mike Clancy would prefer to make a bent fiver rather than a straight tenner any day of the week. I thought he was just messing. Top jockeys don't need to stop them, especially not in the top races. But I was wrong, wasn't I?"

"Oh yeah?"

Physically I towered over him but he didn't budge an inch. Not a flicker of doubt crossed that hard, creviced face. He finished arranging his elastic bands and only then looked me straight in the eye.

"I've no idea what you're talking about," he said finally.

Around us the mêlée of sounds, shouts and PA announcements made it impossible for anyone to eavesdrop on us. The nearest people were just a few metres away but they might as well have been at the Guineas start.

"What made you stop him? You haven't done it before. I'd have twigged it. Or maybe you have, just better than today."

He grinned at that. You had to credit him with coolness, if nothing else. Here was his employer's manager accusing him of cheating and the prospect didn't faze him even slightly. He just kept looking at me, grinning. Finally he stepped even closer, his finger jabbing my chest.

"I've no idea what you're talking about, mug," he said. "You really should watch your mouth. There's no knowing what sort of trouble it could get you into. Well, I know. But make no mistake, you don't – mug."

5

I parked in the usual spot outside the cottage but didn't get out. Everything was the same. Dark-green creepers covered much of the red-brick front. During the winter, light from inside caught those leaves closest to the window and seemed to make them translucent, distorting mass and colour and pulling focus towards the glass. It was bright now but the pull remained.

The six-foot-high hedge that enveloped our house into its own little cocoon from the rest of the farm had been trimmed that morning. So had the grass on the wide expanse of lawn. Martin Mooney, the stud's gardener, livestock boss and all-round handyman, must have been busy. He'd even weeded the two big flower-beds running parallel to each other on either side of the gravel driveway. That was something Cammie usually liked to do for herself, but Martin's unmistakable touch was all over the pristine neatness.

On the other side of the hedge, Annagrove Stud stretched all round for two hundred acres. Thirty of Jake's best-bred mares called it home. The aim was to breed from them the next Kentish Town. Jake never shirked from splashing out at sales for the right horses but this farm, and another he owned in Kentucky, were especially close to his heart. Owning a good horse was always a thrill but breeding it as well added a layer of propriety that he always mocked himself for.

"As if we own these animals," he told me once. "Who's running after who here? Their pedigrees will be remembered long after ours, never forget that!"

The main yard was half a mile from the cottage, an old-fashioned set of stone stables from the nineteenth century that might have been a logistical nightmare compared to modern barns but pulsed with the genes of over a century of breeding racehorses. At the other end of the farm was another, smaller yard where horses injured from racing, or in need of some rest and recreation, were kept. The Weinbergers had first come here twenty years previously, taken one look and told everyone to tamper with things at their peril. The focus though was always the mares' yard with another of Martin's pristine lawns in the middle. In the middle of that was the final resting place of a great stallion from the early twentieth century, another reminder of how we were all just passing through.

Ranging out from that yard in all directions were paddocks that allowed any amount of space to the matrons who in the spring and summer kept an eye on their foals as they tore around the undulating grassland of north Wicklow. At night the glow of the lights in Dublin were visible and to the west lay the sombre mountains dividing Wicklow in half. On the other side of them was the Curragh and any number of other famous tracks around the country that would be the proving ground for our tiny future racehorses. But Annagrove might as well have been in another world for all the relation it had to competition.

There was a flicker through the window, probably of the television being turned on. Six o'clock was news time in our house. Except it wasn't really our house.

Three years earlier, after pay and conditions had been sorted out, and I'd stopped waking up in the middle of the night at just the thought of what I was diving into, we'd arrived at this place belonging to this exotic American billionaire and taken a deep breath.

I'd lifted Cammie up and walked over this new threshold. She'd laughed, called me an idiot and demanded to be put down. Except with Cammie there were demands and then there were demands. The greater the volume meant the less serious she was. The shrieks of false outrage that day had to compete with a joyous laugh. It was when Cammie got quiet that you had to watch out.

Her social instincts were much more developed than mine. She was altogether a much more accomplished individual anyway, but people liked her. They responded to her, recognising a generosity of spirit that put most everyone at their ease. Trying to get to grips with Annagrove, and with the new job generally, had been a tough task that was eased considerably by my wife's ability to get on with people almost immediately. I'm not a social misfit or anything. A liking for my own company doesn't mean sweating up before social occasions. But everyone follows their natural inclinations and mine favours holding back a bit.

Sitting in the car, waiting to go inside, I wondered if it would have been better to have obeyed that inclination at Newmarket.

Clancy got to me. No question. All that arrogance on

top of the earlier deceit had my blood boiling. Outside the Newmarket weigh-room was no place to exercise that frustration so thankfully the jockey had just turned on his heels and walked. Maybe he was banking on me not informing Jake of what I suspected. The connotations of the word *informer* were deeply ingrained in Ireland. There were few things more despised. Or maybe he was all set to brazen it out. It was one man's opinion against another's after all, and he'd known Jake for a lot longer than I had.

My admiration for Jake Weinberger was immense, but I'd invited him to take a big step by telling him my suspicions. This would be the ultimate test of his trust in me and my judgement. If he didn't act upon it, then my position would be untenable. It was a lot to dump on a man who'd just seen his classic favourite beaten.

"You mean he stopped my horse from winning?" he'd yelled involuntarily, making me glad I'd taken him outside the box to the fresh air of the balcony.

It was after the last race and the racecourse was mostly deserted. Inside his guests didn't react. Still, I made sure the sliding door was closed.

"Are you sure?"

"Yes," I said. "I can't prove it. Nobody can. But he stopped him."

"Jesus Christ. I can't believe it. Why would he do that?"

"I asked him. He wouldn't say."

"So, you've spoken to him?"

"After he won the sprint. Said he didn't know what I getting myself into."

"What does that mean?"

"I don't know. He denied it, but he was . . ."

"What?"

"Smirking the whole time he was saying it. Called me a mug."

I could see Jake calculating. How much of this was personal animosity between his jockey and his manager? Could he put his faith in one man's judgement? How come Gerry hadn't mentioned anything?

"How can you be so sure, Lorcan?"

There was the question. I was sure. Even before Clancy's reaction, I'd been sure. But how to explain why?

"When I was riding, I used to ride hundreds of races a year. That was thousands of races in total before I retired. It got to the stage where the actual physical riding got to be second nature. Ninety-nine per cent of the time I could tell you what the horse would be doing, feeling or running like two or three miles later.

"What really counted was being able to guess what everyone else in the race would be doing. How they were going. So you developed an instinct. That's the best I can come up with. I know it's not precise, but that's the reality. Mike Clancy will tell you the same, except he's so much better a rider than I could have even dreamed of being. And everything he did out there today was diametrically opposite to what he should have done.

"I'll bet you anything he got Kentish Town's head in a lock just before the gates opened. That would be completely alien to the horse and he reacted as such. But even if that wasn't the case, all he had to do afterwards was re-gather, get him balanced and stick to the outside of the field. He was practically there anyway. It wouldn't have been ideal but your horse was so superior to that lot he could easily have overcome a lack of cover. Except Clancy knew that. And that's why you got the race you did."

Jake turned away, leaned against the rails and stared towards Cambridgeshire. It was then that my phone rang. Gerry's name flashed up.

"Lorcan, I've had a couple of calls, from people whose judgement I wouldn't dismiss completely, telling me there might be something dodgy about Kentish Town."

"What do you mean 'dodgy', Gerry," I said, catching Jake's eye.

"I mean that it almost seemed like Clancy was looking for trouble," he replied. "I haven't looked at the race again, have you?"

"I have."

"And?"

"I'm not sure, Gerry. Can I get back to you?"

"Okay. It's bollocks anyway. Who the hell would be at it in a Guineas?"

Jake had momentarily gone into the box to say goodbye to a guest. There was a lot of smiling and back-slapping but he returned frowning.

"That was Gerry," I said. "Apparently some of the wideboys on the Curragh have been on to him, wondering if there was something dodgy about today."

"Right. Okay, I'll have to think about this. Thanks for telling me, Lorcan. You promised you'd be straight up with me and you have been. I appreciate that, kid. It's just a pity not everyone is the same."

"Do you want me to arrange a meeting with Clancy?"

"No, I can do that. I have to think things through but whatever happens is best face to face. I think I'll come back from France tomorrow evening and stay in London, meet him before flying home on Monday. You get going or you'll miss your flight. Give my love to Cammie and Max."

And here I was twenty-four hours later to do just that. There was a toy truck on the passenger seat beside me, the absent father's classic bribe to instantly win a child's affection. Hanging from the ignition was the front-door key. I could just walk in but it had been too long for that. Ten days, in fact: long enough for me to knock on the door. The prospect was enough to make me consider driving back down the long avenue to the security gates and back to Dublin. But I was here, and I desperately wanted to see Max. Time then to front up.

6

Max sat at my feet, engrossed in taking bits off his new toy and showing them off. Each item had to get sufficient gasps of awe or the tiny blond figure would raise the volume until there was no alternative but to "ooh" and "ahh" appropriately. It was probably imagination but he looked to have lengthened since I'd last seen him. There seemed to be more of him. That plump, dimpled face, crowned by blond curls and dominated by an azure pair of eyes, looked a little more worldly. No doubt that was guilt talking, but it didn't make the consequence feel any less real.

Not that Max gave the slightest sign of noticing his father's absence. It was the toy that got the reception, and quite right too. He tolerated a hug for just long enough to get his hands on the truck and then toddled off through the empty DVD cases strewn on the living-room floor.

The protective urge towards the little figure was almost physical in its intensity. His birth had been a shock on so many levels and thrown so much on its head. And yet the primary result of this new arrival was a realisation that I was no longer the most important person in the world. Of course theoretically I was under no illusions about my place. It was no more significant than anyone else's. But I also suspected that embedded deep within everyone was the delusion that everything really does revolve around us. It was a delusion probably shared by everybody in the deeper recesses. However, seeing that purple, screeching creature emerge, totally helpless and looking to me for everything, flipped everything on its head. Weirdly enough, it kind of helped, reduced things down, made everything else manageable. This lad was the centre; everything else was just flotsam. And that's what made this situation so awful: the impact on the little guy of his parents' inability to behave properly. He didn't deserve this.

"Tea or coffee?" Cammie asked.

I hadn't even heard her come in, I was concentrating on Max so much.

"Whatever you're having. It doesn't matter," I replied.

My wife walked back to the kitchen. She was wearing a black sweater and black leggings that clung to her shape. There was a tall elegance to her stride that never failed to stir me. Many times the struggle to keep my hands off her had been useless and even mundane tasks around the house had a history of provoking behaviour that had my wife fighting off her over-amorous husband. They were good memories: probably all they were now.

"I'm sorry Kentish Town didn't win," Cammie said, placing a tray on the coffee table. It had a plateful of chocolate biscuits she kept for when visitors came. "Is he okay?"

"He has a few scrapes but he'll be alright," I replied.

"Better luck in the Derby then," she said, sitting down and grabbing Max's hand to hold him close.

My wife's knowledge of, and interest in, racing was negligible at best yet we spent five minutes talking about the Guineas and Clancy's antics.

"That's terrible. What are you doing to do?" she asked.

"Not a lot. It's Jake's call. But you can't have a jockey you can't trust."

"Will Jake sack him?"

"I don't see how he can't," I replied. "Put it like this – if he doesn't, it kind of puts me in a spot."

"I can see that. So, you're going to have to come up with a new rider, then."

"It looks like it."

"I'll make us some more coffee."

Max asked for Daddy to put him to bed. I looked at Cammie and she nodded. He felt heavier in my arms than he used to as I carried him down to the little bed that had taken most of a day, and lots of swearing, to put together from a flat pack. The familiar smell of Vaseline, talcum powder, dirty nappies and little-boy pee enveloped me like a guilt-ridden blankie. I sat on the floor, stroking his hair until he was asleep, and remained there as he started gently to snore.

Cammie was sitting on the sofa, knees tucked under her chin, and staring at the drone on the television. She looked stunning – a little drawn around her eyes but composed and in control.

"The girls in the office were wondering when you were coming back. They need things signed," she said.

I'd told the two secretaries I was going to be away for a while, visiting trainers and checking out Jake's string.

Vicky and Siobhán were hugely efficient. If they were asking about my return it was because things were getting seriously behind. It was time to return to some kind of normality.

"I'll come back in the morning. Catch up on things in the office."

"Right," she said, not moving her gaze from the screen.

"Would it be okay if I took Max for a night? I thought I'd take him down to see my parents. They'd love to see him. And he'd love being spoiled."

"If you like."

"That's great. Thanks."

I stood and watched the TV for a few seconds. There didn't seem to be much point in remaining.

"I'll head off."

"You can stay – if you want."

That was the question: did I want to? My call, my choice. Except was it any kind of choice? Stay and our lives would resume. We could remain a family. This wound would always be there, but walking away would allow it an influence on our lives it didn't deserve. Why did Max have to suffer like that?

"Why, Cammie?"

She kept looking at the television, although I noticed she brought her knees up even closer to her face. That wonderfully expressive face that had reduced me to stammering the first time I'd seen it was unreadable. There was silence for so long I figured she didn't want to answer.

"Because I wanted to," she said. "Isn't that what you want to hear?"

"I don't *want* to hear any of this," I said. "But I deserve to know."

Cammie turned the television to mute, its garish colours darting obtrusively through the low sitting-room lights. Standing up and facing the fireplace, looking at my reflection in the mirror, she caught my eyes with her back to me.

"Don't you ever get bored, Lorcan?"

"With who? You? No. You don't bore me, Cammie."

"Jesus. You can't tell me you've been completely happy either. Not with the way things have become."

"I don't know what you mean. What things?"

"Really? You don't know?"

"No, Cammie, I don't. Tell me."

She turned around and looked at me, eyes filling up. Instinctively I went to her but she stopped me, holding my lower arms in her hands and staring at me, almost beseechingly, wanting me to understand.

"It was getting so terribly fucking predictable," she said. "I woke up one morning a while ago and I knew exactly what was going to happen for the rest of the day – exactly. Trying to get on top of the house, cleaning up after Max, trying to pile so much into the hour when he naps, seeing you in passing, you saying 'Everything okay?' giving my bum a squeeze and then barely stopping before heading off again.

"And I know it's my problem. And that marriage is like that. And that I should grow up. But Lorcan, I don't want to grow old before I grow up. And when I met Paul, it felt so amazing to be the focus of someone's attention, not just another item to be checked off by the man in charge."

"That's not fair, Cammie. I never did that."

"Maybe you didn't mean to. But it felt like it."

"Why didn't you tell me this? If you were so unhappy,

why didn't you just say so? I would have done anything you wanted, anything we needed to do."

"Like another problem to solve?"

I shook her hands off and we switched around, me standing at the fire, staring at the flames, trying to take in this obvious unhappiness and my role in it. I'd had no idea. My wife was a cerebral woman with an appetite for life that was one of the most attractive things about her. Sure we didn't get out much any more, but we had a kid. And yes, I was busy, but so was she. Sometimes it did feel like we only brushed up against each other in passing, but that was the life we'd built for ourselves. And how bad a life could it be to wilfully risk it like this?

"I don't love him. I don't really much like him," she said. "But it felt wonderful to be wanted again."

"I've never stopped wanting you, Cammie. I've never stopped loving you."

"And I love you," she replied. "But everything has got so . . . When you touch me, it feels like my own hand."

To which there was nothing much to say. I picked up my jacket and rifled through the pockets for keys. From down the hall, Max yelled for his mother and she hurried off.

"I'll take him to my parents after finishing up in the office tomorrow, if that's alright," I called after her.

"Yes, that'll be fine," she replied, stopping at Max's door. "I'm sorry. I hope you can forgive me."

As I drove away, the light in Max's room was switched on.

7

It was seven in the morning when the phone rang. I was driving to Annagrove, having left Max sleeping in my mum and dad's house in Dublin. They were insistent that he stay. The previous night I'd told them about Cammie and me having problems: no specifics, just enough for them to worry and give their grandson even more fervent hugs as he went to bed.

Repeated phone calls to his mother about him staying another night had gone unanswered. She was probably using the opportunity anyway, to head out, go shopping, meet *him*. No doubt there would be a scene when I got down there about taking liberties and having Max for longer than planned. And no doubt I would respond along the lines of no dutiful mother not answering the phone. It was all so bloody predictable what we were turning into.

Except it wasn't Cammie ringing.

"Lorcan, can you talk?"

"Sure, Jake, just driving."

It was the middle of the night on the east coast. I knew

Jake and Judith had gone straight home after London. He'd told me it had been a particularly unsettling confrontation with Clancy. The little man hadn't said anything when Jake accused him of stopping Kentish Town. He hadn't appeared surprised or indignant, didn't even attempt to argue his case back. There was just acceptance, Jake had told me. More than that, in fact: it bordered on boredom. Nothing had been decided then, but our boss slept on things for a night and then informed his jockey that he wouldn't be riding for him again.

That had been last evening. Jake rang me immediately afterwards and asked me to prepare a press statement. Nothing too specific, just a general expression of regret at things not working out; everyone could fill in the dots themselves. I agreed and gave silent thanks for being backed up.

Initial whispers on the racing grapevine about Clancy's Guineas ride were increasingly turning vocal. There were more and more nudge-nudge comments on the television channels and more and more explicit articles in the various papers about the ineptitude of the jockey's efforts on Kentish Town. As for the website forums there was nothing reticent about the criticism of Clancy and increasingly of the Weinberger empire for appearing to protect their jockey. Yet again Jake's timing was spot on.

"Ringing at two in the morning is not usually your style, Jake," I went on. "Is everything alright?"

"Never mind that. Have you released that statement?"

"No. I was going to do it later this morning. It's a bit early yet. Why?"

"Don't release it."

"Why not? Is something wrong?"

"I don't have to explain myself to you. Just do as I say, and tear it up."

He was badly rattled. His voice quavered and I could hear his footsteps clattering as he walked around the mahogany floors of his office. I'd never heard him like this.

"Jake, let me ring you back on video phone," I said.

"Never mind that. Just don't release anything. Clancy stays on my horses, including Kentish Town in the Derby."

"You can't be serious!" I said, too quickly.

"Lorcan, I would like you to continue working for me, but don't presume too much. If you feel unable to continue, then I'll understand."

His voice caught at the end of that. It sounded nothing like the man I knew. Something was badly wrong. Seeing his face would be such a help. We usually communicated on video phone but he'd rung on a different number to normal.

"Is everything alright?" I asked. "Forget about the horse – are *you* okay?"

"Of course I am!" he shouted. "Just do what I say."

"Okay, I won't release any statement about Clancy," I said. "Jake, would it be any help if I came over there?"

There was a sharp intake of breath at the other end of the line. Then there was nothing. I looked at the screen on my phone to see if we'd been disconnected. We hadn't. Instead I used the chance to turn the volume up. I could hear him breathing quickly. Then there was a deep thud that sounded like he'd punched something.

"Jake. What's wrong? Talk to me, Jake."

Nothing came back. He was still there. I could hear him. At one stage it sounded like he sobbed. Eventually he spoke.

"Thank you, Lorcan, for everything. You're a good man."

Then he hung up.

I rang back repeatedly but there was only a disconnected message. Mobiles were switched off too. It was impossible.

I drove into Annagrove and made straight for the office to try again. He had sounded badly spooked about something, which was not the Jake Weinberger I knew. But there was still no reply. The only other option was Judith but I rarely spoke to her on the phone and Cammie had mentioned something about her changing her mobile recently. Apparently it was some state-of-the-art technological marvel that could fly you to the moon and make a cup of tea when it got there. If it could get me through to my friend then it would have served its purpose in spades.

I drove loudly to the front of the cottage in order to tip off any visitor Cammie might have at home, Thorpe or otherwise. Even if she was alone there would be the fallout from last night but Jake had put a fear in me. It could have been somebody else I'd been talking to compared to the usually calm and composed man I knew. The niceties with my wife could wait.

There was no reply to the bell. I banged the front door with my fist. Still there was nothing. I found my key and let myself in, prepared for something but not an arm around my neck and a disgusting rag over my mouth and nose. There was a pungent stench that somehow made me think of tequila. I struggled but the arms around me were strong and I could hear another body just behind me too. There was a sudden urge to vomit and after that I couldn't remember anything.

It was the sound of crying that first got through to me. My head ached, and everything felt so off-kilter that the snuffling could have been mine. Tentatively opening my eyes revealed nothing. Everything was still dark: some stale-smelling heavy fabric was over my head. I could taste it when sticking my tongue out. Moving my head about was sore but doable. Not so everything else. Both legs were clamped together by some kind of strap I could feel biting into my calves. And my arms were clamped behind my back by another tightly fitted piece of something. Lying on my side on a hard concrete surface, trying to sit upright seemed impossible.

"Lorcan, are you awake? Please wake up!"

"Cammie? Is that you? Are you okay? What's happening?"

"Oh, thank God, I thought you were dead," she sobbed. "Where's Max?"

Our son, safely tucked up in bed with my parents last time I was conscious – before this lunacy invaded our lives.

"He's fine, he's safe." I was afraid to say more, unsure whether I might be overheard. "What's going on, Cammie? Can you see? Are you blindfolded?"

"No."

"Are we alone?"

"Yes."

"Where are we?"

"I don't know!" she shouted, almost hysterically. "I don't know, I don't know!"

I could understand her panic completely. It was all I could do not to cry out at the pain in my bound limbs, never mind the disorienting terror of having no idea of where I might be, or what time it was, or what surrounded us.

"Cammie, you have to look around for me, tell me what

you see." I scrambled somehow into a sitting position and felt my back leaning against a wall.

"What? I can't see anything."

"Please, babe, try. Just tell me what you can see."

"It's just an old room, like a cellar, and the walls are all stony and sticking out," she said. "There's five steps leading up to a door. That's it, I can't see anything else."

"Is there a window?"

"No, just walls and this cold floor, and my hands and feet tied up. I'm so cold, Lorcan, so cold."

"Are you hurt? What happened to you?"

"No, I'm okay. I'm just so cold," she said, taking a deep breath and obviously shivering. "I went to bed early last night, just knackered, looking forward to a bit of sleep. I don't know what time it was, but I woke up and these men in masks were standing over me. They dragged me out, put something over my eyes and lifted me out to a car."

"Jesus Christ," I said uselessly. "You didn't recognise anything before they blindfolded you? Clothes, or a voice?"

"No. But I did hear them shouting about how you weren't there – or Max. They were going on and on about how Donovan or the kid weren't around."

"So, there were more than the ones who took you?"

"Yes, it sounded like there were half a dozen voices. They stuck me on the floor in the back of a car – put their feet on me to keep me still. And they kept saying Pinkie would be angry with them. I could hear them on phones making plans for some of them to stay in the house in case you showed up. You and Max."

"You didn't tell them where we were, did you? Where my parents live?"

"No. Give me some credit."

"I'm sorry, babe," I said and tried to take in what Cammie had said.

They had been looking for me as much as her, maybe more. It was just chance that I wasn't there. Why would anybody want to kidnap my wife? It didn't make any kind of sense.

"Who's this Pinkie?" I asked.

"How should I know?" she snapped in exasperation. "They must think we're someone else. It's all a huge mistake. I kept telling them. But it was useless."

"You've been incredible, Cam. You just have to keep being strong for a little while until things get sorted out. I promise you, we'll get this fixed up."

It sounded a lot more confident than I felt. This was no mistake. For one thing, they'd known my name, and how many of us were supposed to be in the cottage. Plus nobody got into Annagrove and negotiated the mile-long avenue just on a whim. And they had managed it without tipping off anyone. Every night a couple of security guards patrolled the place that contained millions of dollars' worth of Jake's best bloodstock. There hadn't been a squeak from them: unless they too had been taken on the hop by this gang. It was hardly out of the question. There was a seriousness and a proficiency to all this that worried me even more than the burning pain coursing through my arms and legs. But there'd be time to find that out later.

I strained against what was binding me but it was useless. Shaking my head had a similarly negative result with what was covering my eyes and just made me feel ill. Pretty soon all that I could hear was the sound of my wife's teeth chattering and a faint hum of traffic from above us. There was a faintly acrid, almost burning smell.

"Can you hear cars, Cammie?" I asked.

"I think so."

"There seems to be a lot of them. And in a low gear. How long were you in the car, babe?"

"I don't know."

"Could you see anything?"

"No, I couldn't. I told you."

If it had been a short trip, then we could be in Dublin, or somewhere around it. At least that was something. Having some sort of bearing stopped my mind leaping off in any number of tangents. It was while considering the uselessness of 'if' that the door above us opened.

Cammie started whimpering and I heard her being pulled to her feet, which made me shout uselessly, which in turn led to a kick in the belly that doubled me over on the ground again. Picked up under both arms I was dragged to my released feet and all but lifted up steps that made me stumble and fall again. That got me what felt like another kick in the ribs. It didn't matter. Over the years some much harder kicks from much more powerful legs had connected with most of the bones in my carcass. This was nothing, I told myself; just keep thinking straight. We were marched for at least a minute, Cammie ahead of me, until something obviously heavy and metallic was slid open and I was pushed forward and down into a seat. Only then was the cover on my head taken off.

The unaccustomed light was blinding. But it was fluorescent, not sunlight. Through squinting eyes, I made myself look around. It was a huge area, like some empty factory space, with the same sort of stone walls Cammie had described. Huge lights hung off the towering ceiling and shone on half a dozen men, some in jeans, some in track suits, all of whom were large and physically capable-looking. They stood around an obviously terrified young man who was sitting on a chair at a desk, looking ridiculously like a student being bullied over the contents of his lunch box.

"Lorcan, I'm over here!"

Cammie was also sitting in a chair, about ten yards to my right, dressed only in the baggy *Rolling Stones* T-shirt that had over time morphed from a concert souvenir into my wife's favourite nightie. She looked desperately vulnerable, her bare legs shivering and terribly exposed in front of all these men, two of whom stood guard over us. My automatic impulse to go to her was rewarded with a slap around the head and a hefty shove back down.

"Give the bastard another one, Pete, make him know his place."

The familiar voice came from behind, and then Mike Clancy swaggered in front of me, leaning into my face and laughing out loud.

"Not so fucking high and mighty now, are ye, Donovan?" he said, lips curling with contempt. "Why don't you try running to Weinberger now? You mug!"

I watched him ball his fist and drive it into my cheek-bone. It made a loud noise and sent my head backwards but it wasn't harmful. I knew there was no bone broken.

"Here, stop that! If there's going to be any clattering around here, it'll be done by us."

One of the heavies in the middle of the room marched over and towered over Clancy. He must have weighed at least three times more than the jockey and there was a hardness written all over his heavily stubbled face that contrasted with the perfect sheen of his bald head.

Clancy didn't look in the least concerned. "Don't worry about it, Anto, I was just getting re-acquainted with my boss." He walked towards Cammie. He looked at her in a way she understood only too clearly.

I made to move again but Anto stood in front of me and briefly shook his head.

"You're a lucky man, Donovan," Clancy said, his eyes poring over her. "She's a bit skinny for my taste – I like a nice big arse and something you can hang to. But she's a quality mare."

Cammie kept her gaze down and concentrated on covering as much of herself as the meagre T-shirt would allow.

"You were always good with the women though, I seem to remember," he continued. "The gentleman jockey: the bitches gobbled that up."

I wanted to tell him to shut up, and to keep his eyes off my wife, and that I'd do a proper job on his face given an opportunity. But caution got in the way. This was off the wall: what the hell was the champion jockey doing here with a bunch of muscle, threatening me and my wife? It made no sense. And until it did, I resolved to keep my mouth shut.

Clancy had no such inhibitions. "You're about to find out what happens when you get in the way of something so much bigger than you can even imagine," he said. "You're about to find out what happens when you fuck around with Pinkie Duggan."

He practically strutted, taller than he appeared on the racecourse. His shoes had lifts on, a not uncommon affectation of flat jockeys. Blessed by nature with the physical stature required for their job, they were also cursed by being immediately identifiable as such. Over the years

I'd noticed how so many had been terrier-like in their approach to life. There was a hair-trigger temperament common to jockeys that owed at least something to being hungry so much of the time but could also be attributed to a fundamental insecurity about their height. Clancy didn't appear particularly hungry, although he kept looking at Cammie with a disturbing intensity.

"You're going to find out what happens to those who get in Pinkie Duggan's way!" he practically screamed, eyes locked on my wife.

"Will you shut the fuck up?" Anto bawled in his harsh Dublin accent, making everyone start. "You know what your problem is? You fucking talk too much – give it a rest."

Clancy barely seemed to notice the big man, but just kept moving his gaze between Cammie and me. I found it unsettling; God knows what it was like for her. My promise to get us out of this mess was looking more and more over-optimistic. This was no mistake. It was about me, and Jake, and Kentish Town.

There was another sliding sound from behind me and three more men in casual clothes walked past, a couple of them idly glancing at me. Then a large figure in a pinstripe suit and gleaming black shoes strode towards the group in the middle. I noticed his feet were almost comically splayed when he walked, nearly at quarter to three. He was approaching sixty years old and the expensive-looking suit struggled to contain his bulky figure. There remained a physical power there though that was nothing compared to the presence he brought with him. Everyone deferred, one of the heavies almost tripping over himself to get out of his way.

"How's about ye, Pinkie?" Clancy shouted, practically scampering towards him. "Everything alright?"

There was no reply. Instead the central figure leaned on the desk and looked at the terrified young man who stared back and pleaded.

"Please, Mr Duggan, I can get your money – I just need a little more time," he begged. "Please, you have to believe me!"

"I do believe you," the older man almost whispered in a northern accent similar to Clancy's. "You will get me that money. Because if you don't, you will be found in a ditch out by the airport. Your carcass will probably be well rotten by the time it's found, but you won't really care about that."

There was a sudden stench of urine, and steam rose from the front of the young man's trousers. He didn't even register it, never taking his eyes away from the figure looming over him. Duggan's thin lips curled in disgust. The gesture rippled through his bloated face. Already mottled cheeks turned even redder and a sheen of sweat glistened on his forehead.

He turned suddenly and walked to a sink that was incongruously placed in a corner, isolated from anything else. It looked like it had been recently installed, all modern glint, totally at odds with the surroundings. Duggan plunged his hands under a stream of steaming water and began washing. Soapy lather grew under the ferocity of his scrubbing and he resolutely kept his hands under water that was clearly piping hot. The concentration that had been trained on the heavily breathing youngster behind him was now fixed on this process. Only after a number of minutes did he finally turn off the tap and carefully towel down his scalded red hands.

"Now then, Dean, if you think I have the time to be coming down here every time you or some other scumbag manages to fuck up, you have another think coming. I'm an important man, Dean. That's not bullshit. It's just fact. I've just come from a meeting with a cabinet minister, Dean, discussing potential deals worth millions. The few grand you owe me isn't worth a shit. But, Dean, and this is an important point, Dean, so pay attention: if I let you away with your few grand, Christ alone knows how many other scumbags will try it on. So, Dean, you are going to get what you owe me, and I'm going to focus your mind for you. Now, try and be a man and not be too objectionable."

One of the heavies put an arm around Dean's neck and grabbed his hair, pulling it backwards. Another took a hold of his left arm and two others took the right, holding it rigidly out and on the desk.

"Oh Jesus, please, don't. Please!" Dean shrieked, quite obviously shitting his pants. "Please, Mummy, please!"

Duggan pounced on the hand, prying a finger loose and reaching around for a large and lethal-looking kitchen knife that shone under the lights when handed over to him. Where there had been only disgust and resignation before, there was now a glow of anticipation on the big, flabby face. I glanced at Cammie who looked appalled and was as pale as a sheet. She turned away just as Duggan started to cut into the man's finger.

Shrieks of agony and terror appeared only to increase the speed of Duggan's assault. He held the hand down and cut. Blood squirted all over his face and clothes and provoked a growl of what might have been disgust, but also more than a little excitement. The knife was clearly deadly sharp and cut through muscle and bone in seconds. Duggan straightened, breathing heavily, and holding the severed finger up to the light. Dean was released and barely moved in his seat, just whimpering and looking up at the ceiling, not wanting to look at what had been done to him. I heard Cammie crying quietly but kept my eyes on what was happening in front of me.

"Now, Dean, that wasn't pleasant for either of us. You especially," Duggan said. "And I don't ever want to have to go near a dirty wretch like you ever again. So do as you're told and get my money. You've got a week. Now get him out of here."

Dean was lifted up and carried past us. The door slid open again.

"Here, you can give him this – if he wants it," Duggan shouted, throwing the bloody finger over my head to one of his henchmen. There was an oath as it was caught, then dropped, and picked up off the ground.

"Good one, Pinkie," Clancy laughed. "If he wants it! I like that."

Duggan favoured the little man with a slight smile and looked over at me. Then he briefly glanced at Cammie before clicking his fingers. The one called Pete appeared with a fresh suit on a hanger and hung it near the sink. Duggan stripped to his underwear, consigning with obvious distaste the blood-spattered pinstripe to a heap in a corner. He stood at the sink in boxers and white vest that struggled to confine his paunchy belly. With black socks pulled up almost to his knees, he could have been a comical figure. But no one was laughing.

He went through the cleaning-up process with the same diligence as before but with more to wash. Water pooled at his feet as he scrubbed his face, chest and hands. Removing his socks he towelled himself down.

"Now then, to you, Mr Donovan. What did you think of our Dean? Not saying anything? I'm not surprised. It's a distasteful exercise. But some of it was for your benefit. You see, Mr Donovan, I need you to realise that I'm serious."

He held his hands up and a black hold-all was handed to him by Pete who busily piled the discarded pinstripe into a plastic bin-liner. Duggan fetched himself a chair and sat down to put on new socks he'd taken out of the bag. Then came a pristinely pressed white shirt, complete with tie and cuff-links, before he unveiled his new pinstripe suit. It was exactly the same as the previous one. He started getting dressed.

"You're a horsey guy, Mr Donovan, one of the fashionable crowd I guess, like Mike there. He's some operator, isn't he? Came up from nothing in Belfast, like myself, made something of himself. I read these articles about him in the paper and they tell me he's a genius on the back of a horse. Isn't that right, Mike?"

"If it's in the papers, it must be true, right, Pinkie?"

"I suppose so, Mike. Although how much of a genius would you be if you weren't such a short-ass?" He smiled, then turned to me. "You were a jockey too, weren't you? Won the Grand National, right?"

Almost despite myself, I nodded.

"Yeah, what was the nag's name again?"

"Granite Top," Clancy said. "A fucking farmers' race, just whoever survives the longest."

I remembered back to that sunny afternoon at Liverpool when Granite Top showed a granite constitution over the famous Aintree National fences and carried his relative journeyman rider to ten minutes of fame. Whatever fortune it produced lasted even less time and yet the memory was always enough to make me smile at the sheer unbridled excitement of it all. Or at least it used to.

"Mike is not a man accustomed to doubt, Mr Donovan, and neither am I," Duggan said. "What you horsey types do with your nags is of no interest to me. It's fucking ridiculous really: all this excitement about a bunch of dumb animals running around a field."

He nodded to Pete who handed him a bottle of mineral water. Then he nodded to Anto who jerked his head at the other henchmen. Suddenly Cammie was picked up and marched towards the door.

"Where are you taking her?" I shouted, and got an inevitable slap around the back of head.

Cammie said nothing until the door was sliding again and all I heard was "Lorcan!" before it closed. Then there was nothing.

"Relax, Mr Donovan, nothing is going to happen to your wife – if you play ball," Duggan said.

I chanced a look around and there was only Anto standing behind me. Everyone else had left. I weighed up my chances against Duggan, Clancy and the massive man mountain idly sucking his teeth and calculated I hadn't a hope even if my hands weren't tied behind my back.

"The less people listening to this, the better," Duggan said, pulling a chair in front of me and sitting on it back-to-front. Such proximity made me draw back. There was something reptilian about his bald paleness.

"I don't give a fuck about your horses. But I do give a fuck about those who want to bet on them," he said, taking a pull on the water bottle. "Bookmaking never interested me, Mr Donovan – just a bunch of sad bastards hanging around an office to stay out of the rain. But there's bookmaking, and then there's bookmaking, isn't there?" He gave a brief smile. "There are people out there, Mr

Donovan, extremely rich people, who like to have a bet – a real bet. And plenty of them like to bet the gee-gees. But there isn't a bookmaker in this country, or in Britain, who's willing to take the sort of bet such people want to put down. We're talking shrewdies backing their judgement with hard cash, or just fucking eejits with more money than sense. Either way, they want to bet, and bet big."

He was close enough for me to hear him swallowing the water he was drinking; close enough to hear the sound of his Adam's apple moving.

"It's very simple. There are people here in Ireland who think they're big gamblers. They're not. Certainly not compared to the Far East. You know, I was told that Chinamen would bet on one fly going up a wall, just for the hell of betting on it. I thought it was all bollocks. But it's true. They're mad bastards. It doesn't matter what it is, they'll bet on it. And they're superstitious as hell too. The colours the jockeys wear are a huge thing – so is the name of the nag, even what colour its fucking tail is. Even the smartest, most clued-up, hard-bastard Chinaman can turn into a nutcase when it comes to the gee-gees. Which is where some associates of mine come in. They're based in Hong Kong. Chinamen too, but clever ones. Clever enough to know the real power in gambling is with the bookie, especially one who knows what the result is going to be. So I'm out in Hong Kong on a business trip, talking to one of these people who's explaining to me the millions – yes, millions – his clients are willing to bet on races. Of course, you know over there it's all Tote betting, officially. But the real stuff is done behind the scenes, and these guys are cleaning up. And then it struck me: who do I know in the horsey game?"

65

He looked sideways at Clancy who took a theatrical bow.

"We're both from the same street in Belfast," the jockey said. "My older brother was Pinkie's best friend. They fought the Brits together, side by side."

"Now, now, Mike, let's not give the shop away," Duggan interrupted. "Actually, I think I might have left my wallet in the other suit. Can you find Pete and have a look in the pockets before the prick puts it in the bin?"

Clancy gave me a scornful look and left. Duggan waited for a few seconds.

"He really does talk too much. But he has his uses. He's a bit of a genius on the back of a pony. It's just when he's on the ground that things get a bit complicated for Mike. He is now making straight for a toilet where he can snort another bit of Columbia up his nose. Loves the coke, does Mike, it's all he lives for. I'm amazed he's still allowed ride. But lucky for us, he is. It's quite simple, Mr Donovan. I give Mike all the drugs in the world, plus any other side benefits he might desire – he's mad for the birds too – and a percentage of the profits. In return he stops one every so often. Not regularly or anything, just when it suits me and my colleagues. It's been remarkably lucrative over the last few years. And no one has guessed a thing."

He stood up suddenly, making me start. That got a smile. He fished another bottle of water out of his black bag and took a sip.

"And then, Mr Donovan, that damn nag of yours, Kentish Town, ran so fast that it was all Mike could do to pull it back. In fairness, he did warn us: told us the thing was a monster and not to go at it in a race that would be such a focus of attention. But my colleagues in Hong Kong have noticed over the years that it is the big races that some clients really like to get stuck into. So I told Mike to pull the thing anyway.

"And it backfired. You twigged it straight away, and told this Weinberger fella who bulleted Mike. And apparently now there's all this talk about how the Kentish Town thing was iffy and the authorities are sniffing around, asking questions. So now we have a situation, Mr Donovan."

He fiddled with the top of his water bottle and gestured to Anto who moved away to the end of the room out of earshot. Then he moved even closer to me.

"My colleagues have a lot of liabilities already on this Derby race that's coming up in three weeks' time. And as the race gets closer, those liabilities are going to multiply by any number you care to mention. It's the race everybody wants to win, even if it's just with a bet. The people around the world, especially in the Far East, who will want to back Kentish Town will be – how can I put this – significant. So here's what's going to happen, Mr Donovan. Mike is going to ride your horse in the Derby and he's going to do what has to be done. And then that will be it – job done – and everything will go back to normal. No need to push our luck, is there?

"Weinberger is on board. He's more than happy to let Mike ride the horse. But Mike guessed you would be a different matter, figured you might get thick and go on a solo run, get all high and mighty. So we're going to hang on to your wife, Mr Donovan, keep her here with us until after the Derby, just so your conscience doesn't get in the way. Once we get the result we want, she can be on her merry way and no one's the wiser."

We stared at each other, me with horror at the idea of

Cammie being with these people for three weeks, and him with the absolute knowledge that he was going to get his way. It was written all over his face. The idea that I might counter him in any manner was so ridiculous as not even to enter his reckoning. He was playing with me, all this 'Mr Donovan' stuff, and all the supposed reasonableness of explaining at least part of what was going on. It was just a game. And even then I knew it wouldn't be over after the Derby.

"Not saying anything, Mr Donovan? I suppose not. That's not your style is it? Anto."

A massive hand went over my mouth and I got another taste of tequila.

8

There was a small area between the two doors leading into the Intensive Care Unit. Hanging on the wall was a row of white plastic gowns of the type that tied at the back and always left part of your ass showing. I tied a knot as good as I could and then spent a minute examining what looked like two plastic bags. It took a nurse on her way in to point out they were to cover my shoes. One deep breath later and I opened the stiffly heavy door into an ICU that had just one bed. Jake lay in it, in a coma.

The desperately lifeless, antiseptic stench of hospitals had always made me sick. Even the anticipation of going into hospital made me queasy. But this large room on the thirtieth floor of New York's finest hospital was different. It was fresh, and airy, and the last place I ever wanted anyone I cared about to end up in.

"You can sit next to him, if you like," said one of the nurses on duty.

"Okay," I replied. "What do I do?"

"Nothing. He's comfortable. His vitals are stable. The doctors say it's a matter of waiting and hoping."

"Okay, thank you."

I sat down, petrified at the idea of knocking into any of the pipes, drips and catheters that intrusively protruded from him. He looked desperately old all of a sudden, lying there, grey hair all over the place, hands spotty and wrinkled, all the famous gusto deflated out of that powerful body. No wonder Judith and the kids outside looked as if their world was caving in. It was.

I suddenly thought of my own father and what it would do to me to see him like this. Such vulnerability didn't bear thinking about. All the same, another stab of guilt and worry hit me. It had been half an hour since I'd rung him, to make sure, again, that he and Mum and Max were okay.

"Will you relax?" he'd sighed. "Max is having a ball."

"Are you sure?"

"Of course. Why wouldn't he? This is a fabulous hotel, right on the beach, the sun is shining, he's got ice cream and sand and his granny all over him. It's very generous of you, kiddo. Sending us out here with everything paid for."

I'd asked my parents if they could take Max away for ten days while me and his mother tried to work things out. There was nothing to be gained from telling them what was really happening. How could they understand when I barely did?

It was less than forty-eight hours since I'd woken up, thrown over a ditch into a paddock in Annagrove. It was nearly dark and a curious foal got the surprise of his young life when the funny mound he was sniffing groaned and staggered to its feet. I found a spare key to the cottage, took care of various cuts and scratches and tried to figure out what I was going to do.

The idea of Cammie at the mercy of those people made me want to vomit, and I did, loudly, until there was no more to come up. Reaction also produced sweats, shivers and a desperate sickly feeling in the stomach that no amount of heaving could get rid of. My wife, the beautiful mother of my child, the girl who'd torn the heart out of me, had no one else in the world to rely on except me. Going to the police was not an option. Duggan would inflict an awful retribution. But how could Cammie survive three weeks unscathed? I'd seen enough to realise how fragile she was. It wouldn't take long before she unravelled completely.

At the end of a night spent patrolling the fields, trying to use night air to clear my head into some sort of constructive use, all I came up with was the absolute necessity of getting Max out of harm's way. A phone call to a wealthy owner I used to ride for got the best room in a five-star hotel in Crete for two adults and a child. Another phone call to an aviation company that Jake used when in Europe resulted later in the day in a private jet landing at Dublin airport specifically for the use of one very excited child and two only marginally less excited adults. I charged it to the Weinberger account. Explanations could come later. It was while driving away from waving goodbye that an American number flashed on my phone.

"Lorcan, I need you," Judith said in a voice I barely recognised. "Something awful has happened to Jake."

It's all she said. I recalled Jake's phone call, how desperate he sounded. How long ago it seemed now. And then I remembered Duggan: 'Weinberger is on board.' I swung the car around and begged, threatened and cajoled my way onto the next flight to New York. And here I was now.

"Jesus, Jake, what have you done?" I almost whispered.

A stupid question. We knew what he'd done: swallowed a massive amount of sleeping tablets, washed down with half a bottle of whiskey in a cocktail of anguished despair. It was a miracle he wasn't dead. Judith, normally a deep sleeper, woke up with a feeling of dread in her belly, saw her husband wasn't with her and went searching. She found him unconscious in his office, somehow controlled her panic enough to perform some fundamental mouth-to-mouth, and rang the emergency services. The surgeons said he should have been dead given the quantity of barbiturates in his system. But he didn't die: whatever sub-conscious determination still lurked inside the old man refused to cough him up. At least not yet. But who knew how long he could last.

I stayed with him for half an hour until one of his daughters, tears only a gesture away, came back in and resumed the family presence. She gave me a kiss of gratitude which I hardly deserved and asked if I could take her mom home for a change of clothes. Judith wanted to drive but I insisted, telling her she could navigate me out of New York's insane traffic. After five minutes she was asleep, exhausted. I pointed the big, heavy vehicle northwards and somehow managed to find the right freeway.

What had Duggan done to make my boss do something so appalling? There was no doubt it was Duggan. I didn't believe in coincidences anyway, and certainly nothing as big as this. The owner is on board is what he'd said. But how? Kentish Town was more than just a racehorse to

Jake. He almost represented an ideal. Gerry had told him the year before there wasn't a fault in the colt: temperament, constitution, speed, stamina, it was all there. To someone with Jake's appreciation of the breed and its history, there was no getting away from the significance of such an athlete. Hundreds of years of time, money, passion and desire had created the thoroughbred. Perfection might be illusory but Kentish Town was the closest any of us was ever going to get to it. Jake Weinberger wouldn't besmirch that for all the betting money in the world. What had Duggan threatened him with?

Judith woke up when the car stopped, looked briefly as normal until the realisation of what had happened came crashing back in on top of her.

"I'm sorry for dragging you all the way here, Lorcan. I don't know why I asked you. It just feels easier with you around."

"I'll do everything I can."

"Jake thinks the world of you. He really does. Says you're one of the most capable people he's ever known."

I could see the effort it took for this delicate-looking woman not to break down. We went inside, her upstairs and me sent to the kitchen to make coffee. After twenty minutes there was still no sign of Judith. I didn't want to go to Jake's office but there was a remorseless pull towards the room in the house I knew best. There was no sign of what had happened. Everything was back in its place, the waterfall outside still falling noiselessly, the understated opulence untouched. Some paperwork remained on his large desk, an almost old-fashioned feature next to the state-of-the-art computer that dominated the desk. On top was a printout of a pedigree I'd sent him of a mare we might be interested in at an upcoming auction. Its position was an untypical moment of enthusiasm getting the better of duty.

"He was there when I found him," Judith said behind me. "On the floor."

I turned. She was pointing to the large window.

"You're an amazing woman," I said, giving her a hug. The little figure squeezed back tightly. "Judith . . . did Jake say anything before . . . What made him do this?"

She stiffened in my arms, then slowly disentangled herself. Drawing herself up to her full height she looked at me as if coming to a decision.

"It's something to do with what happened in Newmarket, isn't it?" I said.

She nodded. Before I could say anything else she turned on the computer and clicked on a file. It was piece of video, grainy and obviously amateurish, the type used by undercover reporters who put cameras into bags to tape people. Judith moved to the massive wall of glass by the waterfall, allowing me to sit down and watch.

A naked man walked past the camera. He was squat and powerful and the paleness of his hips clashed with the deep brownness of the rest of him. I was about to tell Judith she had clicked on the wrong thing when Jake's face came into focus. He sat on the edge of a bed and smiled at a young blonde woman who suddenly came into shot and knelt in front of him. She was dressed in a flimsy black piece of lingerie and began performing oral sex on him just as he turned around and beckoned. A dark-haired woman, completely naked, walked past the camera and began kissing Jake. After a minute she moved the blonde out of the way and straddled him.

My attention was drawn to the blonde though: she made

a big performance out of kissing the brunette's shoulders and neck but kept making eyes at the camera and grinning. The other woman was clearly having sex with Jake but glanced conspiratorially at the camera too. I had a strong impression that he had no idea they were being filmed. After another minute it was equally obvious what I was looking at so I switched it off. Judith was staring out at the water.

"I'm sorry," I said.

She continued staring out for some time before replying.

"I love my husband completely. This is nothing," she said, her voice steady. "We have an understanding."

I said nothing. Jake and Judith's sex life was no one's business except their own. Peeping under the duvet was not my style. But she came over, leaned her hip on the desk and smiled crookedly.

"I won't bore you with the details. Suffice to say some years ago my sexual drive disappeared. It was embarrassing and difficult and in the context of our marriage relatively unimportant. Jake couldn't have been more understanding. But just because my interest in sex disappeared didn't mean his had. And it was ridiculous that my problem should also rob him. So we arrived at this . . . understanding."

"You don't have to explain anything to me, Judith," I said.

"I know. But I'm going to anyway. Jake is a normal, healthy man with a normal, healthy man's desires and impulses. So for the last ten years or so he has catered for those desires and impulses. All I ever wanted in return was discretion. And it worked. We've actually never been closer."

I must have looked at her a certain way because she grinned.

"You're probably still too young to appreciate such things. Sex is built up too much these days. Marriage is about much more important things. Jake did what he did, mostly I believe with prostitutes, because he didn't want any emotional ties. He had more than enough of that at home. It was just a physical release for him, one that I didn't want to perform any more. And it worked. I know you won't believe me, but when we kiss it means more than anything sexual."

She stared wistfully past me for a few moments. And then focused on me again.

"We were sitting up in bed talking and reading when that dreadful little man, Mike Clancy, rang Jake on his cell phone. His face just fell. I can remember that. I asked if everything was alright when he hung up and he just jumped out of bed and went downstairs. He wasn't long. And when he came back he didn't seem too different. Maybe a little distracted, but he can get like that sometimes with business. I asked if everything was alright and he mumbled something about a weird email and just told me to go back to sleep."

There was a pause to gather herself together, no doubt cursing herself for having indeed gone back to sleep. I grabbed her hand, gave it a squeeze and told her how lucky Jake was that she'd woken up in time.

"Just the thought of that film getting out made Jake do this to himself. There were just a couple of words on the e-mail: 'Or else.' He's a proud man, Lorcan. He's done a lot of good. He doesn't deserve to be ridiculed for something like this." She finally gave in to the tears. "And this dreadful thing is bound to get out. They always do, on the net. It's so intrusive. Nothing is private any more."

"This will stay private, Judith," I said, hopefully sounding more confident than I felt. "This is all to do with that race in Newmarket, and Kentish Town, and my inability to keep my mouth shut, and me putting Jake in a terrible position. These people are ruthless. But they're not stupid. And they're after something specific. Believe me, I know."

"How can you be so sure?"

"Because they've taken Cammie," I replied.

"What do you mean 'taken'?"

"This gangster, Pinkie Duggan, has kidnapped her. He's holding her now. And they're going to keep her so I won't do anything about Clancy riding Kentish Town in the Derby."

Judith looked at me incredulously. The facts sounded incredible even to my ears as I relayed them. Even in the midst of her own misery, shock was written all over Judith's face.

"Dear God, Lorcan, why didn't you say?" she said, grabbing my hand. "How long has she been with these people?"

"A few days. They took me too, just to make sure I got the message."

To her immense credit, she removed herself from her own horror and gave me a hug.

"We have to do what they want, Lorcan. People like this don't care who they hurt as long as they get their own way. If we don't, then your wife will at the very least be hurt, and my husband's reputation will be destroyed. All that matters is getting Jake better and Cammie free. Promise me that, Lorcan. We can't thumb our noses at them: they're evil."

It sounded odd yet appropriate to use such a word.

Duggan's actions were certainly illegal and undoubtedly corrupt. But evil was a better description, I figured. Jake lay on the edge of death in a hospital bed, driven to a state of mind that calculated it was better to end his own life. Cammie lay on a cold floor somewhere, scared out of her wits and on the brink of caving in on herself. And for what? Just so some faceless rich people on the other side of the world could fill their empty lives with a brief thrill, shovelling money that had probably long ago lost all relevance to reality on a race that didn't really matter to them at all. The Derby took two and a half minutes to run; what Duggan and Clancy were doing was destroying lives. The evil of that was suddenly all-consuming. I felt affronted by it. Anger was hardly an emotion I was unacquainted with but this was colder than anything else.

Judith looked at me, looking for that promise. I nodded. And knew I couldn't keep it.

9

Jocelyn Bryce Mountclifton De Beaufort, Knight of the Realm, and trainer to princes and sheikhs, drew himself up to his full lean six-foot-plus height, stared disdainfully down his long aquiline nose and shook his head. The famous mane of hair, still perfectly blond at the age of sixty, barely rippled at the movement. It wouldn't dare. The stiffly upright guardsman's posture from when he was a young captain in charge of a company flying in and out of South Armagh by chopper was perfectly intact.

"Tell them all to fuck off!" he announced in a tone that suggested he had decreed and so it would be done.

For once, it wasn't me that had provoked Sir Jocelyn's splenetic fury. Normally it was. My presence anywhere near racing's most notably patrician trainer was guaranteed to get that taut jaw grinding. He regarded me as an inter-ference, and a nuisance, and would in the course of most other things have quickly advised me to toddle off back to whatever bog-hole I'd crawled out of. But since I was

Jake's man, the civilities were just about maintained. And it was only my phone that was irritating him this time.

"Blasted parasites – should be all put against a wall," he mumbled before suddenly bolting down the yard to bawl out some unfortunate stable lad who had earned his disfavour. "If you're going to scrape water off Lady Marigold's back, try not to do it like you're scraping barnacles off your mother's arse, Jenkinson!"

Sir Jocelyn's parasites were the fourth estate: the members of which he viewed with lofty disgust and who in return regarded him with a mixture of loathing and fear. Another reason the man whose family estate and stables dominated this picturesque part of the Wiltshire Downs just about tolerated me was that I kept the press guys off his back on a day-to-day basis. But news of Jake's stay in hospital – the details of which were still happily vague – had my phone hopping with reporters wanting updates on one of the world's leading owners and any impact his illness might have on the whole industry. That it kept ringing during morning stables though was an impertinence my host could do without.

I kept details to a minimum – Mr Weinberger had collapsed at home and tests were being carried out to find out why – and so far there was no hint that there might be more to the story than that. As for the racing side of things, it was a straight-bat response of everything goes ahead as per normal. What the impact of Jake's health status was going to be on the business world, I thankfully left to others. There was already enough on my plate.

I'd flown direct to Heathrow the previous night having taken Judith back to the hospital. She had resumed her position next to her husband and her family and I had returned to a world that demanded attention no matter how irrelevant it seemed.

The plane trip had provided time to do some research on Duggan. Once I'd established his real name was Kenneth, even a basic Google search came up with plentiful references to him. He hadn't been boasting about his political connections. There were puff-piece newspaper stories about the successful entrepreneur and his business exploits. What his businesses actually were seemed to be vague, but usually ended up under transport and construction categories. A plentiful supply of pictures was also available: Duggan smiling benevolently at the world, shaking hands with various political notables, arm around showbiz types. Nowhere was there a hint of what I'd seen.

But most people presented a version of themselves to the world, the public face. I did it myself. As a jockey, it had become second nature to be composed, professional, pleasant and yet a little detached every time I went racing. Riding meant being under scrutiny, whether from owners and trainers or just punters with a gripe. It was important to keep a little distance. And it wasn't an untrue picture I presented: just not the whole one.

There were, however, a few oblique references to how much Kenneth Duggan was keeping to himself. One tabloid newspaper reporter I noted had a few stories about gangland and crime-related activities by the big man. He also used the "Pinkie" nickname, although didn't refer to its origins. There were also references to links with Sinn Féin and the IRA, how Duggan was supposed to have been a volunteer in Belfast in the 1970s, although he consistently denied it. But there were pictures of him in matey situations with Sinn Féin politicians, those new pillars of public propriety who not so long ago were pariahs. I finished up my searches amazed that I'd not heard of Duggan before, and sure that the great information-soaked general public had no idea of the reality behind the image. I'd driven to the De Beaufort stables with a lot more than horses on my mind.

Far from relishing any inattention, Sir Jocelyn's mutterings to others about how I kept postponing visits to his yard had got back to me, no doubt with some of the colourful phrases thoughtfully deleted. And he was right. I had been putting it off. It might be the last thing on my mind but the duties had to be done, even if just to maintain the illusion of normality that might yet get everyone out of this lunacy.

"Mr Donovan, would you care to join me?" Sir Jocelyn shouted from his Range Rover.

We drove up a dusty path to the top of the gallops. It was a wonderfully bright, sunny morning that allowed us to peer over the south-of-England view for miles around. It was impossible not to take a deep breath of appreciation as we got out and waited for the string of horses climbing towards us. There were ten of them, apparently slowly coming towards us against the stiff incline. The slowness was illusory. Eventually the snort of their breathing reached us. De Beaufort strained his eyes through binoculars, taking in as much detail as he could.

"The colt on the left of the second pair is one of yours – Giocondo. Did nothing as a two-year-old but he's a different proposition now," he explained unnecessarily.

But he wasn't wrong. Even the naked eye could detect how Giocondo was able to maintain the gallop without any effort. In fact the work-rider was having to take a pull while the horse next to him was being rousted along to keep up. Giocondo was out of an Annagrove mare that Jake was especially fond of. He had made a point of asking about the colt just a week before. It seemed like another lifetime. But Giocondo looked great. He strode out eagerly, making light of the rider on his back and the severity of the gradient. There was a barely restrained joy about the way he came towards us, blatant well-being exuding from his every movement. They flashed past us at the top and there was no doubt Jake's horse was the most impressive of them.

"He's turned inside out over the last month," the man next to me said with justifiable satisfaction. "If he keeps improving like this we could have a Group-class horse for Royal Ascot. Or we could keep him for one of the handicaps. A nice tidy little handicap win beforehand would get him a big enough penalty to get into a decent mile-and-a-quarter handicap. I suspect he would be something of a penalty kick in one of those. What do you think? Which way would Jake like to go?"

I'd barely heard him. My mind was on Cammie, and Max and severed fingers and hospital beds.

"I'm sorry – what?"

"What way do you want to go with Giocondo? Straight into Group races or work his way up through handicaps? Do try to keep up – this is important."

"Sorry. I suspect you'd rather go the handicap route, right? Tackle black type races later in the season?"

He nodded and trotted out a well-used argument for not over-facing a progressive young horse too soon: better to build up his confidence in an easier class first. I agreed, and didn't mention how such horses also were useful in battling the bookies. Making use of a lenient handicap mark was just what Sir Jocelyn loved. Behind the hauteur, everyone knew he loved to get a couple of really good bets on every year on what he considered to be certainties. Bookmakers had learned to their cost that a De Beaufort handicap starter could be expensive to them.

It was a struggle as old as racing and one completely removed from what Pinkie Duggan was doing. The haughty man now climbing into the jeep to get back to the yard and debrief his riders was making use of his knowledge and ability. That ability essentially revolved around moulding talent, something so relentlessly positive as to be outside Duggan's understanding. Sir Jocelyn's betting was a touch of roguery; Judith's word still applied more than ever to Duggan. I'd looked briefly on the computer at stories about illegal betting in the Far East, and Hong Kong in particular, a place I was familiar with. Criminal betting was worth billions every year, and it was tied in with every other kind of criminal activity that turned a buck. Links with the feared Triad gangs were mostly unproven, but only the most naïve believed they weren't involved. The whole operation was international, complex and worth a fortune. None of which made it any less distasteful.

"Yes, I think that Hampton Court Stakes might be the thing to go for," he said as we bounced back to the stables. "Tell Jake he'll have something to look forward to. He loves Ascot."

"I will. He'll be very happy with the job you've done with Giocondo."

"How actually is he?"

"He's not well. But it could be worse. He's in the right place."

"Yes. Good," Sir Jocelyn said. "Tell him we're all pulling for him. Tell him, I'm pulling for him."

"I will."

He arrived into the yard with a great squealing of brakes, almost in an attempt to distract from any sentiment that might have been revealed.

It was a scene I'd spent most of my working life in, an understated panic to get these skittish animals out and exercised, cleaned and groomed, fed and watered: hard, physical work mixed in with an almost quixotic belief that the next horse or the next race could pay-off big time: the whole exercise a triumph of hope over experience.

"Marian Heights will be ready in time for the Oaks Trial at Goodwood. She's potentially very good," Sir Jocelyn said, his eyes not missing a detail of even the most mundane task taking place in front of him. "Do you want to see her?"

"Yeah, that would be great."

We walked around the corner of the American-style barns into a more old-fashioned yard where he kept the fillies. It was warm enough to provoke bees into buzzing us and there was little else to do except listen to them.

"What are you going to do about that little fucker, Clancy?" De Beaufort suddenly asked out of the side of his mouth.

"What do you mean?"

"I appreciate loyalty as much as the next man but that little shit doesn't deserve Jake's. There are a lot of people who think that Guineas ride stank to high hell and I'm one of them. And I've told Gerry Gunning the same."

"Jake has made his decision. Newmarket was just one of those things."

He looked sideways at me and decided that was insufficient.

"The owner's word is final, of course. But I have a

certain reputation to protect as well. And reservations about that man that I've kept to myself in the past are out in the open now. I presume you'll note my concerns."

"They're noted. But Clancy is the retained rider and nothing has changed."

With points duly made, we continued in silence. Marian Heights was pulled out of her box and trotted up and down for my perusal. She looked good, all bay muscle and an inquisitive eye that testified to the general health and wellbeing of the De Beaufort team.

"She'll improve for Goodwood but unless that moron Montgomery runs that filly of the sheikh's in the same race, I think yours should still win. And it will bring her on heaps for Epsom," he said, looking at me. "I get the feeling that there's more to this Clancy business than meets the eye. Am I wrong?"

I met his gaze and said nothing.

"Hopefully you know what you're doing, young man," he said and invited me into the house for tea.

As we walked back into the main yard, a putrid smell came from a stable in a corner. It smelled like hair burning and was enough to have Sir Jocelyn blowing his cheeks out in disgust. I looked over at the familiar figure of a farrier hunched over a horse's bent leg. He was hot-shoeing the animal and the smoky fumes from the shoe being fitted on the hard hoof rose up and spread its stench around. It always amazed me how most horses didn't react to the unmistakable aroma. What amazed me even more was that I hadn't recognised it in the cellar.

10

Some familiar landmarks, mostly pubs, helped me navigate. A girlfriend from years before had studied law, which meant her jockey-boyfriend used to travel from windswept racecourses to the inner city to pick her up at Blackhall Place. Often the car got parked and the pair of us just followed the student throng to one of the boozers that dotted the red-bricked side-streets leading away from the Liffey. It had made for a curious mix: well-bred youngsters mixing with professionals living in the vast blocks of newly built apartments and hardy local born-and-bred types looking down their noses from the bottom of the social ladder. Quite where a jockey with no interest in college and no familial financial nest-egg to sit back on fitted into all of it was a question for when having a good time wasn't the only focus.

Now that all the easy money was gone, the area was reverting to what it used to be. It took only a short walk behind the apartment blocks to rediscover the untidy streets and feel an air of neglect creeping back. It was just past seven in the evening, and still broad daylight, but already the hookers were starting to venture out to work. As I slowly drove around, searching for my own target, there were a number of hands waved at me. It was impossible not to notice their desperation, tiny skirts revealing pale, shivering legs, assorted bits of revealing clothes and all topped off by a hard-eyed determination to do what had to be done. As I turned a corner for the third time in half an hour, a figure jumped out in front of the car, forcing me to brake. She banged her fist on the passenger-seat window to make me lower it.

"Are you shy or something?" she asked in a heavy Dublin accent. "Let me in and I'll do it all. Whatever you want. Just a hundred quid."

"Look, I don't want to do anything," I said, making sure the central locking was on, and taking a quick peek in the rear mirror to make sure a police car wasn't taking down details. "But I need a steer."

"Seventy-five, then," she said.

I noticed the blotches and bruises on her skinny arms. She was obviously a junkie, feeding her habit any way possible.

"And no rubber, alright?" she added.

"Stop. Just listen to me," I said, scrambling in my pockets for cash. I pulled out a fifty-euro note and a tenner. "I've sixty quid. It's yours if you can tell me if you know a building around here, maybe a warehouse, or an old factory. It's got big old grey stone blocks that jut out a bit."

"Stone wha'?"

It hit me how ridiculous I must sound, asking for a grey building in a city of a million people. There was no point stopping now though.

"Stone blocks. Big stone walls, that stick out. Old style."

"Gimme the money, and I'll think."

I didn't have much choice. I leaned over with the notes and she snapped them out of my hand, stuffing the cash into a pocket in her jacket.

"Do you know what building I'm talking about?"

"There's loads of old places round here. They all look the same," she said scornfully.

I was about to wind the window back up and continue searching when she volunteered a little more information. It sounded like something she wouldn't normally do.

"There's a big one down by the army barracks. I suppose the walls are grey."

"Thanks."

"Give us another sixty and I'll suck you off."

"You're okay, thanks."

"Then piss off. You're scaring punters away. And you're fucking mad."

I couldn't disagree with her. How sane was it to be cruising around Smithfield looking for a grey building just because of a faint smell I thought I might have detected days before. The stench of hoof being hot-shod was unmistakable. But it could have come from anywhere. What I was banking on was the suspicion – and it was no more than that – about being in Dublin. There had definitely been the sound of traffic travelling slowly. The quays were a notorious bottleneck. There was also a hunch – and it was no more than that too – about the place being an old industrial place. And I'd checked out with the city authorities and found out that the famous monthly horse fair in Smithfied had taken place on the day I'd been lifted out of Annagrove. But the more I looked, the more tenuous my hunch seemed.

Only when on the verge of giving up did I get a break. An unmistakable figure emerged from a tiny shop as I was passing by. He was laden down with bags but they looked like trifles in Anto's enormous hands. The shock of seeing him was enough for me to accidentally gun the car's accelerator, making a noise that sounded like a rocket to my ears, and which had me checking the rear-view mirror as I sped down the street. However, there was no reaction from the big man as he turned a corner. I frantically turned around and had to fight the urge not to take the corner on two wheels. Instead I pulled in and watched Anto walk another hundred yards before entering a building. I gave it five minutes before driving slowly past. It was grey stone, and the dimpled pattern was as I remembered. There was a ridiculous feeling of accomplishment which quickly faded in the face of the problem of what to do next.

Figuring out a course of action hadn't even occurred to me. Finding this place was such a long shot that the practicalities didn't arise. I suddenly felt woefully inadequate. What was I going to do? Put on black gear and drop from the sky like some skinny James Bond? It was pathetic. It wasn't like I could call up a bunch of hotshot mates who'd join me in some vigilante assault: my mates were teachers, a dentist, a couple of computer geeks, fellas I'd known since primary school. And anyone I knew from racing wouldn't exactly possess the bulk to take on Anto and his pals. A wave of embarrassment swept over me like I hadn't felt since as a teenager a horse had run away with me at the Punchestown Festival. All I'd lost then was face. The stakes were a lot higher now.

I parked at the top of the street with a direct view of the building. It was a huge mass of grey but less of a factory and more of a mill. Either way it dominated this street. The square where the horse market was held was the guts of a mile away but the stench of horses being shod had carried all the way. Unless of course Cammie was being held in another grey-stone cellar.

It required almost a physical effort to put the thought out of my head and concentrate on something practical that could be done. Plans for the interior design of this place would be available somewhere in the Dublin City bureaucracy. The question was how long would it take to organise a look at them. And what would it achieve anyway? Doing nothing was impossible but doing something for the sake of it was plain stupid. It was then that a young guy on a moped pulled up outside the building, pulled what was clearly a pizza box out of a voluminous bag strapped across him and went straight inside – just pushed the door open. He emerged again a minute later and drove off. Doing something for the sake of it might be stupid but I found myself walking down the street anyway.

Riding racehorses had provided me with a reputation for courage that I never felt entitled to and which seemed ridiculous now. Racing was a choice, and the consequences of a freely entered-into activity were small cause for pity when they went wrong. The dangers on a racecourse were spread out in front of us, the same for everyone: fences, fallers, stray hooves, ground shooting up to meet you. There was an artificiality to the whole thing and a democracy to the risk. There was nothing remotely fair about what was happening to my wife and the concept would be alien to those holding her. My legs felt like they belonged to someone else as I approached.

Sure enough the door swung open easily. A short tiled

hallway was directly ahead and led to a wide elevator. To the right was a narrow stairway. I climbed some steps and looked up. There wasn't a sound. There didn't look to be any CCTV cameras hanging on the walls either, although that didn't mean there weren't any around. It felt like my heart was trying to burst a hole in my chest. I ran back down, wanting the comfort of the door and the possibility of escape it offered.

There was no certainty about it, but Cammie had said it felt like she was in a cellar. The sound of traffic had come from above too, or so I thought. Who knew what sort of distortion there might be. I tentatively approached the elevator, keeping an eye out for cameras and an even stronger ear out for any sound of someone approaching. Almost out of sight to the left was a door. It opened outward and there was a descending stairs into what seemed pitch-black darkness. I stood there staring into it when the elevator bell rang and its doors started to slide open. There was nothing else for it but to slip down the first few steps and close the door behind me.

Even standing there, desperately trying to adjust my eyes to the gloom, there was the realisation that I was in the right place. That whirr of the lift doors opening was exactly the same as when I'd sat with my back to the elevator, taking in every sound I could as Duggan's horror unfolded in front of me. There were voices outside but they quickly disappeared, probably outside to the street. That option seemed very attractive. It seemed to take an age but slowly my eyes started adjusting to the dark.

The place was massive. It must have been a store of some kind because the stairs descended twenty feet and it was the same distance wide. I gingerly went down and peered to my right. There were faint lights in the distance. But they could have been a couple of hundred metres away. Claustrophobia shouldn't have been a problem and yet the sensation of going down into such a vast area had me sweating like a pig. It was time to pull out of this funk. My shoes sounded loud. The sound reverberated off thick walls that shone like ones soaking in some terrible Victorian sewer picture and yet were completely dry to the touch.

After walking about fifty yards, a heavy iron door appeared to my right. The temptation to rap on it and shout for my wife was overwhelming but instead I kept going. Sure enough, ten yards later was another door. As my eyes adjusted even more, I could see there were corresponding doors on the other side of the passageway. There must have been at least twenty of them if the ratio was correct. And who knew where this vast cavern kept going to? There could be a bend at the end of this straight bit, leading off somewhere else. It was then that the familiar whirr sounded again.

I dropped to the floor, pressing my face into the hard surface. A light was switched on around a bend and a man I didn't recognise turned the corner. He was carrying a pizza box, presumably the one I'd seen dropped off earlier. He strolled down, giving the impression he was put out at having to perform such a menial task. I prayed his attention wouldn't suddenly pick up. He stopped at a door and started rooting out a set of keys from his pocket. The clang as he inserted them in the steel lock echoed around the subterranean gloom.

"Coming in!" he shouted.

Would he extend that courtesy to a man, I wondered. He disappeared from view. His shoes sounded like they were descending stone steps. I jumped onto my heels, still crouching, and sprinted to just outside the door as silently as possible. There wasn't a murmur from below and it felt like an age before steps started climbing towards me.

I sensed rather than saw him. He was a blur, just a shape filling the doorway. My fist caught him square in the mouth. I could hear and feel teeth being broken. Fighting had never been my thing but I knew the first strike was all-important and any fancy big swings were a waste of time.

He fell back down the steps and had barely hit the floor before I was on him. His automatic reaction to fight back was quick but just not quick enough. I caught him with my fist again into the side of the head, then another one into the eye. The swings were wild with desperation now but enough of them got through. And when I sprang to my feet and caught him with some kicks to the head, he wasn't going to recover. I dropped to my knees next to him, utterly exhausted.

"Lorcan?"

I couldn't say a thing. She was huddled in a corner, clearly frightened out of her wits, and staring incredulously at her blood-spattered husband desperately trying to get his breath back. Her clothes were different: a cheap blue tracksuit instead of the flimsy T-shirt. That wonderful long hair was straggled and dirty but she looked to be alright. She practically crawled across the floor and I grabbed her in my arms. We clung together for a few seconds until I pushed her away.

"We have to hurry," I said, getting up stiffly with the heavy keys in my hand. "Just stick with me, alright?"

She nodded. We climbed the steps and I glanced fearfully both ways outside. There was nothing there. A low groan from behind us made Cammie jump. There was no time for niceties. I kicked him in the head again, grabbed Cammie's hand and bolted. It didn't seem possible we could get away without being seen. But then it hadn't seemed possible getting this far. She stuck to me like glue. We got to the door leading out to the hallway. There were voices. I pushed her back a couple of steps and kept the door just ajar enough to hear.

Anto's voice echoed around. "I'm getting really tired of those two pricks arguing with each other over every little fucking thing," he boomed.

"They're just bored, baby-sitting that bird," another voice said.

"That's what they're being paid to do," Anto responded. "Jesus, how cushy do they want it? All they have to do is sit there."

The lift doors opened again and they stepped inside. As soon as it started whirring upwards, I grabbed Cammie's hand and ran.

Nothing had ever tasted sweeter right then than the inner-city air as we dashed down the street towards my car. We got there by the time Anto's shouts reached us.

"Wayne, grab the car now!" he bellowed, pushing one man on his way and grabbing another. "You, get up there after them!"

My hands were sweating and I was acutely aware of the figure sprinting towards us. Cammie whimpered with fear. I gunned the engine into life and careered towards the man running towards us. He tried to swerve. I didn't. There was a thud and a blur as the heavy figure bounced on to the bonnet at the last second and bumped onto the windscreen before falling sideways. I could see Anto stepping nonchalantly onto the footpath and staring at us as we sped past.

"Keep an eye behind us and tell me if you see them," I told Cammie.

"You think they're going to follow us?"

"Bound to, if we can't slip them."

I turned right and made for the river, glancing in the mirror every few seconds. We both swore as a white Mercedes swung after us and started to make ground. I swore again when lights at an intersection turned red and a car in front of us dutifully obeyed the signal to stop. There was nothing else for it. We pulled out to overtake. I pressed the horn and prayed nothing was coming too fast. Speed didn't turn out to be a problem. A car turning left into our path was barely doing twenty. But it was enough to make me bounce onto the footpath. Thankfully no one was walking there. Cammie screamed and various horns blew as we bounced back onto the road. Even more luck meant we avoided everything.

The Mercedes wasn't as lucky. It squeezed between the two cars and made for a gap between two others travelling across its path. Our pursuers made the gap but were then ploughed into by a large van going the other way. The last I saw was the van driver getting out, gesticulating wildly, and Anto banging his fist off the front passenger dashboard. It would be an unfair contest if it came to blows. But that was someone else's problem. I turned left and drove.

11

She clung to me as never before, wanting me like never before. There was a wildness to us that was almost scary, a primal need to hold and touch and taste. Cammie said little, simply looked at me in a way I remembered so well, and poured her fear into banishing the world away from us for even just a few hours. Everything was so wonderfully familiar and yet different. No doubt it was a reaction to so much fear and anxiety, a fundamental need to renew some control over our lives. But such cold analysis could wait.

There was nothing gentle about our love. She urged me with an unambiguous need that I responded to aggressively. There was a desire to punish as much as comfort. Too much had happened in such a short space of time to leave anything but a maelstrom of emotions that threatened nearly to hurt us.

I woke up slowly and looked around. It was another hotel room, standard plain, and on the outskirts of the city. It was light outside but only streaks of it beamed through a gap in the curtains. A noise had woken me up but I didn't know what. Then the knock on the door came again. I got up silently and padded towards it. A glance through the peep-hole didn't reveal any menace, just an elderly gentleman in a white shirt and black tie.

"Sir, you insisted on getting a personal wake-up call at five thirty," he said, leaving no doubt that I was being indulged.

"Thanks," I replied. "We're up."

He strolled away and I turned and tried to stretch the stiffness and tiredness out of my naked body. In the middle of a stretch that had me contorted on the floor, Cammie woke drowsily.

"That's a hell of a vision to wake up to," she said.

That long brown body that had tantalised me to distraction just a few hours previously was spread across the bed, just a thin sheet covering her bottom half. She pushed herself up on her elbow with a smile on her face.

"Sorry," I said, standing up. "If I don't stretch a bit, all the old racing injuries play up."

"I know," she said.

I went to the bathroom for a towel to tie around my waist.

"We have to get ready," I said to her. "The plane will be at the aerodrome in half an hour. Have you tried on that stuff?"

We'd stopped the previous day for clothes and essentials. Going back to Annagrove was not a runner. Neither was making contact with family or friends. There was no point putting them at any sort of risk. Cammie understood only too well. All she wanted was to see Max. It wouldn't be long before she did. I had got in touch with my parents and told them to get on the first flight to Paris. My dad sounded more than a little miffed at being steered around Europe. He wasn't a man used to being told what to do. But I promised to explain once we met up in France and my mum had seemed to pick up on the anxiety in my voice. They had booked a flight into Charles De Gaulle that would land early in the afternoon. We would be there to meet them in plenty of time.

The idea of Duggan having people at the airport wasn't so unlikely, I reckoned, and I'd abused the Weinberger account with the private plane company again. They would have an aircraft available to take us to France at one of the tiny airfields near the city at six in the morning.

We left the hotel after I'd paid a month in advance to keep the car in the underground car-park and got a taxi. Sure enough the sleek, white jet was literally pulling to a halt at the same time as us.

"Good morning. Welcome aboard," said the pilot whose name I couldn't remember.

"Good morning, Claudio. How are you?" Cammie enquired.

"Very good, thank you, Mrs Donovan. It's always a pleasure to see you."

She couldn't have flown on this thing more than twice before and yet she remembered the pilot's name. It was that kind of touch that made people warm to her. I admired her for it too. Damn Thorpe. And damn her too for being so stupid.

We strapped in and waited for take-off. Cammie hated flying: not enough to stop her getting on planes but enough usually to insist on a couple of swift vodkas before take-off. There was no alcohol here. Instead she leaned over and put her hand on mine. It felt extraordinarily intimate, much more so than anything that had happened the previous night. I hesitated – just for a second. She sensed it too. She kept her hand there, though, and it felt completely normal to entwine my fingers in hers as the powerful engines gunned down the runway.

Marc-Pierre met us at the tiny airstrip. The familiar battered jeep was waiting on the runway. Clearly the normal rules of customs, clearance or any other bureaucracy didn't apply to a Dutroit. Behind the scruffy jeans and nondescript vehicle lay an indifference to appearances that came from being a member of one of France's oldest and wealthiest racing families. I'd phoned him the previous day, desperate and unsure of what I wanted or needed. The response was immediate and unequivocal: get our Irish asses over there.

"Ah, Cam, you look as gorgeous as ever," he smiled, guiding her down the few steps and delivering a big hug.

I followed quickly, waved to the pilot and strode to the jeep. I jumped into the backseat, behind the other two.

"Right, you are coming with me to Chantilly. It is only half an hour away. You can wait there until you go for Max. Then, when you are all united, you will head for Normandy," Marc-Pierre said.

"I'm sorry about all this," I said.

"Nonsense. I have a place on the coast near St Aubin-Sur-Mer. It's been in my family for years. But my ex-wife never knew about it," he grinned. "Or at least I thought she didn't. It became an expensive secret."

Cammie smiled back. I shifted about uneasily in the back. I'd told Marc-Pierre I needed a quiet, out-of-the-way place for a few weeks. He hadn't asked why. I'd also made a couple of other strange requests. He said he'd see what he could do. As we drove through Chantilly, I gave thanks for the French ability to live and let live.

French racing's equivalent to the Curragh and Newmarket was typically busy. The thousands of racehorses here required the same amount of intensive labour as anywhere but everything was being carried out at a different pace: a speed dictated by the importance of morning coffee. Marc-Pierre waved to, and beeped his horn at, various people, wound a window down to others, and generally gave no impression there might be a couple of hundred horses back at the yard requiring his attention. When we pulled to a halt in front of the chateau that had housed Dutroits for a couple of centuries, he even helped us with a couple of bags and informed the housekeeper to brew up coffee.

"Out there," he said, pointing out a window to a much more modern SUV. "That's yours for the duration – however long you need."

He was playing a blinder, more than enough to warrant some sort of explanation.

"I think I should tell you at least something of what's going on –" I started.

"My father always said nothing good ever came of being told only part of a story," he interrupted. "Just so long as the blood and the footprints don't lead back here."

Cammie was practically vibrating with anticipation so we didn't stay long and instead made the short journey to the airport. Nothing was said on the trip. Normally she liked to grab my hand and place it between her thighs in a gesture that was as sexy as hell when we first met and had over time become as much of a reassurance as anything else. We didn't do it now. We made our way through the crowds and checked that the flight from Athens was on time. It was. Another quick cup of coffee later and we joined the crowd waiting at arrivals.

Max looked bigger, his face lightly tanned, and a little more knowing, as he bounced through the gates between his granny and granddad. When he saw his mum he ran towards her with a solidity I hadn't noticed before. She swept him up and covered his face with kisses until he protested.

"Hey, you little bugger, don't be giving out about kisses!" my dad said, clasping my shoulder.

I kissed my mum on both cheeks and hugged her.

"You look thin, Lorcan, are you okay?" she asked.

"I'm fine, Mum. Thank you so much for everything."

"Don't be ridiculous. We had a great time. I just wish you were as well behaved at the same age as our grandson. Hello, Cammie."

"Hi, Susan. Thank you so much for taking such good care of my little man."

"Well, we have to take care of our men," my mum replied.

"Now then, what's next on this tour of Europe?" my dad interjected. "I trust we won't have to indulge in anything as dreary as driving."

"I'm afraid so," I said. "How do you guys feel about a week or two in Normandy?"

There weren't any objections, although it was plainly on the tip of my father's tongue to ask what the hell was going on. I gave him a look which hopefully suggested to the two of them that I'd fill them in soon. I would too.

We piled bags and people into Marc-Pierre's SUV, which even had room to spare at the end. Max insisted on helping me, never stopped getting in the way, and earned the tightest hug in history at the end.

"Okay, let's go," I said, and pointed the vehicle north.

A couple of hours later, and despite a number of coffee and toilet breaks, we started to circle Caen and make for the sea. Since Jake had hired me, I'd made any number of trips to Normandy, scouting the many stud farms that dotted the flat landscape. The neat square fields and tall cypress trees gave a distinctive look to the area that had my art-loving mum cooing about light. She sat in the back with Cammie, Max strategically strapped in between them. After that initial thrust at the airport, the two women appeared to settle on a temporary truce, chattering away and clucking over the little boy demanding their attention.

Dad was in the front passenger seat, pronouncing the French signposts, and relishing the sounds. After getting around Caen, the roads got smaller and slower and signposts started appearing, giving directions to various World War II cemeteries dotted around.

"You know, this St Aubin we're going to is where the Canadians came ashore on D-Day," he said.

A career spent working in a bank hadn't come close to providing enough of an intellectual challenge to a sharp brain that soaked up historical detail and political nuance like a sponge. This area was like a paradise to him, except it didn't seem like one he was overly enjoying.

"Everything alright?" I asked.

"Yes," he said, quietly. "We really are a bloody awful creature though. Look at what we're capable of doing to each other. God knows how many thousands are lying here. And for what?"

There didn't seem much to say to that. Cruelty wasn't exactly unique to any period. The only difference here was scale. I noticed an American military cemetery was just a couple of kilometres to our right.

"Would you like to see it, Dad?"

"Yes."

We parked. Cammie said she'd stay with Max who'd fallen asleep. But Mum came with us. It was remarkable the mix of emotions the place provoked. Admiration at how perfectly kept it was couldn't come close to diluting the overwhelming sadness and regret that hung over us like a heavy pall. The massive lines of small crosses seemed never-ending. The scale of it all was overwhelming.

"Mum. Dad. I'd better tell you what's been happening."

They turned from gazing at the crosses and stared at me, apprehensive.

I hated burdening them but it was necessary. It sounded more than a little surreal but I ploughed on, leaving out some of the more grisly aspects of Duggan's behaviour, playing down some of the implications, but basically spelling out the picture. Mum's thin, elegant face dropped a number of times and she grabbed my hand almost in reassurance that I was okay.

"Dear God, poor Jake!" she gasped. "What can we do?"

"You're doing it. Believe me," I told her. "You can't believe how valuable it was knowing Max was safe with you."

"I was wondering what the hell was going on," Dad said. "It's not like you to be ringing up in a flap and sticking us on to private jets. Not that I object to the last part."

He grinned and gave my shoulder a squeeze and left me grateful yet again for having them as parents. How valuable had it been growing up knowing they were there – how valuable it was still. Max deserved the same. We walked straight back to Cammie who got a heartfelt hug from my mum.

"How awful for you! Lorcan's just told us. We're here for you, darling. Don't ever doubt that."

It was a lot more voluble in the back as we drove on, Mum asking questions and declaring the world wasn't half settled. Dad kept his questions minimal and they were basically a variation on asking what I was proposing to do now. I shrugged a few times for the simple reason that I didn't know.

Marc-Pierre's love-nest wasn't so much a hideaway as a replica of his chateau in Chantilly. But it was secluded. The small town of St Aubin was just a couple of kilometres away but it might as well have been a hundred. A long avenue brought us to the front door, which was shielded on all sides by high, thick hedges that were at least a dozen feet high. I pulled up next to a big car parked outside the front door.

Two men climbed out. Both had military tight haircuts and looked to be about the same age as me. Physically they were very different. One was short and wiry, his deeply tanned face taut with the evidence of extreme physical fitness. His colleague was huge, biceps and chest muscles straining at a T-shirt he wore on top of jeans that looked like they were specially made to accommodate years of accumulated body-building. Together they looked eminently frightening and capable.

"Monsieur Donovan. I am Manolo and this is my colleague Sebastian," the shorter man said, shaking hands with me.

Sebastian barely acknowledged my nod and stared off into some unknown distance, hands stuffed into pockets. Manolo was a lot more chatty, shaking hands with my father and saying hello to Cammie and my mum.

"Monsieur Dutroit gave us minimal instructions. Simply told us to come here and you would explain your requirements," he said in good but heavily accented English.

Marc-Pierre had taken me aside earlier in the day, informing me that an idle if desperate need expressed by me less than ten hours previously, to have some muscle of my own, would be met at St Aubin.

"A family like mine makes connections that might not be suitable for public consumption but which are nevertheless useful," he said. "These men are very useful. The best of the best that our armed forces provides. It has been to my good fortune in the past that they now operate on a more private basis."

I moved aside to talk to Manolo, just as Max trotted up to the enormous Sebastian and looked up. The big man didn't budge. But there was an almost imperceptible wink and my boy grinned in response.

"Thank you for getting here on such short notice," I said to Manolo. "I don't know how much you've been told but basically I need my family protected. For the next three weeks. There are people in Dublin who aren't above harming them to get at me and to get what they want."

"What kind of people? Criminals? Or more political?"

"This is purely criminal."

"Who knows you are here?"

"Just Marc-Pierre. I've told no one else."

"Good. Maintain that, please."

"I don't know what the arrangement is financially," I said. "Or how you want to be paid."

He pulled out a card with bank account details written on it.

"We cost two thousand euro a day each. If you can

transfer one week's pay, twenty-eight thousand euro, into that account immediately, then we will begin work. The rest can be paid once the job is over. Agreed?"

"Yes, I will do it straight away. And thank you."

"Don't thank us. This is our job."

The house was magnificent. It stretched backwards from a vast, open area inside the front door that easily accommodated a wide staircase leading up to six tastefully furnished bedrooms. The sweep of the house was backwards rather than sideways, making it physically much larger than might be guessed from the outside. It was enough to have my father chuckling with appreciation.

"We bags this bedroom!" I heard him shout, quickly followed by Max yelling: "Like this one!"

I spent some minutes arranging for the money to get into Manolo's account – Jake's credit card was really taking a battering but I could repay later – and by the time I finished, Mum had managed to produce a pot of coffee in the vast kitchen.

"I think we might be able to survive here for a while," she smiled. "But you and your father need to go and do a shop for some essentials."

"Sure thing," I replied. "Thanks again, for everything. It's terrible putting you guys in the firing line like this. But you've been great."

"What firing line?" she said. "This place is beautiful, we have our grandson and we're being useful. This is wonderful. Those gurriers back in Dublin might as well be on the moon. They wouldn't even think of coming to a place like this."

"Thanks, Mum."

"I'm very proud of you, Lorcan," she said, coming

round the kitchen island to put her hand on my face. "Cammie filled me in on what you didn't say happened. This Duggan man sounds dreadful. And what he is doing is deplorable. But if we keep our heads, it will be over soon."

"I know, Mum," I said, squeezing her hand. "You'd better write out a list of what we need. And I'll go get it."

Max and his granddad were too busy exploring the garden to consider getting back into the SUV but Cammie said she would cook dinner that night and didn't trust me to get all the ingredients right. We were walking out the front door when Manolo appeared in front of us.

"Your payment has been confirmed, Monsieur Donovan. *Merci*. Where are you going?"

"We have to get some groceries for the house and to keep everyone fed," I said.

"Then I will come with you."

"Please, there's no need," Cammie said. "What we really need is for Max and his grandparents to be looked after. We don't need bodyguards."

"She's right," I said. "I don't think there's any danger for us in St Aubin."

Manolo shrugged and stepped aside.

Late evening sunshine was almost blinding, making the heavy air feel like a physical thing to have to battle through. Even the fat bees seemed to be buzzing in a low gear, lazily lifting off from the vast diversity of flowers around us. Max ran around a corner, laughing delightedly. I waited to ask his granddad if he had changed his mind about shopping but instead Sebastian lurched around, bent over, clucking like a chicken with his hands outstretched. He straightened up with a scowl on his face when he saw us but, after Max grabbed his hand, waved goodbye, and dragged the big man over to where Granddad was furtively puffing on a cigarette, there was a base rumble that was a more than adequate impression of laughter.

It took only minutes to drive into the small town, find a car-park and walk down the thankfully shady narrow streets onto the promenade at the sea. We turned our faces to the cool sea breeze and took the first breaths in some time that weren't full of stress. The tide was out and the beach stretched away for a couple of hundred metres, probably the same as that fateful morning when Canadian soldiers lumbered off their landing craft on D-Day and tossed their lives to the fates. It hardly seemed credible that such madness could occur in such a place. Behind us, a café served a number of elderly men and women carefully wrapped up against the evening sunshine and wind.

"You've thought of everything," Cammie said, finally. "With the bodyguards, I mean."

"It's all Marc-Pierre's doing," I replied.

"I would have said before that it was all a bit much, but not now."

"Was it awful back there, in Dublin?"

"It wasn't great. I was just so scared. They didn't actually harm me or anything. It got a bit better when they gave me that tracksuit to wear. At least it wasn't so cold all the time."

"You did great."

"I couldn't believe it yesterday. God, it doesn't even seem like yesterday. When you came in like that and pounded that awful man. I was so scared he'd get back up."

"You and me both."

We walked along the promenade for a little bit, then I

asked a woman in schoolboy French where there was a supermarket, which we found with little difficulty. After off-loading our packed trolley into the car we returned to the café on the beach. We didn't say much, but the silences were comfortable.

"We'd better get back and feed everyone," Cammie said eventually.

We walked back to the car. She put her hand in mine and I let her. Behind us there was a shadowy flicker, the same as I'd noticed a couple of times earlier, darting down streets but keeping us in view the whole time. Manolo mightn't have remained invisible but considering how my senses were so on edge his trailing abilities were impressive. They were also reassuring.

Max was about to fall asleep by the time we got back, exhausted from all the running around. His granddad promised to take him to the beach which earned him a "God bless Granddad" in night-time prayers. There was even a "God bless Sebastian". That had us grinning and by the time we had got to the bedroom door the little man was already asleep.

It took Cammie no time at all to rustle up a curry that we ate, with German lager, in the vast garden as darkness started to fall. She insisted on our two protectors joining us. Manolo dithered but it was the big man who mumbled thanks and manoeuvred his massive frame into an almost amusingly small and rickety garden chair at the end of the large wooden table.

"Sebastian tells me he was in the Foreign Legion," Dad announced. "La Légion Étrangère. Spent his time pounding around bare sand in Chad and any other number of god-forsaken dumps."

This provoked a slight grin and little else. Manolo sat at the other end of the table, chatting easily to Cammie about curry ingredients, and looking much more to the manor born in the same smart sports jacket he had worn while tailing us in St Aubin. I noticed a strap on his left shoulder when he leaned forward to get some bread. It hardly took a genius to figure out what it was carrying.

The two men finished up, told us one of them would be patrolling the house during the night, and not to worry. There was such an air of competence about them that I was prepared to take them at their word. Despite everyone's exhaustion we stayed outside in the increasing cold and drank another couple of beers. They tasted wonderful. I looked at my parents squabbling amiably over something silly and wanted very much to feel that ease again with the woman sitting opposite me at the table. A lot of the stress and anxiety had left her face, to be replaced by an understandable fatigue. But the smile was back. She indulged my father's awful jokes, drank enthusiastically from a bottle and glanced often towards an upstairs window where Max's nightlight cast a blue glow against the glass.

"I'll say one thing for you two. You certainly lead more exciting lives than banking," Dad said, standing up, stretching and nodding to Mum. "I'm knackered, and there's an extremely expensive Norman pillow in there with my name on it. Goodnight, folks. Don't worry. Everything will be fine."

There were a couple of bottles left. I opened them and we sat there, drinking in this new tranquillity. It felt so good, just to be able to sit, and drink, and listen. The only interruption was a flurry from bats launching expeditions from a nearby outhouse. And Sebastian's vast frame occasionally coming into view. He'd obviously drawn the first shift.

"I'm going to bed," Cammie said suddenly.

She walked into the kitchen and shortly after a light come on upstairs. I sat and looked around this oasis of calm and ached for it to be real. The mobile phone in my pocket was off but switching it on resulted in instant lists of messages and missed calls from the outside world clamouring for attention. I looked at a few of the texts. One was from Judith. Jake was still in the ICU – no change. Even the luminous impersonal letters seemed tired as I read. There were any number of messages from reporters and the office back in Ireland. There was even one from Gerry Gunning, reporting Kentish Town to be flying in his work and noticeably making no reference to his race jockey. There was nothing from angry gangsters promising to wreak havoc.

I finished my drink, and tried and failed to find Sebastian before slowly climbing upstairs. Max was snoring soundly in the massive double-bed that we'd put spare pillows around in case he somehow made it to the edge and fell out. The wooden floor creaked loudly when I took a step inside so I backed out, not wanting to risk waking him up. My parents' room was directly across. There was no sound from there.

The room I'd thrown my bag into a few hours earlier was at the end of the corridor. Cammie's room was before it. A light was still on and the door was ajar. I hesitated outside, just stood there. And then went in, closing the door behind me.

12

Clancy strode towards me in the Lingfield parade ring with the same cocksure strut as always. There were only five runners in the upcoming Derby Trial race so the big green area was pretty empty. I stood on my own, watching Jake's runner, Royal Armada, stalk around. He was a big rangy chestnut we had bought in Kentucky as a yearling for over a million dollars with the aim of moulding him into a Derby contender. Bartholomew Montgomery had got him to this stage, now the colt had to go and earn a Derby place.

The trainer wasn't present, having succumbed to a bout of glandular fever that meant complete rest and a rare hiatus in a life where horses comprised every waking thought. A brief phone call the previous day contained instructions to Clancy that lasting out the mile-and-a-half trip was not a sure thing, and to nurse him home. Then Bartie had hung up abruptly to face some high-temperature misery. On the whole it appeared a better option in the misery-stakes than facing the squat figure approaching.

There was no scornful grin this time. And there was no mistaking the anger in his eyes. All around us, civilised people in civilised hats made civil conversation at this picturesque and leafy racecourse in affluent Surrey. Nothing like pretence existed among the Royal Armada camp, although nothing obvious to the outside world.

"You stupid cunt," he growled.

I glanced down into that hard face. Clancy wasn't the brightest but he wasn't going to attract attention to himself by doing anything here. Nevertheless, there was more than just contempt in the way he stared back. If I hadn't known better there almost seemed to be some anxiety mixed into his temper.

"Why the fuck did you do that? All you've done is make him angry," he seethed under his breath.

"Bartie wants you to be patient with this horse and —"

"Fuck this horse, fuck Bartie, and fuck you, you stupid prick!" he blurted out, face redder than I'd ever seen it before. "There was nothing to it. Just wait until after the Derby and everything would be fine. But you have to go all fucking Lone Ranger. Do you have any idea what you've done?"

"I got my wife away from you, that's what I did. And you can tell Duggan there is no way I'm going to damage Jake. So he can relax about the Derby."

The crowd around the parade ring was sparse but there was still no need to be drawing attention to ourselves by having a stand-up row. And my reference to the Derby seemed to mollify Clancy enough that he didn't say any more. Instead we waited for the bell to ring for mounting up and he was legged up on to Royal Armada's back.

As he left to canter the short distance to the start, I felt relieved at Clancy's display. Such obvious temper indicated he, and presumably Duggan's other people, had been wrong-footed. If they'd known more, like about where Cammie was now, then the little man would hardly have been so angry. But that was a presumption, and uneasiness at leaving them behind in St Aubin just a day after taking them there still bubbled in my stomach.

My hand was forced by increasing media speculation about Clancy that my lack of contactability was only fuelling. In my absence, Gerry Gunning had been plagued by queries about the jockey's Guineas ride and his view on who should ride Kentish Town in the Derby. Gerry's increasingly terse "no comments" only increased the information vacuum that any amount of wild speculation rushed to fill. It was helping nobody, least of all Jake in his New York hospital bed, so I'd come to Lingfield, where I knew all the top racing hacks would be for the Trial. After a circuitous journey, by train back to Paris, the Eurostar to London, and a taxi to the racetrack, I'd materialised in Lingfield's Press Room trying desperately to appear unconcerned.

"Ladies and gents," I announced, light-heartedly, "apologies all round. I've been out of commission. Glandular fever, I'm afraid. In fact you might all want to keep your distance."

There was no such luck. I grabbed a chair and invited them to ask whatever they wanted. By and large I liked the press crowd. There were a few buoyed by pomposity, others who operated on a hair-trigger propensity for believing the worst of everyone's motivation, but there was also a passion for the game that was impossible to ignore. I'd known plenty of them in England from winning the National and once the tape-recorders were off there were plenty who were a good laugh. Even when the recorders were on there was usually a good-natured decorum to their enquiries, underpinned by the realisation we weren't exactly dealing with a subject of vital public importance. Interest yes, but hardly life and death – usually.

"Lorcan, what's the Weinberger take on Clancy's Guineas ride?" asked the old gent from *The Times*, lobbing in a gentle opener.

"I think if Mike had the race to ride again, he'd do it all very differently," I replied. "He'll tell you himself it was hardly his finest hour, but there were many glittering hours before that. We're not going to finish a long and successful partnership over one ride."

"Don't you have a duty to the betting public to be less blasé about this?" chipped in a young tabloid reporter whose name I couldn't remember but whose speciality was a mannered righteous indignation on behalf of the betting-shop punter.

"I think the Weinberger horses are just the type that the betting public like," I said. "They are always trying, always run to win and have been an adornment to the industry for years now. How many races have you ridden in?"

I hated taking such a tack. It was a hoary old argument, that you had to have ridden yourself in order to criticise jockeys, and one that would have cut the ground from underneath any number of good judges whose opinion I respected completely. But needs must, and it was important that a good front was put up. My interrogator said he'd ridden none, and I tried to lighten the atmosphere.

"Look, jockeys make mistakes. No one wishes more than I do that Clancy had picked a handicap at Pontefract to mess up in, rather than a classic, but that's the reality."

"But the rumour-mill is full of –"

"Full of what?" I countered. "Whispers that he wasn't trying? Come on, you know those kinds of suggestions are always out there."

"Clancy seems to attract a lot of them though," said a sharp-eyed columnist from the trade paper. "There are plenty fellas out there, Lorcan, who will tell you he's as bent as an S-hook."

"Any of them prepared to go on record?" I asked, in as neutral a tone as possible. "You throw enough at the wall, some will stick."

"So you're happy for Clancy to ride Kentish Town in the Derby?"

"That's the plan. Mike Clancy rides Kentish Town," I said, and left it at that.

A few of them thanked me for going out of my way to come in and brief them and I said no problem while feeling like any kind of louse. Credibility was an ephemeral thing in racing, a sport where believing the worst wasn't just the preserve of tabloid journos. A punter with a losing docket never had a shortage of people to blame: the jockey stopped the horse, or the trainer couldn't get it fit, or the owner was stroking the odds for another day. There was hardly a need to encourage such prejudices and yet here I was feeding these people bullshit about mistakes and a great partnership while all the time Jake was lying in a hospital bed with only technology keeping him from death because a little scumbag and his gangster handler wanted to get their hands on more dirty money.

The little scumbag could still ride though. Sublime talent can reside in the most inadequate of vessels, I thought as I stood in the stands, peering through binoculars.

Watching Clancy nurse the half a ton of wilful thorough-bred that was Royal Armada was like witnessing a piano virtuoso manipulate keys to his will. The horse broke from the stalls with all the gusto that eight months of a racecourse absence could generate. But without changing his hands on the reins, Clancy eased him back to the rear of the small field, subtle signals and an absence of movement managing to subdue Royal Armada's instinctive wish to run.

Coming down the steep hill into the straight, the little figure didn't rush, allowing the colt under him to figure out the unusual gradient and tight bend for himself before only then asking a question. Far from stamina being a problem, Royal Armada appeared to relish the long straight and after overhauling the leader a furlong out kept galloping to such purpose he was five lengths clear of his rivals at the line. In spite of everything, I could feel my heart racing faster and there was a smile on my face while making the short walk from stands to the winner's enclosure. That million-dollar purchase price didn't seem so extravagant now. Royal Armada might not have the raw class of Kentish Town but he stayed, acted on the track, and would clearly improve for the outing. Team Weinberger had another Derby candidate, it seemed.

The horse came back, sweating, blowing and clearly full of himself. Clancy slid the saddle off, looked at the stamping colt carefully and unclipped his helmet.

"He isn't bad – actually stayed really well. Epsom might come a bit soon but the Curragh a few weeks after might suit him," he told me.

It was similar to any number of post-race debriefs we'd had before: straightforward, professional, dispassionate. None of the hacks standing just a few yards away would have noticed anything different about us – proof, in its own way, that appearances at a racecourse are more deceptive than most places. I turned to my inquisitors, expressed satisfaction with Royal Armada and emphasised my satisfaction with Mike Clancy's ride. On its own terms, it didn't take any effort, which made it even more of a pity that it was only a fraction of the true picture.

"Can we expect to see Jake Weinberger at Epsom for this horse?" one of the journos asked.

"I certainly hope he will be at Epsom. It would be great if his health allows," I said. "But Kentish Town is very much our number one hope."

What I didn't tell them was that the number one hope was going to have his first serious piece of work since the Guineas the following morning. Sunday morning workouts weren't usual but Gerry was keen to keep any prying eyes to a minimum as the horse worked over ten furlongs. It would be another quarter mile in the Derby on top of that but a stiff gallop up the Curragh would tell us a lot about Kentish Town's stamina. That, and some rather plaintive comments from Gerry about all the unwanted attention, was more than enough to send me to a flight from Gatwick to Dublin. But it wasn't the only reason.

I'd called in a favour with one of the racing hacks in Ireland. His paper also employed the news reporter whose name had featured on plenty of the more substantive archive pieces on Pinkie Duggan. It took a few calls to finally get Niall Doherty on the other end of a phone but he'd agreed to meet me in Dublin.

A couple of hours later, a taxi ride into the city centre and a short walk brought me to a quietly fancy side-street café.

Bright evening sunshine had large crowds of people walking past a small seated area outside where a tall, well-built man a little younger than myself was expertly tucking into some tagliatelle.

"You're paying for this, by the way," he said, indicating the tagliatelle, apparently not needing an introduction.

He didn't look or sound how I had expected. His accent was expensive Dublin and the suit he was wearing wasn't cheap off-the-peg either. Niall Doherty looked like he would be more comfortable at a golf club than tracking down gangsters but apparently he was highly regarded for his contacts and ability to nose out a story. I sat down, ordered a coffee, and asked if he'd like one.

"Since you're buying, I'll go instead for a half-bottle of the best Merlot," he said. "I'm sure you can rise to that."

"Of course," I replied, nodded to the waiter and waited until he had left. "Thanks for meeting me like this. I need a steer on an individual you might know."

"Who?"

"Pinkie Duggan."

He shot a glance at me and then applied himself again to his tagliatelle. "Why would someone like you be interested in Pinkie?"

"I'm not. But there's someone I know who is under some pressure from this guy and unloaded on me," I said, lying just as fluently as earlier at Lingfield. "I'd like to help him out but something tells me it might blow up in my face."

Doherty shrugged, not revealing if he believed me or not, or cared. He waited while a waiter poured his wine and paused for a couple next to us to pay up and leave.

"Okay, what do you want to know?"

"How dangerous is he?"

"Oh, about as dangerous as any homicidal maniac, but with the added bonus of intelligence."

"Is that an exaggeration?"

"No." He swirled his Merlot and then looked straight at me. "All this is strictly off the record, right?"

I nodded.

"That guy Moriarty in sport who put you in touch with me says you're alright, so I'll level with you. But if this blows up in *my* face, I'll know who to come to."

"Strictly a steer."

"Pinkie Duggan presents this image of a businessman about town and he has put a lot of his loot into legitimate stuff. But the root of it all is dodgy. You name it, he's got a finger stuck in it, if you'll excuse the pun. You know why he's called Pinkie?"

"Yes."

"Oh. A lot of people put that down to urban myth, but I can guarantee you it isn't. It's like his calling card. There are people out there, real hard men, who're absolutely terrified of Duggan. He really doesn't give a shit. About anything. Anyone who gets in his way either gets hurt or vanishes. I take it you also know his ace in the hole with all this?"

"No."

Doherty looked pleased. He drank deeply from his glass and looked around, a little theatrically, I reckoned, before leaning closer.

"What's the most organised, dangerous and best-armed gang in the country?"

"I don't know. You're the expert."

"It hardly takes expertise to figure that out. The freedom fighters haven't gone away, you know."

"You mean the Provos?"

"Please. We don't use such terms about our new bastions of respectability – these people are our political betters now," he said, grinning slyly.

"What's the link to Duggan?"

"He's a patriot too. Or a volunteer, whatever they called themselves years ago up there. I don't know how high up the chain he was but he did get to know some very influential people. The story goes that he had to break for the border in a hurry and started working for himself rather than the cause down here. He brought some rather brutal methods with him. It didn't take him long to build up quite the empire but he's always flown under the radar. Most of my colleagues are too shit-scared to even mention his name. No one's ever going to admit it but in return for a percentage of all this drugs, prostitution and racketeering money, Duggan gets a nice Republican umbrella to continue doing whatever the hell he wants."

"How come you're not shit-scared of him?"

"Oh, don't worry, I am. I have been informed that the first chance that presents itself will see me get a bullet," he said with a flourish of bravado. He presented the threat like it was a boast. "But what I have on my side is that guy standing over there."

He pointed across the road to a man standing outside a shop window, wearing shades and a suit that looked to be too heavy for comfort in the evening sunshine. Doherty waved but his pal didn't respond.

"Police protection, twenty-four hours a day," Doherty said proudly, with the well-practised timing of someone who had told the story a lot. "Costs the state a bloody fortune, but God bless the Irish taxpayer. I'd be dead without them."

"And it's Duggan who's after you?"

"Not just him. But he is one of the scrotes out there who would just love to shut me up," he said, a little more quietly. "It's almost like a corporate thing they've got going on between them about me and another couple of reporters. It would be a feather in a few caps if they knocked us off."

"And you continue to write about him?"

"Why not? Can't let the bastards win. Anyway, it's too late now. In for a penny, in for a pound."

"Do you regret it?"

"Nah! You can't have these scrotes going around scot-free."

He ordered another small bottle and filled me in on some other colourful pieces of Duggan's history. One tale in particular caught my attention.

"No one's ever verified it, and no one I know has ever seen it, but apparently there's a video tape floating around of a former top Garda officer knocking off a couple of hookers in a hotel room. The story goes this cop was getting a bit too close to the truth for Pinkie's liking so he found out the guy's weak spot. The cop was supposedly un-bribable and didn't like drugs but he was mad for the women. So Pinkie got these young ones to pretend they were mad for a three-way with an older fella and yer man was all over them like a rash. Only problem was a film of him arrived at his desk, along with a note threatening to have a copy sent to his wife, and the Garda Commissioner if he didn't start playing ball.

"So the guy owns up to his superior, shows the tape and decides he isn't going to be blackmailed. The only problem is it doesn't take long for the powers upon high politically to let it be known they would be much happier if the whole matter just happened to fade away. Like I said, Duggan's pals are legion and they're not all Shinners either. Anyway, it dawns on yer man eventually that it's all futile. He's just an embarrassment, to everyone, not least of all himself. So a couple of months later he's found hanging in a wood up in the Dublin Mountains."

"Jesus," was my lame response.

"Exactly," Doherty replied. "Look, I don't know what your involvement with Duggan is. I won't say I wouldn't like to know. And if you ever want to go on the record about something, then I'm your man. But a word of warning: the guy is lethal. People die around him. Much better, I would suggest, to steer clear."

"Thanks," I said, standing up and handing a credit card to the waiter. "After what you've said, I'll do just that."

13

A stiff wind cut across the Curragh, uninterrupted but for a few clumps of gorse and the jeep in which Gerry and I sat waiting for the two horses walking into the distance to turn around and come back. People had been watching horses gallop across this plain for centuries. It was ideal for it, flat, fair and on a surface that at this time of year seemed more cushion than turf. In easier times I'd always looked at Gerry peering into the distance at his horses and viewed the scene as timeless. But nobody seemed to be in an easy mood now, least of all Gerry. Instead of watching Kentish Town's swinging gait as he followed his work companion, the trainer was peering at a paper.

"I see Mr Clancy is getting the benefit of the doubt," he said.

"He is," I replied.

"At least it's put to bed now. I couldn't draw breath for all the phone calls I was getting from reporters."

"Sorry about that. Things have been a bit manic recently and I took my eye off the ball a bit, media-wise," I said.

"It must be desperate alright – Jake stuck in a hospital bed like that," he said generously. "I tried to get in touch with Judith and the family but no one's answering their phones. How's he doing?"

"No real change. And don't worry. Judith knows how much you like Jake. It's just with everything going on, returning calls isn't really a priority."

Especially calls from trainers whose noses might be out of joint about a jockey. They hardly compared to a husband's suicide attempt. But that was unfair to Gerry. Unlike many trainers, he was more than capable of looking beyond racing's narrow, self-interested borders and recognising a big picture. Not that he was thrilled with the idea of Clancy riding Kentish Town again.

"Look, I don't know if the little shit stopped him in the Guineas or if he didn't," he said as a light drizzle started to fall on the windscreen. "No one can know for sure, except him. But it's like anything: once there's a suspicion out there, then it stays there. All I can say is, he's Jake's horse and it's Jake's call, thank God."

We climbed out and surveyed the vast green gallops. Normally, at this time of the morning, there would be hundreds of horses in the vicinity, shouts of encouragement from riders mixing in with even more raucous roars of disapproval from trainers surveying charges either going too fast or too slow. But it was all but empty now on a Sunday. A lone horse and rider in the distance plodded towards a pair of joggers. The only sound came from traffic whizzing by on the motorway that bisected the historic training centre.

Gerry swung his binoculars up and peered down the long straight gallop at the pair of horses that had just begun their work. They were a mile and a quarter away and pretty much a blur. Lines of tiny cones on the ground marked the carefully-tended grass gallops. Optically the horses were little more than brown blobs on the horizon, hardly seeming to be moving. Gerry changed his grip on the glasses, knuckles white as he disengaged from the world and focused intently.

They were moving now alright. Kentish Town's work-rider had a distinctive green helmet with a white bobble on top. It sat reassuringly high as the rider on the horse in front tucked low, cajoling and moving his arms to make his mount go faster. In contrast, Kentish Town was moving well enough for his rider to sit motionless, the only pressure being on his arms as he silently controlled the colt's instinct to go even faster. They flashed past us in a brief thudding explosion of power and energy. Kentish Town was half a length ahead of his hard-ridden rival. The rider had a smile on his face. I remembered that feeling myself. There was an etiquette to gallops, no need to win too far, just enough to confirm superiority and well-being. From what I could see, Kentish Town was feeling very well indeed. The two horses circled back and walked towards us, sweatily stomping around Gerry and myself as the riders gave their reports.

"That Guineas run has really sharpened him up – he was going well before, but he's a stone better now – unbelievable feel he gave me," said Emmett, a veteran work-rider who many years ago had failed to cut it as a jockey but whose judgement of a horse remained priceless.

"And stamina?" Gerry asked.

"He was only getting going there at a mile and a quarter. Another quarter mile won't be a problem at all," Emmett grinned. "Say hello to the next Derby winner!"

There was an almost palpable release of tension in Gerry who delivered a hearty smack to Kentish Town's rump and told the lads to head back to the yard where he'd see them right for working on a Sunday. He practically bounded back to the jeep. I followed, much more leaden-footed.

"Christ, did you see the way he quickened up the instant Emmett gave him the tiniest squeeze. I'd had top sprinters who wouldn't have been able to do that," he laughed. "Can you imagine what that's going to do to the opposition at the end of a mile and a half?"

He was still giddy with excitement as we arrived back at the yard, announcing that no one in his lifetime could truthfully say they'd handled such a talent. All talk about Clancy and the Guineas was forgotten. Once again the only relevant race was the next one. And Kentish Town had just shown us he would have an outstanding chance at Epsom.

"All we have to do is get him there in one piece," Gerry said.

"I've no doubt you will," I replied, watching him take off into his office.

After a lifetime spent living on the Curragh, he didn't even register any more the sounds of artillery batteries getting in some target practice at the army base a few miles away. Right then, though, the dull thuds of the guns were an appropriately ominous soundtrack to what I was thinking.

A horse like Kentish Town was so much more than a talent in his own right. So many people were investing so much in him. Gerry had made no secret he was the best he'd ever trained. The outburst of emotion I'd just seen was a symptom of the self-imposed pressure to do things right by this horse, to prove to himself he was capable of moulding this talent to maximum fruition when it counted most. Gerry would feel a pall on his entire life if any regrets and 'what if's' lingered after the horse's racing career was finished. It wasn't just him. Somebody like Emmett would always be identified as the man who rode Kentish Town. In horse-mad Kildare, that would matter. It would be a tag to define a life. Even lads who just worked in the yard could say they were there at the same time as the great horse. Even I would have a tiny slice of glory by association – the man who bought Kentish Town. How much better that sounded than the man who facilitated the greatest fraud in racing history.

Gerry was behind his desk, wading through paperwork, the high of the gallop already filed away to memory in the face of future plans for a hundred other lesser-lights in the yard. Typically the surroundings were resolutely practical rather than fashionable. It looked more like a builder's on-site portakabin than the nerve centre of a dream factory for rich owners. Perched on top of a pile of old form books was an old kettle that managed to provide us with a couple of cups of tea.

"That two-year-old by Oasis Magic is really starting to blossom, you know," Gerry said. "I think those tiny setbacks in the spring were just growing pains as much as anything else. He might be ready to kick off by the start of July."

What neither of us said was that the Oasis Magic colt doing well was no bad thing considering he'd cost a cool five million guineas the previous autumn, the most expensive price for a yearling paid anywhere in the world that year. I'd no problem remembering. My hand had shaken slightly signing the purchase docket.

"How are Cammie and Max?" Gerry asked. "Any sign yet of that young fella of yours taking an interest in the horses?"

"No. He seems to be more of a football boy. They're away for a little bit, taking a break."

"Very good, very good," he muttered, his brow furrowing at the prospect of teasing out the upcoming meeting at his local track just a couple of miles away. "Look, when you're talking to Clancy next, just emphasise how happy I am with the horse and just to keep things nice and simple at Epsom. A nice position on the outside with a clear run ahead of him will be fine."

"I'll tell him. Well done, Gerry, he's a credit to you."

Traffic was light on the motorway but I decided to head to Annagrove over the mountains. It meant driving on tiny roads but it was more direct and there was still the ever-present need to look over my shoulder every now and again. Coming into Kilcullen there was just a single car in front of me and it pulled to a halt at the lights in the centre of the town. I was mildly aware of another car pulling up behind me. The cold metal feel of the revolver pressed into my neck a couple of seconds later focused my attention rapidly. Suddenly the passenger door opened and Anto's large figure flopped into the seat next to me. In the rear mirror a man I hadn't seen before continued to point his gun at me.

"Now then, I don't want any repeat of the mad driving antics like last time," Anto smiled nastily. "Just follow that motor in front. And if you try anything, Larry here will blow your brains out."

14

It took only half an hour and we pulled up outside a house in Tallaght. A tortuous route through various vast estates left me dazed in terms of a precise location but the mountains in the rear mirror were always visible, next to the looming figure of the man holding a gun to my head.

"I've got to hand it to you, you've got balls," Anto said, almost mournfully. "Let's just hope you hang on to them, eh?"

The streets were mostly deserted, everyone taking advantage of the chance of a Sunday morning lie-in. A couple of small kids were riding bicycles at the end of the road but paid no attention as the driver of the car in front walked quickly towards us and dragged me out. The idea of shouting for help never occurred to me, and it didn't occur to Anto and his friends either. It would have been useless anyway, but there was an assurance to their movements that made anything but obedience seem ridiculous. Clearly they weren't doing this for the first time.

Pushed through the hall into the kitchen, I was manoeuvred onto a chair and tied up for the second time in just over a week. Except now it was my feet that were tied together. Once that was done, Anto filled a kettle with water and organised mugs and tea-bags. They had barely sipped their drinks when the front door opened and feet marched quickly towards us.

Pinkie didn't break step, picked a pan up off the table and struck it across the side of my head. It felt like my skull was caving in. I couldn't hear anything, the room jumped in front of my eyes, all senses seemed to be encased in cotton wool. Instinct took over, hands covering the head, leaving the rest to fend for itself. The blows kept raining in, accompanied by a running commentary.

"What are you? Stupid? Did I not give you that show so that you would take me seriously? Do you think I have time for this shit?" he screamed, all polish lost in a torrent of harsh backstreet Belfast. "You take the piss out of me like that? Do you think I'm going to let you treat me like that, you fucking moron? Do you?"

There was nothing to say and little to do except fall to the floor, curling into a foetal position, leaving my back and kidneys vulnerable to the kicks that came crashing in.

"What, you think 'cos you're some sort of posh cunt that you can shit on me like this? Is that it? I'm just some lowlife for you to shit on? Let me tell you, I shit bigger than you. You're nothing, nothing do you hear, mug, do you?"

I heard alright. I also heard the sound of a pistol being cocked. Some heavy hands pulled me up, grabbed my hair and thrust my face upwards. Duggan half-knelt in front of me and pushed a gun past my lips, forcing my teeth open and thrusting the barrel towards my throat. That was enough to make me choke and cough. But it was the oily stench of the weapon that made me vomit.

"Jesus Christ, you filthy fucking animal!" Pinkie roared, holding his puke-soaked hand as far away from himself as possible, the weapon hanging absurdly by the trigger ring at the end of his finger. He dropped it and flailed at my head with his fists. Spit and vomit spattered my face as the avalanche of blows rained down. Few of them did any real damage. But the seething fury behind them scared me more than anything ever had before. There was an animal savagery to it that didn't leave even the illusion of control. I'd known danger in my life but nothing so elemental. I prayed he wouldn't pick up the gun again. And then, almost instantaneously, he stopped, stood above me, gasping for breath.

"Where's the fucking sink?" he shouted, and Anto turned around and turned on the tap.

Duggan thrust his hands under the water and rubbed them raw with a pot-scourer despite steam rising from them. He took off the blue sports-jacket and began removing his vomit-spattered white shirt before stopping. Sweat still poured off him. But the mania was gone. Instead there was just a grim determination.

"I told you before that if I allow cunts to get the better of me, then I'll be up to my oxters with fuckers like you trying it on. I reckoned a bright guy like you would take that on board but obviously not."

He rolled his sleeves up and motioned to one of the henchmen who left the room.

"You've put it up to me, challenged me. I can't have that. You will do what you're told. If you don't, then forget about tapes and hostages and all that bollocks. I will kill you – and all belonging to you. I promise you that. Don't think for one second I'm fuck-acting here. I will kill you – painfully."

Dragged up on to a chair next to the table, I felt as weak as a kitten, partly because of pain, but also relief that he hadn't shot me. Bruises and cuts will heel, I thought. And then the man returned with a knife. Fear re-energised me. I strained to stand up, legs pushing at the plastic ties. It was useless. Anto shoved me back down and then wrapped his massive arms around me.

He whispered into my ear. "Don't struggle. It's worse if you struggle," he said. "Be a man about it."

But that was impossible. I groaned with terror, not out loud, but low like an animal in pain. That made Pinkie grin for the first time. Another strong pair of hands grabbed my left arm and pulled it to the table. The strength I had left was useless.

"Not so tough now, are you, mug?" Pinkie cried, happily. "Maybe this will get your attention."

It only took a few seconds. I didn't scream, didn't fight, just focused on an air-ventilator at the top of the wall, stared at it like a drowning man reaching for a lifebuoy. I thought I heard Anto whisper something like "Good man" at one stage but couldn't be sure. The thin metal ridges of that ventilator were all I allowed myself to think of. Pinkie was just a dim shape to my left. The others might as well not have been there at all.

"Maybe you're a bit of tough guy all the same," Duggan said, straightening up. "Not a peep out of him, Anto, eh? Fair play to him." He patted me on the head.

Anto released his grip. I looked at the table. There was

surprisingly little blood. Only then did I glance at my hand. He'd cut my ring finger, between the knuckle and the wedding band. With all the motion and sweat the ring had slid off, its gold plate shining in the small pool of blood left behind. There was no fountain of fresh blood from the mangled stump. It wasn't even particularly painful. But the feeling of violation was overwhelming enough to have me choking back sobs of disgust. Pinkie returned from washing his hands in the sink and glared into my eyes.

"Learn this. Don't fuck with me. And just so you don't get any more bright ideas, I'm going to make sure you remember this moment. I've told the lads to get rid of that filthy fucking thing I cut off you. There's going to be no convenient little surgery for you. No little story you can tell your pals over dinner. No, you're going to remember me. Forever."

Everyone disappeared within seconds. The silence they left behind felt unnatural. It took a minute to realise my legs were free again. I didn't move for a bit longer. Some distantly remembered piece of first aid came back to me and I held my hand just under my chin, forcing, hopefully, the heart to pump. I picked up my bloodied wedding ring and stood up. A clean towel was at the sink and I ran water to lukewarm before soaking it, then wrapping it around the injury. Luckily there had been enough blood in my life before to ensure fainting wasn't a problem. Ridiculously I found myself rushing in case whoever lived in the house would come back and blame me for the mess.

Outside the street remained quiet. The two kids on bikes rode past, staring at the figure emerging from the house. I tried to smile reassuringly, but it can't have looked too pretty. They pedalled away fast. Easing into the car, for the first time ever I gave thanks for Sat-Nav. Normally the dislocated tones turned me cold. Now there was a reassurance to them, a reminder that civilisation still existed, even in a world where gratuitous hurt could be so casually dispensed.

Once out of the estate, I quickly recognised a couple of landmarks. After that it took only quarter of an hour to make Tallaght Hospital. A couple of scares with croup and a rash had meant a couple of late-night dashes with Max. I parked and walked a little unsteadily to A&E.

There never seemed an end to the lines of people queuing up. Harassed staff rushed around. There was even a queue for the woman sitting behind the glass reception area. I stood for ten minutes before making it to the top.

"Name?" she asked, and I told her.

"Problem?" she droned, and I held up my towel-covered hand.

"Lost a finger," I said.

It was then that I wondered why the floor was rushing up to meet me.

15

I'd fallen asleep in front of the telly, finally nodding off at some stage of the early morning and getting a few hours' sleep. With the walls of the hotel room coming in at two in the morning, the only option had been to get dressed and go for a walk. There'd been a nip in the night air that had made it necessary to pick up the pace down a deserted footpath towards the nearby motorway flyover. Cars and trucks whizzed by underneath, busily continuing towards wherever they had to be. I'd eventually walked back to slump in an armchair and stare at the telly.

Now, turning the TV off, I got into bed fully clothed and lay there wondering if I'd be able to get back to sleep. The remains of the bottle of whiskey that had kept me company the previous evening sat on the table nearby but even the thought of drinking again made my stomach heave. So did the idea of getting anything to eat.

It was over twenty-four hours since I'd signed myself out of hospital after an overnight stay. There had been some toast for breakfast then that had remained untouched.

Escape was the sole thing on my mind. There had been enough concussions in my life to know when a headache really was just a headache. I'd booked into this small hotel, made a few calls, slept intermittently, watched TV and eventually worked my way through the bottle of whiskey.

Now, every piece of my marrow ached to get on a flight to France. Simply get away, back to my kid, to my family, and forget about racing and horses and cruelty and pain. But it wasn't that easy. They were safe where they were, with me away from them. Who knew what eyes would be watching my movements? Duggan's men had picked me up so simply, almost casually, that it would take very little effort for them to do the same again. Having them know where Max was chilled me more than anything else.

I glanced down at my hand. There was a heavy gauze bandage around it. At first glance it looked like a simple broken finger. And there wasn't much pain any more. But it took an effort to look at it. There were times when it felt like the finger was still there, just like those phantom limb movements that wounded soldiers spoke of. Compared to so many people's fate, such a problem was nothing. The doctor had assured me it would take a little getting used to in terms of gripping things but I was right-handed anyway so that would make things easier. "You'll be functioning at one hundred per cent again in no time," he'd said breezily. No doubt I would. Wanting to pull the duvet over my head and banish the world was more worrying. It was tempting, lying there, nursing a sick stomach, just to turn over, forget about everything and sleep. The problem was that sleep came fitfully and waking up still presented the same reality.

Time then to stop feeling sorry for myself.

It was easy to work the phones from there, ring St Aubin where the sun was shining. Max was having the time of his life and Cammie assured me she wasn't in the least bit worried but would I be coming back soon? Judith answered her phone and offered to fly everyone to New York immediately when I gave her a brief summary of events.

"What are we dealing with, Lorcan? People can't behave like this," she said.

"Unfortunately they can, and do," I replied. "I've got everyone over here in a safe place. But if it comes to it, can we take you up on your offer?"

"Of course, take it up now. Get away from these dreadful people. Put an ocean between you and them."

"Even an ocean isn't enough, Judith. Look at how they got to Jake. How is he?"

"Fighting hard. The doctors are pretty amazed he's still with us. But that's Jake."

Even Jake though had momentarily dissolved enough to try to take his own life, I thought. Even the toughest could bend if pressed enough.

It had been almost a relief to get through the reassuringly normal and uneventful stuff of a regular working day. There were a number of calls from the press about a rumoured gallop on the Curragh by Kentish Town that had blown Camp Weinberger over it was so good.

"The colt is giving every satisfaction in his work," I said as neutrally as possible, giving them an essentially meaningless quote that allowed them to expand on this fascinating gallop to their hearts' content. It was all part of the information game and usually both sides played by the rules. And if they didn't, the only things hurt were egos.

"The plan is for Kentish Town to go for the Derby at Epsom. And we're hopeful he will have enough stamina to last the mile and a half," I concluded, almost picturing the following day's headlines as I spoke.

Epsom was also on Jocelyn De Beaufort's mind, but the Oaks rather than the Derby. When his name came up on my phone, it took an effort of will not to ignore it. Routine was all very well but pandering to the Englishman's moods wasn't exactly an enticing prospect. Much as I admired his ability and skill, he remained a difficult man to warm to. There was also the reality that he'd never bothered to disguise his own lack of warmth towards me. Neither of which mattered much professionally, but it was a pain to talk to him in such circumstances.

"Ah, Mr Donovan. Nothing bad to report. It's just that Marian Heights won't be ready quite in time for Goodwood. It's a bit close to the Oaks anyway, so I've decided it would be best to send her straight to Epsom. We can get her fit enough here, and she's a light, athletic type of filly anyway. I presume that's okay?"

The translation of which was: 'I'm doing it my way whatever you say, but let's just keep up appearances.' It didn't matter. In fact it made things easier when he went to the trouble of maintaining appearances. They didn't matter much in the long run but making things difficult for the sake of it was tiresome.

"Yeah, that sounds fine," I said.

"Good, see you tonight then."

"What's tonight?"

"The Derby dinner in London. You know, the one we are more or less obliged to attend every year."

I swore silently to myself. It was an annual duty to

attend the dinner in the centre of London where the Derby sponsor blew a lot of money feeding and watering owners, trainers, media and anyone even vaguely associated with the race. As a former Derby winner De Beaufort was invited as a matter of course. Since Kentish Town was favourite, there was also no getting away from the reality that my presence would be required.

"Of course," I said. "It should be a good evening. Looking forward to it."

After twenty minutes' driving I found myself on the road south to Wicklow. It wasn't a conscious decision, more a need to move, turn on a radio and create something different for the senses. But keeping going was not a chore. Another twenty minutes and there was Annagrove. Nothing had changed. The place still looked pristine on the outside and in the office the operation was clearly humming along as per normal.

"My God, what happened to you?" Siobhán, the ultra-efficient administration officer asked as I walked in.

I'd been ready for questions about my hand but I'd forgotten about how the rest of me looked. My face was full of cuts and bruises that were swelling up and actually looked worse than they were. It was the rest of me that ached but nothing worse than I'd walked away from at many racecourses when I was riding. That didn't stop me looking like a butcher's window though.

"You should see the other fella," I said, trying to wink but, from Siobhán's reaction making myself even more grotesque. "I wish it was so exciting. I fell down the stairs – genuinely." All this lying was becoming second nature.

Siobhán barely heard me, but seemed to accept the

explanation. She quickly presented me with a folder full of paperwork which thankfully required little more than a succession of signatures. Then there was a much more welcome cup of hot coffee, with a hint of milk, just as I liked it. Its recuperative powers were remarkable. After a few minutes, I told Siobhán and her colleagues I was going for a walk.

It was a warm, calm morning and the mares and foals were out in the paddocks, the mothers hungrily cropping grass and trying to ignore some of the playful boisterousness of their offspring. I walked through a couple of paddocks, some of the mares approaching and brushing against me in the hope of something to eat, most of the foals treating the interloper a lot more gingerly. Just the familiar smell of the animals raised my spirits. So did the simple fresh air of this place.

Climbing over a timber rail into another paddock, I looked around for an occupant and found him in a corner under the trees, availing of some shade and some relief from the ever-present flies. I recognised him as Choirboy, a rare six-year-old runner for Jake whose talent wasn't in the Kentish Town class but who possessed a will-to-win that endeared him to everyone connected to him. He was on a break from training, recuperating from a slight muscle problem that looked all but cured. The change of scenery, and a few weeks of relaxed grazing, had him looking great. Typically he stood still as I patted his neck, felt tendons in his legs that were completely cool, and generally made a fuss of him.

The impulse to suddenly jump on his back came from nowhere and yet had me trotting back to the cottage. A saddle that I'd used on my last day riding was stashed away in the attic. I retrieved it, dusted it off and grabbed a whip that was thrown in a corner.

Choirboy saw me coming but true to form didn't bolt at the idea of being pressed back into service. He stood still as I slipped his head-collar off and slipped the bridle I'd retrieved in the stable's tack-room over his head. As I jumped onto his back he didn't miss a beat and allowed me to drop the stirrup irons a couple of notches compared to when I'd last used them. We circled a couple of times, walking, and then began to trot. It was like speaking a language not used for years. There was a familiarity but also a newness to it that made me forget. Instead it was all back to the fundamentals of trying to get this half-ton of animal underneath me to at least pretend to obey my commands. The language revved through the reins like electricity, informing me of Choirboy's wellbeing and willingness to please while also letting me know that most of that was his choice. Fundamental physics dictated that eleven stone could never be completely in charge. But as always the negotiations were as thrilling as they were intricate.

Choirboy seemed to enjoy the fresh activity too. We trotted for a few minutes before cantering a couple of furlongs slightly downhill to a section of stream that bisected the farm. Surrounded by insects and relishing the warm sun on my damaged face, I let the horse drop his head to take a drink. Once he had his fill, we both stood still examining the bucolic scene all around us. It really was beautiful here, something always known but only now really appreciated. The inactivity bored Choirboy though and he backed off, tugging at the steel bit in his mouth.

"You want to run, do you?" I asked, and wheeled him around.

In front of us was over half a mile of perfect lush grass, practically an invitation. The horse seemed to pick up on the idea at the same time. I only had to click my tongue and he bounded ahead. There was a wildness to it that I'd forgotten. A miler in his racing career, Choirboy reached full speed very quickly and had no difficulty keeping it up. There was nothing for it but to tuck low behind his neck, practically tasting his mane, hardly daring to breathe, concentrating on not getting in the horse's way. Organising the reins felt a little weird with the big bandage but I could hold them well enough. No doubt Gerry Gunning would have a stroke watching me urging his horse on with taps of the stick down the shoulder. There were also some rather elemental shouts that weren't so much encouragement for Choirboy as defiance against the world.

I started to pull up so we wouldn't crash into the railing. There was something about Choirboy that suggested he wouldn't have minded a cut at jumping the thing but that would have taken things too far. Instead he condescended to slowing down and bumped to a halt just in time. It was easy to see why he was so popular. Everything about him wanted to please. He'd lifted my spirits to a level unimaginable just minutes before. Instead of being exhausted at the unaccustomed activity, I felt exhilarated, senses reawakened, muscles almost glorying in being used again.

The exultation lasted through washing the horse down in the yard with a hose, filling a bucket with nuts and walking him back to the paddock where he stuffed his head into the bucket. He deserved it. I stayed for a short while, patting his neck until it was obvious he was becoming irritated by my presence.

"You look a lot happier than when you came in here first," Siobhán said approvingly. "Now if we throw a gallon of disinfectant on you then you might be presentable at tonight's dinner."

"They'll just have to skip their meal if I'm too much for them," I said. "Is everything booked?"

"There you go," she said, handing me an envelope with tickets. "Keep flying the flag."

16

About five hundred of racing's great and good crowded into a massive conference centre ready to praise to the skies the sponsors, the Derby and all who travelled in her. It was hardly a chore and there were plenty of genuine enquires about Jake. Once again, I was startled at the affection the man was able to engender. Even from those who had no professional reasons to enquire after him there seemed to be widespread goodwill for him to pull through. At the cutting-edge of top-flight international flat racing such sentiments didn't usually apply. Weinberger was an exception though, and the focus on Kentish Town was even more than it normally would be on a hot favourite.

Gerry had taken the opportunity to duck the event, given that I would be there, but Jake's two English trainers were present and correct. Bartie Montgomery barrelled his way towards me almost as soon as I was through the door. The short, squat figure always brought a no-nonsense energy with him that could sometimes rub people up the wrong way. And there was a brusqueness to him that sometimes could be open to misinterpretation. But I had always appreciated his willingness to call a spade a shovel.

"Jesus Christ, Lorcan, it looks like someone kicked the shit out of you!" he bellowed, the idea evidently too ridiculous to be taken seriously. "Whose wife were you at?"

I eased towards a corner so we wouldn't be centre stage. Sure enough Bartie didn't waste any time coming out with what was on his mind.

"There's a yearling in Maryland right now that will be for sale in Kentucky in a couple of months. He's owned by that Taylor man that we bought Pellinore off." Pellinore was a horse that Bartie had trained to win the St Leger for Jake. "This colt is a half-brother and I've seen film of him," he went on. "He's a real one, Lorcan. Jake would be well advised to examine him closely at that sale."

He was getting his oar in first, I reckoned, just in case there was any chance he might go to Gerry, or worst of all De Beaufort, if we did buy the horse at the sales. If we did buy it, the obvious place to go, given his experience with the relative, would be Bartie. But I'd learned that it was sometimes necessary to put a stop to his gallop: "I would imagine I'll be at the sale alright, but things are up in the air a bit with Jake's health, so who knows what the state of play might be in terms of horses in a couple of months' time."

His face seemed to crumple. Clearly the link between Jake's well-being and the continuation of his racing empire hadn't struck home before. That it did at the same time as Jocelyn De Beaufort arrived to join us really was a double whammy for the little man.

"Ah, Bartholomew, hustling for more horses, are we?" De Beaufort said with a patrician hauteur. Anyone watching the scene might presume the tall, elegant figure was above conspiring for an advantage himself. But decades of surviving at the top of the cut-throat profession indicated how he could indulge in some judicious use of the elbow himself. "Anyway, you're going to have to release Mr Donovan to me for a while. We're at the same table."

"That's tough on you, Lorcan," Bartie sniffed, moving away. "Getting a bad draw like that."

De Beaufort positively beamed at the insult, delighted at having drawn some verbal blood.

We trooped into the banquet. Sure enough De Beaufort was sitting next to me and we introduced ourselves to the others at our table. I knew, or knew of, most of them, but one space remained vacant. Only when the compère stood up to begin his spiel did the last member of our table arrive.

"Crikey, there's a touch of alright," my neighbour whispered.

I couldn't disagree. Long, straight blonde hair cascaded down the back of a petite figure that beamed a big smile around the table.

"Hi, I'm Danielle Simpson – call me Dani," she said in a soft American accent. Shaking hands all round, she ended with me and said: "I'm going to have to talk to you afterwards."

Absurdly I found myself blushing, and saying that wouldn't be a problem.

"I'm a reporter," she grinned. "My camera guy is at another table."

I could feel De Beaufort smiling at my discomfort. A few others grinned too.

"I live in London, working for one of the racing channels in the States and we just need a few words about Kentish Town and his chance at Epsom," she went on.

148

"There's quite a lot of interest at home, given the horse is owned by Jake Weinberger."

"That's what I'm here for," I told her, and turned to listen to the first of the speeches.

Mercifully they weren't long and the meal began to be served at the same time. It wasn't long though before I was called up to be interviewed about Kentish Town, and Jake, and the wonder of the Derby itself. None of it was difficult. Affection for my boss was widespread and genuine. The horse himself, even in the midst of everything else that was happening, still made my pulse quicken at the depth of his talent and the Derby was always the ultimate. An entire breed, and as a result an entire industry, was built on the great race and the desperate desire for more than a couple of centuries of so many people to win it.

"Apologies for the state of me, but there's no legislating for an ex-jump jockey's clumsiness," I said sheepishly at one point to general applause.

Duty done, I sat back down.

"Very smooth," said Dani Simpson, a smile playing on her lips. She had incredible green eyes, and golden-brown skin, and I really needed to get a grip. "What sort of media qualifications do you have?"

"None."

"Really? You're very good, very fluent."

"It must be an Irish thing," I shrugged.

"Yeah, that accent is a powerful weapon," she laughed.

"Are you one of those Irish-Americans that drink green beer and carry shillelaghs and hate the British?" De Beaufort drawled.

"Nope. Far as I can tell, we're Dutch German," she replied. "I don't like beer, I don't know what a shillelagh is and it's only a certain kind of Brit that I hate."

He loved that. It seemed to me Sir Jocelyn was very taken with the American journalist who looked to be still in her twenties, but also looked more than capable of holding her own in any verbal jousting with the older man. De Beaufort was divorced for many years but had a reputation as something of a womaniser. He spent most of the meal exhibiting his charming side.

Over dessert, I felt my phone vibrating in my pocket. I quickly went to answer, awkwardly spilling change and paper out on to the floor. It was Cammie.

"Is everything okay?" I asked as I got to my feet and walked away from the table.

"Everything is fine. Max is in heaven. Your dad and Sebastian have been taking him to the beach and to playgrounds. He loves it here. He's even saying a few French words. We just wonder when you're coming back. We miss you."

"Not for a little while. I'm sorry, but it's much better you stay where you are, out of harm's way. It was ridiculously lucky to get you out once: there isn't a hope in hell of doing something like that again."

"I understand. That doesn't stop us missing you, though. It doesn't stop me missing you."

"As soon as this mess is sorted we can try to sort out everything else. But this has to be gone through first. Give my love to everyone." I hung up.

De Beaufort had retrieved my papers and change from the floor. Lying on top I noticed a folded-up photocopy of an article on Pinkie that was wrinkled and worn. I had shoved it into my pocket earlier with a small bunch of receipts and notes.

"You alright?" Sir Jocelyn asked, glancing down at my hand.

A little blood had made its way through the bandage. Nothing significant but the sight embarrassed me.

"Yeah, nothing serious," I said, stuffing my hand underneath the heavy linen tablecloth.

He looked at me for a second and then returned to his charm offensive. We finished the meal and then Dani Simpson raised her eyebrows at me.

"Shall we do that interview now?" she asked.

"Sure, where will we go?"

The cameraman decided the foyer with people streaming past in the background offered the best shot and he didn't need long to set up.

"You look a little rough," she said. "What happened to your hand?"

"Ah, nothing much. Long story."

"You up to this?"

"Yeah, I'm just tired. Sir Jocelyn has the edge in the smoothness stakes. Just a pity he doesn't train the horse."

"He's asked me down to his stables, to ride out. I sometimes do some track work at home. Should I go, or is he dangerous?"

"I reckon you'll be well able for him, whatever his motivation," I smiled.

We did the interview. She was concise, to the point and very professional.

"Short and snappy – that's what they want," she said. "So, about Sir Jocelyn, what would you recommend?"

"I suppose ideally you might need an escort," I said.

"Got anyone in mind?"

17

The following morning I found her house in West London easily enough, easier than finding a parking space within a couple of hundred yards of the front door.

"Why don't you skip down and ring the bell, tell her we're here," I said to the quietly hung-over figure coiled in the passenger seat next to me.

"Why don't you do yourself a mischief?" Sir Jocelyn muttered, head leaning sideways, eyes shut. "Or just give her a ring."

He'd booked into the same hotel as me once he realised trying to get home the previous night was not on. Waking him up had not been easy and even the prospect of an hour in a car with Dani Simpson hadn't cheered him up. I'd half expected him to climb into the back seat, leaving me to my driving duties, which I actually wouldn't have minded. Sitting next to Dani held a lot more appeal than a headachy knight with a hangover. But no such luck.

I rang the doorbell and heard a "Hold on!" from inside. Five minutes later and Dani appeared, wearing black jeans that looked like they were painted on, and a black turtleneck that emphasised her blonde hair. Unlike her escort, and her host, she looked magnificent. It took a little throat-clearing before I trusted myself to speak.

"I was going to ask if you were ready to go but you clearly are."

She took my obvious admiration as entirely appropriate and skipped down the steps with a swagger that kept me lazily making up ground on her for as long as was decent.

In the car, Sir Jocelyn briefly rallied when Dani jumped into the back seat but faded quickly as we steered our way out of the city. By the time we hit the motorway he was snoring quietly.

Not wanting to wake him, there wasn't much conversation between Dani and me, but the silences were comfortable. She looked at the countryside, passed an occasional comment about some places sign-posted along the way and clearly didn't feel any compulsion to make small talk. That suited me. I was still trying to legitimise such a quick visit back to Hampshire in such a short time. The previous night Sir Jocelyn had been doing the same thing, glancing from me to his invited guest with a quizzical look on his face, and not buying into the argument at all that Marian Heights was really deserving of another look before the Oaks from her owner's racing manager. In fairness, only the most pea-green innocent would have believed such an explanation, and De Beaufort knew innocence was not a sentiment that Dani provoked.

We drove into the stables as the horses were being pulled out for first lot. The yard reverberated with noise and Sir Jocelyn looked more than a little green as he consulted with his head man and pointed to Dani. A stately old gelding I recognised from many racecourse appearances over the years was pulled out for the visitor and she jumped up with an ease that testified to at least some previous experience.

"Lorcan, you can head up on your own and oversee things," the trainer announced. "I am heading to my bed for a couple of hours."

At the top of the gallops I watched the string in their morning workouts, keeping an eye out for Dani's progress especially. She rode longer than most of the other riders but there was a lack of movement in her hands that indicated more than the usual level of competence. The black-clad figure sat neatly in the saddle, sticking resolutely next to the horse and rider she was paired with and made it past me with a gratifying lack of incident.

"Wow, that was great," she beamed as the string walked back past me. "God, I'm unfit – like a pound of butter."

"You looked okay to me," I grinned.

A voice piped up from the string, in a strong west-country accent: "You should have been behind her then!"

I noticed the good-natured laughter that accompanied the joke provoked blushes that didn't really tally with the super-confident impression Dani had projected up to then. But she tossed her head in mock indignation, straightened her back even more and carried it off with enough style to have her neighbours grinning along with her.

It also didn't seem like a coincidence that such a general display of good humour among the staff coincided with the boss's absence. But I regretted the thought. Sir Jocelyn De Beaufort might have been the epitome of stiff upper lip in many respects but he wasn't humourless. In fact, compared to a certain racing manager recently, he was sun on a stick.

He was waiting in the yard when I got back, sipping coffee and slowly welcoming some colour back into his face.

"Everyone present and correct?" he yelled, and I nodded. "Can the guest ride?"

"She can, and she's turned a few heads too."

"Licentious buggers," he grinned. "Can hardly blame them though. How's your hand?"

"Fine," I said, remembering the distasteful job of bandaging it again the previous night back in the hotel. "Just a scratch."

The string clattered back. Dani jumped off and went straight to the water hose to wash down her old stager and used the scraper over him with an obvious familiarity. She led him back to his box and got to work grooming as the horse buried his nose in the feed-pot.

I stood at the door. "Where'd you learn to do all this?"

"My dad was a trainer, in northern California mostly, but we moved around. I grew up with horses. Strictly third-rate stuff, but he made it pay. Worked like a slave though. I decided pretty early on that it was not for me. What I do now is much easier, and much better paid."

"So, it's all for the money?"

"Are you kidding? Look at the horses here. They're all top-bred, gorgeous animals. Most of my dad's were glorified cripples, held together with injections and hope. And you'd want to be here a long time before getting sick of the sights around here. This place is beautiful."

"Yeah, I guess it is."

"How well do you know it? Got any country pubs stashed away where you can buy me lunch?"

"I'm afraid not. But why don't we try and find one?"

Dani rode out in one more lot of horses, then we went inside for coffee where she made of fuss of De Beaufort who made a graceful retreat and invited her back any time. As we left he even treated me to a wink.

I was very aware of her next to me as we drove vaguely through the countryside. There was a vitality to this woman that made me want to stop the car and indulge in the sort of gymnastics that Dani might or might not have been happy to go along with. However, even the idea that she might was confusing enough to ponder the benefits of driving back to London, dropping her home and speeding away. The temptation to believe I was in some way entitled to play away from home after what Cammie had done was increasing with every mile. There was also no getting away from the fact that I was intensely attracted to this self-possessed American. What in the hell was I doing?

"There's a signpost for the Huntsman's Arms. It says food served," she said. "Let's go there."

It turned out to be a kitschy representation of what an English country pub was supposed to be with lots of brass and beams. But the food was simple and good. Dani loved it all – the atmosphere, the pictures on the wall, the sense that time was going at its own pace.

"Tell me the coolest place you've ever been?" she asked out of the blue.

"That's a tough one," I said. "I suppose the winner's enclosure after winning the National. Except it wasn't very cool, just incredibly emotional and sweaty and crowded."

"I remember watching it. The whole coverage," she laughed. "It was all about this Irish jockey winning the world's most famous steeplechase. You actually looked quite polished."

That had been my trademark when riding. I'd never been one to go in for big rousing displays of effort, legs and arms flailing, using the whip extravagantly. Even on heavy winter ground it always seemed to me to be mostly show. Better to try and make yourself as inconspicuous as possible on the horse, I always reckoned. And being tall meant getting tucked down aerodynamically and smoothly always felt more important than bouncing up and down like a cowboy. The down part was it sometimes looked like I could be doing more. In reality, reaching for the stick was usually the last resort. That didn't make me hugely popular with betting-shop punters but it did result in opportunities given to me by those in the know, which otherwise might not have been the case.

Granite Top in the National had been just such an opportunity: a horse with a touch of class, but also one whose enthusiasm had dimmed with one tough race too many. My instructions had been to leave him alone to make his own mind up about the unique challenge of the National fences. I'd known after just three jumps that he was reinvigorated by them. Even so the prospect of actually winning hadn't entered my head until the last mile as, treading our way through the detritus of the race, we arrived at the last fence disputing the lead. Even up the long run in, I hung onto Granite Top's head for as long as I dared, persuading him that this wasn't as hard as it seemed, encouraging him with thought and sense to make one final effort. There was a lot of praise for my ride afterwards. But it was the horse that had made that final effort. Even now the memory was enough to make me smile.

"Just on the best horse," I grinned. "What about you? Where's your cool place?"

"Oh it was cool alright. Kilimanjaro. A couple of us climbed it four years ago. There were a couple of times I thought I was going to turn my toes up. It was unbelievable. And so damn cold. We were huddling together for warmth."

The idea of Kilimanjaro suddenly seemed pretty cool, but instead I settled for a pot of coffee. We relaxed over that, Dani doing most of the talking, me happily listening. When the grandfather clock in the corner boomed out that it was three o'clock we checked our watches to make sure it really was that late.

"I'd better get you back to London," I said.

"I guess so. But it's a pity to leave," she replied.

It started raining as soon as we got into the car and got heavier the closer we got back to the city. Things also grew quieter in the car the closer we got. Dani directed me down a number of side-street shortcuts and we eventually pulled up outside her door. Rain hammered down and both of us sat silently.

"Hey," she said, and leaned across.

Her lips tasted wonderful. My senses were suddenly full of perfume and promise and yet I pulled away.

"I'm sorry," I said.

"What for?"

"I'm married," I said, automatically holding up the bandaged hand with the missing ring-finger.

She laughed a little shakily and sat back in the passenger seat. "Married men are not my style," she said.

"I didn't think so. If it's any consolation, my wife and I have had problems recently. I moved out."

"You don't have to explain anything."

"I know I don't, but I want to," I said. "We have a son, Max. He's nearly two. I don't know what's going to happen to us but there's no point embroiling you in any of it. If I go in with you now, it will only complicate things for everyone –"

"Whoa there, stud! Where'd you get the idea I was taking you in? I realise you've got a high opinion of yourself, and no doubt you're used to women throwing themselves at you. But I'm not a sure thing. Not by a long way."

"Jesus, I'm sorry, that's not what I meant," I stammered. "Oh fuck it . . ."

Dani smiled, leaned across again and kissed me lightly on the lips. "Thanks," she said quietly, and climbed out of the car. "Let me know when things get sorted out. You might get another chance."

18

Clancy walked towards us, smirking. Bartie nudged me.

"Good to see the little shit in a good mood for a change," he said. "It probably means someone else is in the crap though."

The jockey glanced at how my hand remained resolutely in my pocket but said nothing.

"Everything good, Mike," Bartie boomed around the Newmarket parade ring. "Still keeping ahead of the game, I see."

"Better than some," was the reply.

It was one of those midweek fixtures that didn't attract much attention or attendance. Compared to the Guineas the place was deserted. But these low-key fixtures often saw the first steps of future top-class performers. The three of us were hoping it would be a similar story now. At least I hoped we all did.

Bartie had been raving all spring about a little speedball two-year-old he reckoned was going to light up Royal Ascot. Speedgun was his name, and after burning up the gallops just a few miles away he was now having his first ever race. I looked at him skittering around the ring, the strong wind not helping the lad leading him, but with his nervous energy just about under control. It was all very new to him and the important thing was that Speedgun should leave the racecourse with no bad memories of his first experience of it.

"Just jump and go on him, Mike," Bartie said, looking a little wound up himself. "It's just five furlongs and he's plenty fit enough. Get him balanced and he'll win."

"No sweat," was the response.

Sure enough, there wasn't any. Speedgun jumped from the stalls like an old pro, shimmied across to the rail and made all the running to win by four lengths with Clancy looking around for non-existent dangers.

"That's great!" Bartie said, patting his excited colt. "Coventry Stakes, here we come! How did he feel, Mike?"

"Very good. But he's a bit hot. Maybe keeping him at five for the time being might be a better option? Say, the Norfolk?" Then he turned to me. "After all, it's always good to appreciate what you've got."

"What the hell is he talking about?" Bartie said as Clancy walked back to the weigh-room.

"He obviously just wants to stay at five," I said.

"Yeah, I guess," he muttered.

Jake's only other runner on the evening was in the fifth race: Devil's Glen, a largely disappointing three-year-old. Hanging around waiting for it didn't seem particularly attractive. But De Beaufort trained Devil's Glen and he could be odd sometimes about there being no owner representation when the horses ran. I decided to stay, rang Gerry for an update on Kentish Town and issued a 'steady as she goes' report to the couple of reporters that came looking for quotes.

Sir Jocelyn looked a lot healthier than a few days previously. His tweed suit was perfectly cut and could be seen reflected in the brilliant shine of his brown brogues. The English gentleman image though was undermined by some proletarian language as he jogged late into the ring.

"I hate this fucking horse," he said, nodding dismissively at Devil's Glen. "All the talent in the world but he'll always find a way not to put it in. Fucking pig of an animal! Don't know why I came all this way."

"He'd better start bucking his ideas up alright or else he'll end up not too far from here in the sales ring, getting bought to go hurdling," I said.

"He'll know about punishment then," the trainer agreed. "Speaking of which, are you going to the sales tonight? Isn't there a mare you're hoping to buy?"

"If the price is suitable, then yes, Jake would be interested, ordinarily."

"Everything is a little out of step, isn't it?"

"Just a bit," I shrugged. "But I've not heard anything to the contrary about bidding for this horse. So we'll see."

"I'd be interested to see her," Sir Jocelyn said. "I'll see you there."

We watched the race. Devil's Glen again travelled easily but once Clancy asked him to quicken his head went up in the air, resenting the pressure. He finished runner-up – again.

Not surprisingly I finished second to De Beaufort in the race to the sales ring. He was a famously quick driver. Much more surprisingly, he waited for me. The horse I was coming to look at was a nine-year-old broodmare, well past her racing days, but in possession of a pedigree that could send a seven-figure sum towards a Canadian owner whose business was going down the skids. There was no obvious interest here for a trainer and yet he walked with me through the lines of stable boxes. The chestnut mare was being walked in front by a bloodstock agent we both knew.

"Are you interested in this, Lorcan?" the agent asked. "If you are, just tell me now. I can prepare my client for disappointment."

"We might be, but not at stupid money. What about your guy?"

"I don't know – he's pretty stupid," the agent grinned. "But he's also pretty wealthy. I've been cultivating him for quite a while now, and I've found out he is competitive."

He'd seen enough and headed off, leaving De Beaufort to mutter "Parasite" under his breath, and me to take in a general impression of this matron that in a few minutes would be changing hands. She looked better on paper than in the flesh, I concluded, but maybe she would start to bloom during the summer. I walked to the sales ring doing mental arithmetic.

Spending millions of someone else's money had been a chore at the beginning. The responsibility had kept me awake some nights. Then Jake re-emphasised his belief that all anyone could do was their honest best and I concentrated on the fact I was being paid to spend this man's money. Experience, though, hadn't made me a spendthrift.

Many people liked to try and disguise themselves when it came to buying, skulking behind corners or pressing next to walls. It usually didn't matter since regular buyers generally had a preferred spot to bid from and their rivals quickly realised who their competition was. But instinctively there was little difference between this high-finance auction and a mart flogging sheep and cattle. Everyone wanted an edge, either real or imagined.

Jake's wealth meant I usually went the other way, sitting plain to see in the middle of the auditorium. The alternative seemed juvenile, and there was my own hunch too that the sight of the Weinberger representative bidding could discourage the opposition.

De Beaufort sat next to me today, barely glancing at the couple of horses that came into the ring before the mare. He did check out Jake's potential purchase but made no comment.

The auctioneer's manic chant tumbled into gear and the bidding began almost immediately. There were a couple of hands raised that I knew couldn't realistically hope to buy a horse like this, but the agent from outside was on a balcony upstairs with a phone clamped to his ear. He raised his eyebrows once and the spotter yelped out to tell the auctioneer. We were already at 250,000 guineas. I waited until the figures on the luminous board reached 340,000, along with its equivalents in euro, dollars and yen, before nodding at the spotter nearest to me. I nodded a couple of times more, but they were trumped each time from upstairs.

"Back to you," the auctioneer said to me, when the price had gone past half a million.

I glanced above me and saw my competition whispering into the phone with his hand in front of his mouth. His features were becoming a little strained, gestures a little more jerky. He looked like he was having to encourage his client to stay in the fight. But I looked at the rostrum and shook my head. When the gavel finally came down, De Beaufort and I were already halfway to the exit.

I knew what would be said: Donovan bottled it – again. There had been a few similar battles where I blinked first, mainly because the price had gone way past what I reckoned was in any way value. It wasn't my money, but I wasn't going to flush it away either. In the machismo bloodstock world, a few minutes of bidding could define you. I'd gone fifty grand over the price I'd reckoned would represent value for the mare. And it wasn't enough. Keeping going would be muscle-flexing with Jake's money. People could think what they liked.

"She wasn't worth that kind of cash," De Beaufort said as we crunched over the gravel avenue towards the car park.

"I hope she doesn't produce a Derby winner," I grinned ruefully. "It will probably be Epsom before we meet again. Take good care of Marian Heights."

"Sure," he said. "Have you got a minute? Sit into the car."

It was a Jaguar, top of the range, and sitting into the passenger seat felt suitably luxurious. I readied myself for Sir Jocelyn's pitch. There was some horse somewhere that he felt would suit Jake, especially if it was trained by him. Usually he could be relied upon for a more subtle approach than Bartie but the aim was usually the same.

"Who did that to your finger," he asked, wasting no time.

"What do you mean?" I retorted.

"You're minus a digit, Lorcan. Who did it?"

"It was an accident, at home."

"Right," he said. "So the fact that you're walking around

with paperwork about Pinkie Duggan in your pockets means that you losing a finger is just coincidence."

This was definitely not what I'd been expecting. Sir Jocelyn's aquiline features were as haughty as ever but his expression was neutral and his voice quiet.

"Lorcan, before I started training, I was a military man – did two tours in Northern Ireland. A lot of that was spent scurrying across streets in Belfast, petrified that some bastard with a rifle was going to pick me off from some tower block or from behind a wall. There were any number of times when I was scared out of my wits, eyes out like stalks, looking for faces to fit the pictures shown to us of known paramilitaries. Even thirty years later I can see those faces. They're burned into my memory."

I looked at him and believed him. This was a very different man to the usual.

"A colleague of mine, who shall remain nameless, was a captain, same as me, in another regiment. We've been friends since Sandhurst. His area of expertise was – how shall I put this? – in the intelligence area. There wasn't a pub or a club on the Falls Road he didn't know down to the last speck of dust in the corner. It was bloody nasty stuff back then. Anything went. And the whole thing revolved around information. My friend ran a number of people, informants, individuals who kept him abreast of what was happening in return for substantial cash rewards. He was very discreet, my friend, never uttered a word about his work. Except one night we had nothing to do except get stinking drunk. He told me some stuff that would make your skin crawl, about what was being done to people. And one thing that always stuck in my mind was this little detail, about a lunatic who had a calling-card, this sick fetish for cutting people's fingers off. He was IRA, and deeply in. But the way my pal spoke about him made me suspect he might be on the payroll. Oh, and by the way, his little habit gave him a nickname – Pinkie."

My brain was running a million miles an hour trying to keep up. De Beaufort reached behind him and pulled an envelope out of a briefcase.

"I could hardly credit it when I picked up that stuff you dropped at the dinner. There were a couple of faces in a picture I remembered only too well from the old days. It was like a slap seeing them again. And then in the piece underneath there was mention of a guy called 'Pinkie'. Everything started to make some sort of sense then.

"I don't know what's going on, but there's far too much happening for it to be all coincidence. Jake Weinberger's racing manager is walking around minus a finger, and with stuff about an IRA gangster falling out of his pockets, just a couple of weeks after the hot favourite for the Guineas is stopped by a jockey who just happens to be from the same place as the gangster?"

He waited for me to say something. I couldn't. Everything was escalating too quickly.

Outside there was a ruckus as a horse got loose and galloped into the car park. He went about a hundred yards, adroitly avoiding vehicles and then stopped suddenly, standing there, trembling, and staring back at the stable yard. Three figures ran past us towards the animal, slowing down as they got closer.

"I don't know if this will be of any help but have a look at it," Sir Jocelyn said, handing over the envelope.

I paused for a second, then opened it. It took a little while to get my bearings but eventually it started to make sense. There were a couple of invoices, outlining payments to a bank-account number. They totalled about ten thousand pounds, I reckoned. The dates on them were from 1983 and 1985. The name Duggan cropped up more than once. There was also a grainy black-and-white photograph. It showed Pinkie, with a full head of hair, and considerably lighter, but still immediately identifiable, talking to a pair of men.

"Anyone active from around then would recognise the three people in that picture," Sir Jocelyn said. "My pal is quite a noise now in intelligence. I got in touch with him and mentioned the name Pinkie. You never got this from me, okay?"

I nodded.

19

Max came scurrying out of the house, shouting "Papa!"

I clutched him up and held him tight.

"Present?" he asked.

"Aren't you getting to be the linguist," I said, kissing his sunburnt nose, and grinning at Sebastian.

The big man smiled slightly and stepped aside to let me in the front door. Manolo scampered down the stairs and nodded to his colleague.

"Is everything okay?" I asked.

"No problems at all," Manolo said. "There has been no incident, no unwanted visitors. I think your family is having a good time in Normandy."

They certainly were looking well on it. The parents were in good form, praising their grandson and admitting to a fondness for a certain red wine that was unbelievably inexpensive in the local supermarket. My father even pronounced it in a Gallic style that included a slight arm flourish. Cammie looked spectacular. That tawny skin had browned even more in the sun. She was wearing shorts and a halter-top that reminded me with a jolt how much of a physical hold my wife continued to exert on me.

"Thank God you're back," she said, hugging me. "Are you okay? What happened to your finger?"

"I'll tell you in a minute. How have things been here?"

"Fine. Just missing you. Max is very happy. And your parents have been so helpful. I think they like being useful."

I watched as Dad got down on one knee to help his grandson tear open the toy train I'd bought on the ferry to Cherbourg. It had been a rough trip, a heavy swell making my guts as unsettled as my head. I'd taken the boat, partly as an excuse to get some time to think and partly to salve fears about being tailed. The one reassurance was the family being safe in St Aubin. For some illogical reason the impulse took over that I was less likely to be followed if going by boat. This was as illogical as the presumption behind it. Clancy's confidence in my passivity was absolute. There was no need for cloak and dagger stuff any more. But the fear remained.

I took Cammie outside to the garden and told her what Duggan had done to my hand. She grabbed it and held it in her own. We said nothing for some time.

"Lorcan, you've done so much. I don't know how you got me out of that awful place, but you did. And you brought us here, which is incredible, the more I think about it. But you can't do any more. This man will stop at nothing. You've gone beyond what anyone else could. It's time to stop running. Let them do what they have to do and then we can forget about them. It's just a race, Lorcan. It's just a horse. It's not worth any more."

I nodded. She was right. What mattered was here, my

family, my kid – the little person who'd made sense of my life, who'd pushed all the bullshit stuff to the side in the face of the one glaring purpose to my life which was raising Max the best way I could.

"Come in, and let me make you dinner," Cammie smiled, keeping hold of my hand. "I'll show you how the French eat. You'll never want to leave here."

Max was exhausted by early evening. He even allowed me to put him to bed, which had become Granny's preserve. I kissed his head all over until he was slapping me away in irritation. Within seconds he was asleep. I stayed there for quite a while, watching my innocence breathe lightly into his pillow. Downstairs Mum called out, asking whether anyone wanted a cup of tea. There was an unintelligible base rumble that presumably was Sebastian.

The big man had never uttered more than a couple of words to me, but Cammie said he and Max had become best buddies, traipsing around the garden, my boy on those massive shoulders, getting to touch and experience trees and flowers that must have seemed in another orbit from the ground. Manolo was the brains but tended to keep his distance more. She also said she'd seen them indulge in some sort of kick-boxing moves in the garden that scared the hell out of her while allowing her to sleep better at night.

Max's room was next to Cammie's. Through the wall I could hear her moving around. Her mobile phone rang with the distinctive jangle that always caught me unawares. She answered but spoke quietly and I couldn't make anything out. There was a burst of soft laughter. A minute later she skipped past the door on her way downstairs.

It was time to move myself. I kissed Max on the

forehead, slid out of the bedroom and gently closed the door behind me. Cammie hadn't done the same with her door. It was half open. I went in and her phone lay on the bed. There was no automatic keypad lock on it. I pressed the green button and a list of incoming and outgoing calls appeared. The most recent incoming was an Irish mobile number. My finger seemed to move independently. But I let it ring.

"Can't stay away, huh?" a voice on the other end said lightly. "Hey, we'll be together again soon. A little patience, honey."

I said nothing.

"Camilla? Are you there?" Thorpe asked.

I hung up, put the phone back on the bed and walked downstairs. Everyone was in the massive drawing room, watching a football match, Mum, Dad and Cammie sitting down, Manolo and Sebastian standing but watching the television intently. My wife caught my eye and smiled brightly.

"Would you guys like a night off? Head out somewhere?" I asked Manolo.

"There aren't many options for going out in St Aubin," he replied, smiling. "And you are paying us to do a job. We will continue to do it."

My father tore his attention from the screen and looked me over. "I've been stuck in this hell-hole for nearly a week now. The least you can do is buy me a drink. What about the two of us heading into town and trying to find a decent beer?"

I nodded. He got up and went to his room to change. I asked Mum if she'd like to come and she winked and said she had her eye on a glass of their new favourite wine.

"Cammie and me will stay here and hold the fort," she said.

It looked to me like my wife would have liked a change of scene very much indeed but she said nothing, except to tell us to have fun when Dad appeared again.

We walked along the narrow road into town, high hedges hiding fields of wheat and flax that stretched across the flat landscape into the distance. Long rows of tall apple trees interrupted the view occasionally. Late evening sunshine made us squint but there was a warm breeze from the sea that kept it very pleasant.

Dad glanced at my hand a couple of times but said nothing. He'd learned over the years that I didn't like to discuss being hurt.

"It was Duggan," I said. "He picked me up and showed me why he's called Pinkie."

"You don't mean . . ."

"Yeah."

"Jesus Christ," he said, and nothing else.

We strolled through the town, down cool, shaded back streets to the beachfront. Instead of heading to a café or bar we kept moving on to the broad expanse of hard sand left behind by the tide. It was easy to walk on and the pair of us kept up a good pace away from the centre of the small town on the beach that was assigned as "Juno" on the D-Day landings in 1944. It was a lot more pleasant than when the Canadian troops of the North Shore Regiment of New Brunswick struggled ashore from landing craft into the withering fire of the German defences. The courage required to do that had always impressed me and it seemed almost inhuman now, to come from the eastern tip of Canada three thousand miles away to risk one's life in a struggle that hindsight made one of the noblest in history, but which at the time must have appeared another ritualised slaughter organised by a remote government in a faraway place they must have known little about.

"Why don't you just break this Clancy's leg?" Dad said eventually. "Or his arm, or cut his damn fingers off."

"Don't think the idea hasn't crossed my mind. But all that would do is expose another jockey to all this mess," I said. "Duggan would just threaten or intimidate whoever we get in to replace Clancy. That wouldn't be fair to anyone."

"Okay, what if you announce Kentish Town is hurt. And he can't run. That's Duggan kyboshed."

"First of all, a horse gets one chance at the Derby. There are over a hundred thousand thoroughbreds foaled every year. About fifteen of them get to line up at Epsom. So the odds against having the winner are massive. And the odds against having an outstanding favourite are ridiculously massive. I know it's just a race, but the Derby is history, the basis of an entire sport and industry. Winning it, whether it's the horse, trainer, owner, or breeder, means securing a little piece of that history for yourself, a little piece of posterity. I know how preposterous that must sound to anyone outside the game but, for someone like Jake Weinberger, the Derby and all it means is immense.

"And second of all, let's not kid ourselves. Do you really think someone like Duggan is going to pull a stroke like this, shake hands and never come near us again? He will be back again and again, stretching the boundaries even further every time. It'll be a licence to print money for him, and to hell with everything good and decent that gets in his way."

Eventually we stopped and peered out over the English

Channel. To our right the Norman coast swept eastwards, large industrial buildings in the distance. The sea was flat calm and inviting. It was easy to see why this beach had such a long history of attracting Parisians eager to escape the clinging summer heat in the city. And yet it would always be primarily associated with one cold day decades ago when there was only fear and death and awfulness. I was thinking too many dark thoughts. It was time to stop that. We turned back towards the promenade, facing the wind that rushed in from the west.

"I'll buy you that beer now," I said.

We found a small bar selling good German draft lager and sat outside, sheltered behind an awning that rattled in the breeze.

"Max is turning into a carbon copy of yourself," Dad said. "He told me yesterday he was going to be a fireman, helping me and Granny out of a burning building. And when I asked who'd help him, he said nobody. He could do it all himself. I seem to remember you saying something terribly similar at around the same age. It's amazing how the genetics work out."

"Yeah, the poor little guy has no chance. I –"

"You're taking an awful lot on yourself, boy," he interrupted. "Just remember, the graveyards are full of indispensable men."

"I know that, Dad. I've no illusions about my significance. Don't worry about that."

"It's not that. It's just I don't want you to hurt yourself. Not any more."

We ordered another beer. Dad read a tourism pamphlet that showed a picture of the beach just after D-Day. There was a crashed warplane among the rest of the debris. It was hard to square the image with the peaceful scene in front of us. But if I'd learned anything over the last few weeks it was not to trust appearances.

"I have something on Duggan," I said.

"What do you mean 'something'."

"I know about a part of his past that he would very much not want to get out."

"Jesus, so you can do to him what he's been doing to you. Fuck, that's outstanding. Ha! What've you got?"

"Something that would leave him wide open to his former comrades."

"You mean, the Provos? Christ, that's perfect. You've got him."

"I don't know."

"What's wrong? You're not worried about the fucking morality, are you? Do you think that bastard gives two hoots about morality? He couldn't even spell it."

"No, it's not that."

"What then?"

"If I go down that route, who knows where it might end up? It's a shot in the dark. And I don't like making decisions like that unless I have some idea of what the outcome is. With Duggan, I don't know."

"What do you mean?"

"When this happened," I said, holding up my hand, "he was like this animal, out of control. He could have done anything. He would have killed me without a thought. I've never seen anything like it. He frightened me."

There wasn't much to be said to that and Dad didn't try. We finished our beers, paid up and walked on, stopping to look at a large digger out on the beach pushing piles of sand into a big heap.

"Forget fireman: if Max ever sees that, there'll be no competition for what he wants to do when he grows up," I grinned.

"There'd be nothing wrong with it either. These guys who work diggers and JCBs are able to pick the eye out of your head. They can play those machines like fiddles."

"I can't see you ever working one of those," I said.

"Maybe not – but it wouldn't have been the end of the world if that's how I'd ended up," he continued. "I'm afraid my career was fundamentally based on the need to make a living. Don't get me wrong. It's made for a good life, and it turned out fine for raising the family. But it's hardly been life's young dream either. That's why I've never worried about you. You were doing something you loved. Even when you came home looking like someone who'd done fifteen rounds with Sonny Liston. It didn't really matter because the nags were all-consuming for you. Regrets are the bastard, boy. Never forget that. Regrets are the real bastard."

20

Niall Doherty was still chortling quietly as we snaked our way through Dundalk. The journalist was driving and he navigated his way expertly through the big border town. My own experience of Dundalk was confined to the motorway going past it and the short detour from there to the racecourse. But that was no good for finding the Town Hall. Doherty knew his way around, but I needed him for a lot more than that.

"I'll give you this, you're full of surprises," he laughed. "Here I am ferrying your ass around on the vague promise there might be a story in it for me about Pinkie Duggan – eventually. And not only that, but I have to get you close to the biggest lunatic in Ireland. Explain to me again why I'm doing this?"

"Because you're a patriot?" I grinned.

"Piss off," he said without rancour. "Whatever about being used, I will not be accused of patriotism."

He was right about being used. I clutched the NUJ card

with "Press" written extravagantly across the top. It was photo free and the name on it was Kevin Connolly.

"Kevin also gave me one of his cameras. It's in the boot. You can sling that around your neck when we get there," Doherty said. "And that cost me a gallon of pints to Connolly so you owe me that too."

"I'll subsidise a lake of porter if I can just get close to Duggan," I promised.

Doherty had assured me after I rang him first that I'd been watching too much television when it came to getting access to a press conference. This was Dundalk, not Washington, he'd said. Barring people on the basis of non-accreditation was not the Irish way. But I didn't want any potential problems that could be avoided with just a bit of foresight. So I'd badgered him, and pleaded, and given vague promises about a potentially sensational story if he helped me out. Eventually he relented, partly through exhaustion, partly through curiosity and the promise of free access to an executive box at the Curragh on Irish Derby Day, with unlimited food and drink thrown in.

"You do realise that you being seen with me is not something that's going to earn you a place in Pinkie's heart," Doherty reminded me.

"I just need to get close enough to him to tell him something – quietly," I said. "I'll just follow on your coat-tails so I can get near him and then it's up to me. You won't have to do anything."

"Except watch," he said. "I'm not going to miss this. How's your finger?"

"It's fine. Just an accident with a corkscrew at home. The bandage will be off in a few days."

"Fair enough," he said and looked at me sceptically.

"Keep an eye out for a parking space. And some real patriots. The place is crawling with twitchy ex-heroes from the north who'd just love to get near me."

I took an enormous camera out, hung it around my neck and tried to make it look natural. Doherty took it off and hooked it over my shoulder.

"You're a hack, not some tourist," he said. "And try to look bored. These gigs are always tedious as hell."

The gig was a meeting of a cross-border quango. Various politicians and business people from both jurisdictions were presenting a report into local government co-operation. Normally such events were of little newsworthiness, but several national political worthies had decided to lend their weight to this one and so a decent turn-out could be expected, Doherty said.

We crossed the road and entered the building, Doherty getting double-take reactions from various people, some of whom smiled, others who didn't. I shuffled behind in his shadow, making myself as inconspicuous as possible, trying to fiddle with the enormous camera like I knew what I was doing. A red-haired woman in a sharp business suit was standing at the entrance to a big room, armed with a clipboard.

"Niall Doherty, well, well. To what do we owe this, ahem, pleasure?"

"Marianne, how are you? Looking as splendid as ever," my guide said, grinning meaningfully at her.

She didn't miss a beat. "What are you doing here?" she asked. "Besides being a nuisance? I don't want any hassle today. If you want to be nauseating to someone, do it on someone else's shift."

"Don't be like that – not after everything you meant to

me!" He grinned at me. "By the way, this is my snapper today. His name's, er, Kevin."

She shook my hand firmly, a brief quizzical look flashing across her face. I looked at Doherty and pleaded silently with him not to draw attention to me. But he was having none of it.

"Marianne works for the Department of Justice," he said. "We used to be an item, once."

"Shut up," she responded, looking around to make sure no one else was in earshot. "Once was it. The memory alone is enough to put me off shagging forever."

"Ah, you loved it. I can still see that lovely red thatch bobbing like –"

"What do you want?" she said, daring him to continue.

"I presume Duggan and the other patriots are in here," Doherty said, letting it go.

"If you mean the Minister and his good friend Mr Duggan, then yes, they will be arriving shortly," she said. "No doubt they'll be thrilled to see you."

"No doubt. What do you say I give you a lift back afterwards? We can stop in an airport hotel and I can return that favour," he said, again turning to me as his audience.

"Don't mind me," I said, staring mostly at the floor.

"Niall, the only way you will ever get me into a hotel room again is if your sorry ass is lying in repose in one," she said, before flashing a big smile at a local worthy with a chain around his neck.

"She loves me really," Doherty said, making his way towards a large table with sandwiches and bottles of minerals on it. "Take a look around. There are about half a dozen geezers around here who in most any other country would be behind bars."

"Really?"

"Let me put it like this: when this thing kicks off I might do a runner. Ring me when you're finished and I'll pick you up."

"You really are worried?"

"Let's just say, I'm glad my shadow is in his car outside."

"I forgot about him."

"I never do," he said. "And I never forget how dangerous Pinkie is. I don't know what you're doing and, story aside, I don't really want to know. But be under no illusions about what this guy is capable of."

He looked meaningfully at my hand when he finished, then lightly slapped my arm and left. I tried to look busy, pointing the lens at various people who self-consciously straightened up and lifted their chins at the sight of a camera. Most importantly of all I kept moving. The last thing I needed was for some other photographer to ask who the hell the new guy was, or even worse, ask anything about photography.

There was a commotion at the door, Marianne laughed and suddenly Duggan appeared, side by side with a government minister and a supermarket magnate I recognised from the telly.

They all bounded onto a small stage, along with three others who were on a committee devoted to improving conditions for cross-border commerce. I was so busy trying to remain unobtrusive that it took a few seconds for it to dawn on me that a few snappers were taking pictures of the five men and one woman lined up in front of them. I shuffled towards them, stuck my camera up and kept it there, pressing a button that might nor might not have been the right one.

"Okay, lads, that'll do you," Marianne said, stepping in front of us.

A couple of my supposed colleagues hung around near the front taking shots but I quickly retreated.

The Minister had his own police security. A stocky man in a shirt a size too small for him stood to the side of the stage. There appeared to be a bulge under his suit, or maybe I just wanted there to be one. Being this close to Duggan had me sweating. I noticed my breathing had become heavy. The camera seemed to weigh a ton. Suddenly, getting out like Doherty had done seemed very attractive.

"I'm delighted to be here today at the publishing of our report into . . ."

The Minister gave every indication of settling in for quite a stint at the dais. The committee members had retreated to the side, near the police security man. Duggan I noticed was laughing quietly with his female colleague, lightly touching her arm and giving every impression of urbane charm. As always the suit was pristine, the smile bright, all malevolence tightly under wraps. I moved to the back and circled around behind the audience. Under the guise of wanting a shot of the speaker, I excused my way through and found myself standing just behind Pinkie. His proximity made my hands shake. I prayed such uncertainty wouldn't come out in my voice.

"Can we go somewhere more private?" I said quietly.

He turned around, still smiling, and did an almost comical double-take. His female colleague was rapt with attention on the speaker. No one else appeared to be paying attention to us.

"Or we can talk here," I added.

Pinkie looked around. The idea that Anto & Co might

be nearby had me pondering the possibility of collapsing in a heap, pretending to have a heart attack, and getting out of there via ambulance. But there was no sudden shadow over the sun behind me. I pulled an envelope out from my jacket and held it out to him. He didn't acknowledge it, just stared straight at me. So I opened it.

"Did you know your MI6 reference number was MB270711?" I asked, trying to sound something even close to normal. That eruption of raw anger back in Tallaght was still fresh in my mind. There was no reaction but I could sense his back straightening. "Or that you were known as 'The King'. Apparently that was a term to reflect the importance of the information you supplied for a five-year period in the late 1970's and early 1980's. Your handlers were a pair of spooks you knew as Cook and Wilson. Have I got your attention?"

He turned away, looking ahead, to all intents and purposes rapt in the speech. But there was a rigidity to his shoulders that let me know his attention was on me alright. The drone from the stand was loud enough for me to speak quietly.

"You got five thousand sterling in cash in one payment on April the 27th, 1979. Another five grand in March '81. And ten thousand in cash on December the 5th, 1982 – was that a Christmas present?"

There was a brief burst of applause for the speaker, which Pinkie contributed to. I shuffled the papers to the one I wanted.

"Wilson wrote a report in May 1980, stating that '*The King is a resolutely amoral individual whose only concern is his own profit. He is also the most dependable and valuable provider of data and information on the activities of the Provisionals in West Belfast, particularly the Ballymurphy area.'* He goes on to mention an incident where an escaped prisoner from the Maze was picked up and at the same time an assassination attempt on the Shankill Road was averted with three volunteers arrested. This is the bit I like: *'This reflects the continued input of said informant who right now is an invaluable source for us.'* How do you think your ex-comrades would react to that?"

There was a "sshh" from the woman standing in front of me who turned around and glared. I ignored her.

"You're an informer. You used the money you got from MI6 to start lifting yourself up the criminal ladder. But you're still an informer. And we know what that means in Ireland. Have a look at this."

This time he did glance around to look at the picture I held out from thirty years previously. He flinched. I could feel it, and that boosted my courage. I held out the other picture, more grainy but still clearly Pinkie. Then I showed him ten pages of text, files and account numbers.

"These are all copies," I said, stuffing them back into the envelope. "You can have them."

He ignored the package. The speech finished up to more applause and the audience started moving about again. I took a step closer to him in case we were overheard.

"You've done monstrous things. My friend is lying in a coma. You took my wife," I said, almost whispering. "This is very simple: if you come near me or mine ever again, other copies of these documents will go to a number of people in news organisations. Niall Doherty will be one. Copies will also be sent to some of your former colleagues. I'm sure they'll be interested in them. Hostilities might officially be over but scores are still being settled. And it seems to me there is a large score against you. Also, if anything happens to me or mine, I have arranged for a signed affidavit, outlining everything that has happened, to be sent to the authorities. But I reckon they will turn out to be the least of your worries. 'Informer' is still a very dirty word in Ireland. You won't last. Or if you do, it won't be for long."

"Darling, come and meet some friends of mine," said Pinkie's committee friend, grabbing his arm.

She didn't even seem to register with him. He stared resolutely at me. There was an energy radiating from him though that encouraged me to take a couple of steps backwards. That didn't seem to register either. But the energy off him was almost palpable.

"Darling, are you okay?" the woman persevered. "Has this person been annoying you?"

That was my cue to get out. I noticed Marianne moving quickly towards Pinkie and his friend, then turning around to look at me making for the door. I jabbed at the phone to ring Doherty. It didn't seem likely that Pinkie would go anywhere without having some muscle nearby. The last thing I needed was to get caught up in a spontaneous expression of rage before realisation of the new lie-of-the-land dawned.

He was snookered. I'd run every permutation possible through my mind a hundred times. There was no getting away from it. His reaction alone told me the evidence of his youth was a nightmare he'd never expected to have to revisit. Up to then there had been inevitable doubts bound up in the simple reality of being scared to death of him. But it wasn't just being in front of loads of people that prevented Pinkie going for my throat. He was many things, but stupid wasn't one of them – I hoped. I jogged a couple of hundred yards to the end of the street and Doherty pulled up next to me. I swiftly got in.

"Did you get what you wanted?" he asked.

"I hope so," I replied. "Now, if you could, will you get us as far away from here as possible?"

We were halfway back to Dublin when Judith phoned.

21

I sat quietly by the bed. Judith had left to get a shower, exhausted and thinner than seemed possible. She looked like she would barely have the strength to lift a cup of coffee. Once again, how deceptive appearances could be. This supposedly frail little woman was the rock on which everyone else leant.

I'd explained to her on the phone what had happened with Duggan. It was while waiting to board the flight in Dublin. She said how marvellous I was, and how stupid, and brave, and how recklessly irresponsible I was to put my family at such risk. And could I please hurry.

"There's no need for you to wait here. I can let you know," a nurse said to me.

"No, I'll wait. It's the least I can do."

The words were barely out of my mouth when Jake slowly opened his eyes. They took a few seconds to focus in on the array of medical equipment above his head and then he looked sideways.

"I thought I heard your voice," he whispered. "Reckoned I was at the track there for a second."

He moved his finger about an inch to touch my hand on the bed: a tiny gesture that moved me more than I could ever have imagined.

"You old fuck," I said, eventually. "You had us worried."

"Sorry about that, kid," he said.

It was still a whisper. His throat was raw from the number of tubes stuck down it at various stages. But it was steady enough and clear enough. The fact it was there at all was miraculous. Judith hadn't told anyone, but on the first day she had been told by surgeons that her husband had just a one in ten chance of surviving. But he's always liked beating the odds, she said to me before leaving to go home to change. The first thing he'd said apparently, after emerging from the coma, was to ask when was the Derby. She'd wept with relief, almost collapsed with released stress and started ringing around to say her husband had come back to her.

Jake had slept for much of the time since but it was genuine sleep, the real deal. The doctors kept remarking on how tough the man was: all his vital signs were encouraging. He wasn't going anywhere for quite a while but was over the worst.

"Thank you, Lorcan, for everything," he said.

"Relax, just get better."

"What a stupid thing to do, huh?" he persisted.

"Put it out of your head. Just concentrate on getting better."

"I'm so ashamed, kid. What a cowardly thing I've done. Running away like a scared schoolboy from a bully," he said, his voice catching.

I made to shush him but he ploughed on.

"Even when I was swallowing those pills, I wanted someone to stop me. Do you know that? Like I needed someone to make my mind up for me. How pathetic is that?"

"It doesn't matter, Jake. It's like anything. The only thing that matters is the end result. And you're still here. You've fought your way back. None of us ever figured you wouldn't. We know what you're like," I said softly.

"Jesus, what a mess I've made," he said, staring up at a ceiling that must have seemed crowded with recrimination.

"Jake, what's done is done. You did what you did. But you did it after being put in a situation not of your making. If you weren't thinking completely straight, then welcome to how the rest of us feel most of the time. No one is unbendable, Jake. Not even you. The only thing that matters now is that you make the most of this second chance. You'd better get well."

Giving a pep talk to my boss felt both right and wrong. Maybe it was wealth or power, maybe even his age, but it almost felt like a liberty talking like that to him. I meant what I said, but it sounded strange to my ears. I half-expected a jokey put-down but instead he turned his face away, trying to compose himself. I liked this man very much.

"Judith has been telling me bits and pieces about what's been happening," he said. "But I want to know the full picture."

"There's time enough for that."

"Lorcan, fill me in."

So I did, leaving out nothing. There was little or no reaction from Jake, even to those events that sounded incredibly melodramatic in the retelling. It all seemed fantastic, were it not for the fact that it was painfully real. The only time Jake moved slightly was to look at my hand.

"This Duggan doesn't know who he's dealing with," he whispered.

"He scared the shit out of me. Still does," I replied.

"I don't blame you. Only a moron wouldn't be frightened. He sounds desperately impulsive."

"He is."

"You look even thinner than usual, kid. It's been a tough time for you. What do you weigh now?"

"I've no idea."

We didn't say anything more for quite a while. The nurses came and fiddled about with wires, checked charts, took Jake's temperature and told him he was talking too much when he tried to flirt with them.

"There's not much wrong with him, huh?" one of them grinned to me. "We're going to have to watch this guy."

She scribbled something on his chart, asked me if I wanted anything and said I would have to go soon. The patient needed rest.

"I don't care if it gets out," Jake said a minute later. "That damn tape. As if it matters to anyone. It's just embarrassment. And I was going to . . . Judith is wonderful, isn't she?"

"Yes, she is."

"She told you how things got to that stage?"

"Nothing specific."

"I'm a lucky man."

"Yes, you are."

"So are you," he said. "Nothing else matters except those closest to you. You do know this man is capable of anything?"

"I do."

"You've blindsided him something wonderful, thanks to good ol' Sir Jocelyn. But there's no guarantee he's going to play by the rules. Even if he does, who's to say associates of his will? And nothing is worth having your family put at risk."

"That's true," I said. "But they're in a safe place for the time being."

"And?"

"And I don't like being pushed around."

"That stubborn streak is going to get you into trouble," Jake said, smiling at me. "But thank God for it."

Again we didn't say anything for a bit. Whatever about the patient being tired, I found myself almost nodding off. Jake was right: if I looked as knackered as I felt, then I was a sight for sore eyes.

"We're going to have to hide Kentish Town," he suddenly announced, jolting me awake.

"What do you mean?"

"If this guy is up to his neck in betting liabilities for the Derby, then the obvious thing for him to try is to get at the horse. If Kentish Town can't run, then all bets are off. There's no knowing his reach. It doesn't matter if it's threats or money. He can get to people. And with Clancy in his pocket he would know exactly who to go for, and where. We have to get the horse out of the yard."

"Okay. But you can't just take him away. Gerry might be a little put out."

"If Gerry is put out, then put him on to me," Jake said. "I can talk on the phone to him. But it won't come to that. You're in charge, Lorcan. You're the only one I trust. I hate to put you through more of this. And if you want to back out, I'll more than understand. But if you're willing to stick with it, then we have to presume the worst of people. It's a damn thing to have to do. But there's no other option."

"That's okay."

"One more thing."

"Yeah?"

"Ask the nurse for bathroom scales."

"Why?"

"Just do it."

I asked for scales and got the inevitable question about what a man in an ICU bed wanted to weigh himself for. But even in hospital the American habit of doing what the man with the money said came through. Within a couple of minutes, a shiny bathroom scales was handed to me.

"Okay, Jake, what do you want these for?"

"Step up on 'em," he ordered.

I did what I was told. The needle hovered just past the eleven stone mark. It was amazing what a dietary aid rampant stress could be, I figured. Nearly ten pounds dropped in a couple of weeks. I hadn't been this light since my riding days.

"Eleven stone one," I said.

"Think you could lose a stone?" he asked.

"Why on earth would I do that?"

"Because you'll have to ride Kentish Town in the Derby."

That knocked the air out of me in a way that hadn't happened since hitting the ground at thirty miles an hour was an occupational hazard. The idea was ludicrous. My spin on Choirboy had been my first time on a horse in a couple of years. Even in my prime, I was a good middle-of-the-road jockey, polished enough to hold my own. But even the real top jump jockeys could put me in my place. Just the idea of mixing it with the sleek polish of the best flat riders in the world, in the most famous and important race in the world, made me queasy.

"Jake, let's get real. I can't do that. I'm not good enough. I'm not fit enough. I'm not light enough."

"Every horse carries nine stone in the Derby, right?"

"Yes. And even allowing for the lightest saddle imaginable, paper-thin everything, that means being eight stone eleven stripped. I'm too big and too old. I'm too . . . everything."

"You're the only one I can trust. You'll have to ride him. Even if another of the top jockeys isn't bought off, it wouldn't be fair to place him in a position where he could be vulnerable. And if he was compromised, the first we'd know about it was after the race – too late then."

"But it's asking too much of Kentish Town," I said, scrambling to try and make the man see sense. "You're asking him to give the best horses in Europe a stone: that's like giving them a ten-length start. He's good, Jake, but he can't be that good."

"If he isn't, then he isn't. But I need to know that he's trying for his life. So do you. How can we know that for certain if anyone else rides him? You're going to have to, Lorcan. Whether you like it or not."

"But the papers will go spare, wanting to know why."

"Tell them it's at my insistence. Tell them on the QT that I've gone bananas."

"I think you have," I said. "And Gerry might have an opinion on it too."

"It's what I want. Kentish Town is mine. If anyone is

upset, then remind them of some home truths – like who pays the bills."

"You're letting yourself wide open, Jake."

"Fuck that. Look at where worrying about what other people think has got me. I need you to ride my horse. If you lose, so be it. But my horse needs to try. Will you do it?"

I nodded.

"Good man. Now, go start starving."

22

In his quietly measured way, Gerry Gunning was having an episode. It was hard to blame him. Having the racing manager of his most important owner arrive at his front door at three in the morning was unusual enough. To have that same manager announce he was taking away the favourite for the Epsom Derby would have induced apoplexy in most of his colleagues. It was to Gerry's credit then that he looked at me with only mild incredulity. What he felt inside I could only guess at.

"This is mad, Lorcan. You can't be serious. Where are you going to take him?"

We strode through the yard, a chill night air smoking our breaths as we walked. The two night-time security guards who'd caught me in their flashlights when I first arrived and were all set to get heavy until peering into my face, had been sent home early, Gerry assuring them everything was fine. His face though said everything was very far from fine.

"Lorcan," he said, seriously enough to make me stop,

"I am the trainer of this horse. He is my responsibility. We're talking about the Derby favourite here. You can't just take him away."

"I know this is highly irregular but . . ."

"Highly irregular is a serious understatement. It's – it's mad."

"There's a lot of stuff going on here, Gerry, believe me. This is necessary. I can ring Judith and she can put Jake on to you, if you like. It's his idea."

"No, there's no need for that. But at least tell me where you're going. As his trainer I need to know. And I need some of my people there with him, people he knows and trusts."

"He's not a particularly quirky colt, is he?"

"No."

"Then, I should be able to look after him."

"Jesus Christ, this can't be happening."

I understood that sensation only too well. And if Gerry was having a breakdown now, I didn't like to think what his reaction was going to be to the real doozy I was putting off. I asked him to reverse my four by four, and the horsebox attached to it, near to the hay shed. Most thoroughbreds ate whatever was put in front of them. Some were more finicky. Gerry got to work filling the store area of the box with bales and nuts. He even put in a barrel of water, just in case. While he did that, I fetched Kentish Town.

The most valuable racehorse in the world was asleep, lying luxuriantly on a deep straw bed, happily oblivious to everything going on around him. Even the racket of me unlatching the stable door, and standing there looking, resulted only in him opening his eyes and delivering an almost exasperated snort at this unexpected interruption.

He had a lightly padded rug strapped around him and it was almost comical the air of resignation he exuded when climbing stiffly to his feet.

"Sorry about this, Chief," I whispered, clipping a lead rope to his head-collar and leaning down to pick out bits of dirty straw from his feet.

Kentish Town stood there dozily, thankfully as far from the clichéd snorting stallion as it was possible to be. I led him outside and we walked to the box. Gerry had helpfully lowered the back of it. The horse took a long look at the unaccustomedly cosy accommodation but clumped noisily up and settled in for his unexpected trip.

"You're taking him to Annagrove, right?" Gerry asked.

I said nothing. He took that as an affirmative.

"I'll bring his lead horse over tomorrow," he said. "And I'll bring Luis, his work-rider, over too. He doesn't need anything strenuous. We'll just keep him ticking over with a few canters. All the serious work is done. All this is mad though. And all because Jake is afraid someone is going to try and nobble the horse? I can double the security here, triple it, if that's what he's worried about."

"It's nothing to do with that, Gerry. Jake has complete faith in you. But he wants to be completely careful with this horse. You know what Kentish Town means to him."

"He kinda means a lot to me too," the trainer said, almost wistfully, peering over the horsebox at his champion's broad brown rump. "You know, I think he's gone back to sleep in there."

We both grinned. He really was an exceptional individual. The world deserved to see how exceptional. Responsibility weighed down on my shoulders again.

"He's not going to Annagrove, Gerry. I'm not sure

where I'm taking him yet. In fact neither you nor anyone from here can see him until Derby Day," I said. "I'll keep in touch. You're still in charge of his preparation. Just think of it as if you're sending one to race in America. The guys you send out there are on the ground with the horse but you're still the boss. This is the same thing. You tell me what to do, and I'll do it."

"Except I at least know what part of America they're in," he said.

"There's one other thing."

"What now?"

"I'm going to ride Kentish Town at Epsom."

"No, I don't like my horses to work on the track," Gerry declared. "If they're going to come down that hill properly, they're more likely to do it first time of asking,"

"No, not in work. In the race."

Even in darkness it seemed like his face drained of colour. He looked at me first as if I was joking, then realised too much weird stuff was already happening for me to embellish it with a gag. Ireland's champion trainer was too stunned to say anything. It appeared as if his senses were briefly numbed, only returning to allow him to look me over silently and do some quick arithmetic in his head. The sum didn't work out satisfactorily.

"But you're . . ." he said.

"I know, Jerry, but these are Jake's wishes. I don't like it any more than you do."

"But you're a jump jockey, *were* a jump jockey."

"Yeah."

"You haven't ridden in a long time, not even work."

"Yeah."

"And what do you weigh?"

"I aim to make ten stone for the Derby."

"That's a stone more than the others!"

"Yeah."

"Unacceptable," he muttered. "Completely unacceptable. The poor horse has no chance."

"It's got to be this way, Gerry," I said.

"Not for me, it doesn't. I'm going to be a laughing stock. We're all going to be ridiculed. A retired steeplechase rider against the best jockeys in Europe. It's completely ridiculous. And what's Clancy going to say?"

"It doesn't matter what Clancy says. He isn't riding for Jake ever again."

"Then what are the Press going to say? Jesus Christ. They'll have a field day. I'm not sure I want anything to do with this."

"Gerry, please don't make an issue. It will be to no one's benefit. If everything goes pear-shaped, I'll let everyone know this was done against your wishes."

"But I've spent years building up a reputation," he said. "That sounds up my own ass but nonetheless it is true. I wouldn't go along with something like this if it was a ninety-rated handicapper, never mind the best horse I've ever had. And you won't even tell me why this is all happening. It's unacceptable."

"Fair enough, but Kentish Town is Jake's horse. Ultimately what the owner wants, he gets, and Jake wants it to happen this way."

He didn't say anything to that, instead busying himself with a latch on the back of the box that didn't need a fraction of the attention Gerry was suddenly lavishing on it. After what seemed an age he spoke again.

"You're right, of course. Kentish Town is Jake's. But I

want it on the record that I believe this to be insane behaviour. And once the Derby is over, and Jake is well again, I will demand a meeting to review our relationship. More immediately, I demand to be kept informed of every step this horse takes."

The carefully worded language spoke of the chasm that had just opened between us. Gerry was not going to be hung out to dry. I could hardly blame him.

"What do I say to the press?" he asked.

"Nothing. Refer them to me."

"Okay. Just stay in touch. I don't care when you ring. Just ring. Even if it is the middle of the night." He grinned, slightly. It was a tight, forced grin, but at least he'd squeezed it out from under his deep unease.

"Don't worry, I will," I said. "And you never know: maybe Kentish Town is good enough to overcome everything – even me."

The look on Gerry's face clearly suggested I was dreaming. I drove off with the trainer stolidly staring after us.

We caught the dawn driving through the outskirts of Dublin, making the M50 in good time and circling round to the north side of the city. Traffic was very light and there were no hold-ups on the way to the airport. Away from the main passenger terminals, it felt eerily quiet. The entrance to where freight and other business flights operated was manned by two security men, one of whom remained in a fluorescently lit office while his colleague yawned and examined my paperwork.

Horses were regularly flown in and out of Dublin airport so there was nothing to excite the guard's attention. Kentish Town's name didn't appear anywhere but my desire to keep his identity secret had made me put a noseband and a pair of cheek-pieces on him. Unaccustomed to this headgear, the colt had momentarily started at this new equipment but thankfully quickly settled down. To add to the effect, I'd also thrown a tatty old rug from Annagrove on him – anything to make him seem like just another horse flying out of Ireland.

The guard barely looked over the back of the horsebox, clearly not interested. But my paranoia about Duggan's reach was absolute. Everything depended on maintaining our anonymity. I'd driven Siobhán to distraction aiming to make sure every aspect of the documentation was perfect, ignoring how she had been doing it perfectly competently for years. We were waved through after I signed a lengthy document testifying to how the airport wasn't liable for any damage to the jeep and horsebox while it remained in the airport until someone from Annagrove picked it up later in the day.

The plane waited close by: Siobhán's logistical ability proved yet again. Far from the pristine ultra-modern aircraft that usually carried Jake Weinberger's bluebloods, this was something that I might have flown in a couple of decades previously when escorting British-bound runners for the trainer I used to ride for. Even the sight of it was enough to provoke a queasy feeling in my stomach at the memory of one shuddering two-hour-long journey where we had dipped and swooped in a rattling cacophony of sound and mild panic that had the humans on board offering grateful thanks when we landed. This was no suitable vehicle for a Derby contender but it was the only thing available on such short notice, and more importantly it was hardly likely to generate unwanted interest in its cargo.

"What have we got here then?" said a polished English accent from the cockpit window.

"Just the one," I shouted up. "He's late for a vet's exam. That's why we're in a bit of a hurry."

I jumped out and quickly dropped the back of the box. A young man ran down the gang-plank from the plane and waited as I backed Kentish Town out. The colt stood and peered around at the scene. His ears pricked and took it all in but he was unconcerned at the noises and sights. I noticed the man from the plane had a deep tan and when he asked if I wanted him to lead the horse on board his broken English came in a South American accent that might have been Brazilian. I pulled an old black beanie further down my skull and pulled up a coat collar. It didn't seem like he recognised me, nor did the pilot look at me differently as he waited for me to lead Kentish Town up. That was not too surprising. Pilots were hired to fly, not to handle bloodstock. Thankfully this guy had the look of someone who wouldn't know the front part of a horse from the back.

"Welcome aboard!" he shouted over the racket of the propellers that roared just yards from us.

I positioned Kentish Town into a stall, tied his head-collar, patted his neck reassuringly and ran back down the gangway, forcing myself to not look back. After parking the jeep in an out-of-the-way spot, I sprinted back to the plane, trying to reassure myself that what I was doing was logical and correct and not the result of paranoia run wild. Everything revolved around keeping Kentish Town hidden and safe, and that meant flying under the radar as much as humanly possible. If I could tell the pilot to do that literally, then I would have.

As it happened, the flight wasn't too bad. Everything rattled and the noise was intense. But there were no dramatic turbulent dips. I sat on a bale of straw in front of the colt whose temperament really was amazing. Take-off and the noise didn't budge his equilibrium at all. Within minutes of being in the air he was picking at a twist of hay and he even drank a couple of times from a water bucket.

"He is very relaxed!" the young guy shouted at me.

"Yeah, he's really good!" I yelled back.

"He like old mare!" he laughed.

The landing at Southampton airport was smooth and it was a sunny morning as Kentish Town clumped back down the gangway. I led him a couple of hundred yards away to where a small shiny green horsebox designed for just two occupants waited with a representative of the hire-company Siobhán had spoken to the day before. It had been necessary to take Siobhán into my confidence – to an extent. It was safer that way: someone had to be entrusted with the vital task of fielding any enquires about my whereabouts – and, if it came to it, the whereabouts of Kentish Town.

"I take it you are the Dunne party?" he asked cheerily.

Dunne was the name I'd told Siobhán to use. I nodded, pulled my coat collar up a bit more and said as little as possible.

"The customs chap said he might be a minute. He shouldn't be long."

It took a long ten minutes for a customs official to show up. He looked at the horse as if it were an exotic creature.

"We don't get many of them through here," he said, almost hopping backwards when Kentish Town's hooves scraped on the tarmac.

He signed and stamped his forms and I took the keys of the box, led the cargo on board and tried to drive out of the airport as carefully and as un-dramatically as possible. I marvelled at the colt. Through everything, he hadn't turned a hair, just behaved like a schoolboy on a school tour, taking it all in. I stopped about ten minutes down the road, climbed in the back, filled his water bucket and gave him a heartfelt pat on the chest.

23

Wasting had always been a pain, a daily struggle during my riding career to stay as light as possible. Like most jockeys cursed with a body too heavy for the job, I'd tried everything to lose weight: some healthy, some not so. In the end it usually came down to deprivation – basically not eating. As one trainer ruthlessly pointed out to me years previously, "This hole," pointing to his mouth, "is bigger than this one," pointing to his backside. The joy of riding racehorses and being able to compete at something I loved meant the demands of making weight were always met. It wasn't always easy, but in a world where choices were denied to so many, the decision to go without much to eat never seemed like much of a sacrifice. But sometimes the effort made me want to hide away in a dark room and face the wall.

It wasn't that bad now. There was a target, and it was short-term. The real headwreck came from looking too far down the line and knowing there was no relief from the daily ordeal of hunger pangs, aching muscles and incessant sweating. It was a cocktail to warp the strongest mind, if you let it. I'd forgotten how much an empty stomach could colour your view of the world, even if it was voluntarily empty. At least this was going to be over at the end of the week.

Ever since leaving Jake in his bed, I'd resorted to the old regime of vitamin pills, bird-like sips of water and fresh air. It still didn't taste great. Just a few more days, I told myself. Then, at least, I could gorge again. Typically I never did. But knowing I could was important. Culinary fantasies usually began with a real burger with pickles. And ended with a milkshake. It was proletarian stuff, but it was also paying off. Ten stone was not an unrealistic prospect, if I kept starving and sweating.

As I drove Kentish Town, ears alive for even the faintest movement or disturbance in the back, a parade of emotions danced through my mind on the prospect of riding him in the Derby: trepidation at a gumshoe jump jockey being shown up by some of the best riders in the world, not to mention a real queasiness at what the wider media response would be whenever I made the announcement. That was something that could hold until final declarations forty-eight hours before the race.

The prospect of embarrassing myself in front of tens of millions of people worldwide watching on TV was bad enough. But over a hundred thousand would be at Epsom in person, eager to see if a great horse could overcome being ridden by a fat, middle-aged relic. I was fit enough in ordinary Joe Bloggs terms. But riding was a very different matter. Muscles I hadn't used for years were starting to ache at even the idea of riding Kentish Town. How was I going to be of any assistance to him for the two and a half minutes it took to run around the world's trickiest racecourse?

But despite all the worry, stress and hunger, there was something else and it was like an old pal come back to visit – excitement at the prospect of racing again. Given the choice, I'd have preferred one of those veteran charity races where jockeys indulged in a puffing nostalgia for their youth and the only fingers burned were those soft hands getting re-accustomed to reins. I'd discussed with Jake the outcry there would be from punters who'd already backed the horse for the Derby, only to find him carrying over weight, and probably in their eyes, deadweight. His response was blunt.

"No one forced them to bet. The horse is my property. All of mine try their best, every time. Who rides them is my decision, not some taxi-driver's in Hartlepool. Plus any prize money we get, even if we win, will go to charity."

Yes, pulsing underneath all the unease was excitement. The potential for turning into a laughing stock was huge, but there was a small bit of me that already relished the chance to ride in the greatest race in the world, maybe even win it. Sure every other jockey in the race would be more stylish than the long-legged veteran, better in a finish, better judges of pace, fitter too – everything in fact. But still it was impossible not to imagine whizzing around Tattenham Corner and facing into the famous cambered straight that had been like an unimaginable fantasy-land for all my life with horses and now remarkably was becoming very real indeed.

It wasn't like jockeys hadn't mixed flat and jump riding before. It might have been decades previously, but riding in both the Derby and the Grand National was not unknown. That might have been a more Corinthian age, definitely more amenable to what was being proposed now, but still there was precedent. And there was no getting away from the competitive urge. Everyone might well write us off, but we might show them yet.

Every so often, my fears would win out and I'd stop at the side of the motorway, jump out and check him, make sure he hadn't stepped on some rogue stone in the straw or banged his head off something. Each time Kentish Town would look at me, nonchalant and unconcerned, thankfully still in one magnificent piece.

"Not long more now, kiddo," I said. "Then we can relax a bit."

24

De Beaufort was leaning on the gate in boots and an old oilskin jacket, a million miles from the tailored racecourse elegance he favoured. He jumped into the passenger seat and directed me for a mile along a winding road that took us into a small wood. Bright sunlight speckled through the trees until we came to a clearing that contained a small stable block. It was a functional block of concrete with four boxes and a sloping corrugated iron roof. Outside one of the doors were a few bales of straw piled up and an empty wheelbarrow thrown up against the wall.

"This is the isolation yard where I keep any horses I suspect might be coming down with something," the trainer explained. "I've disinfected it completely. The only time people are here is when there are horses to look after, so you won't be bothered."

We jumped out and I backed Kentish Town out to take a first look at his temporary lodgings. The only sounds as he peered imperiously around, ears pricked, nostrils flaring at these new smells, came from a pair of pigeons cooing in the trees. His host, I noticed, was peering intently at him, slowly placing a hand on his shoulder and running it down to feel a taut but perfectly cool tendon.

"And to think I turned this one down," Sir Jocelyn, muttered, shaking his head. "He looks good, even if he has been treated like some hurdling screw brought over here on the sly to pull off a stroke."

"He's actually been brilliant, cool as a breeze," I said. "Thanks for doing all this at such short notice. But Jake wants him out of the way. And the fewer people who know, the better."

"I can understand that," he replied. "Are things any clearer after those documents I gave you?"

"Much clearer – they've saved the day, in fact. I'll never be able to thank you enough."

"Don't bother," he said. "I hate bullies."

He followed me as I took the horse over to a clearing and allowed him pick greedily at some long grass.

"My main yard is five miles away. The best way to do this will be to canter him in the morning before anyone gets in. My head man is in at six every morning. You'll have to use the gallops before that, and after eight in the evening. I'm going to give my security guard some time off. His mother's not very well so I'll look like the kind-hearted boss. The gallop should be fine, but you might want to take a quick look for stones or something that might have blown on to them," Sir Jocelyn said. "No one should see you. But if they do, they'll come to me first. I'll tell them some cock and bull stuff to keep them off the scent. It's Monday now – we just have to keep things under wraps until Saturday. That should be doable."

"Gerry says all the work is done. I just have to keep him

ticking over. A seven-furlong pipe-opener in the morning maybe, and a gentle canter in the evening, just to get him out."

"That sounds about right. What's happening with Mr Clancy?"

"Clancy is out of the picture."

"So I guess you're going to import a jockey. Anyone in mind?"

"Yeah. Me."

"I see."

I was glad he did. I was even more glad that his reaction was not to burst out laughing. It was almost possible to hear his brain whirring out the calculation of how much was at risk that it required Jake's manager to ride Kentish Town in the most important race on the calendar. Typically, though, he didn't say anything about that.

"What do you weigh?"

"Right now, about ten and a half. I need to ride at ten."

"So you've got to get to nine stone twelve stripped."

"Minimum."

"Okay," he said. "There's a kitchen at the back of this place, and a toilet. Very basic. No bathroom though. If you need to get a sweat on, just ring me and you can come down to the house and run a bath. I'll stay with the horse if necessary."

"Thanks again."

"Are you a jogger?"

"Yeah."

"These woods go that way," he said, pointing eastwards, "for about a mile. And there are various tracks through them. You can juggle them about for variety. And the pine cones at least will make the ground spongy: save those geriatric joints a bit. I take it you won't require much grub?"

"No."

"Right, anything you need, you have the mobile number. Just ring."

He walked off through the trees. Kentish Town got another five minutes' grazing and then got to know his new box. It was big and roomy with a high ceiling and felt cool after the sunshine outside. I poured some nuts into a feed pot which he attacked hungrily. A bucket of water fitted neatly into another pot and there was a deep bed of straw on the floor. Closing the half door behind me, I reckoned our stretch of isolation would be quite tolerable. The phone rang. It was Judith.

"Everything is fine here," she said immediately. "The doctors even reckon Jake might be able to leave the ICU in a few days. He just wants to know how you and Kentish Town are. That's all he's talking about."

"Tell him we've arrived and are settling in."

"Okay. I will. Lorcan?"

"Yeah?"

"Be careful."

25

There was little or no heat in the dawn sunshine, but I put on running gear, topped off with a heavy winter sweater, and started pounding out some miles. De Beaufort was right. There were any number of trails and even when there weren't there was easily enough space between the thin evergreens to make detours easy. But I never went out of sight of the block. It meant going around in circles for the guts of an hour but I was sweating enough without having to worry about what might be happening back at base.

After peeling off the gear and washing myself as much as possible from the cold-water tap, I changed into jeans and a T-shirt and gave Kentish Town a rub-down for twenty minutes. He really was in superb condition: muscled, toned, and yet totally relaxed, just idly picking at some more grass I'd pulled for him while I brushed away. I fetched a saddle. The horse stood patiently until the saddle was tightened, a process his lad had told me before was guaranteed to get him skittish. There was no reason for it, no pinching, but sure enough the big tough colt suddenly got very delicate indeed and skipped around a little in his box. A final pick-out of his hooves and I pulled him out.

Kentish Town clambered back into the horsebox without hesitation and I slowly drove the short distance to Sir Jocelyn's gallops. The man himself buzzed us through the gates and directed me out of sight from the yard where I could reverse out of the way and go on to the all-weather gallop. All the major fitness work was done with Kentish Town. All that was left was keeping all that toned muscle supple and prepared. It was a different story with his rider though. This would tell a lot.

It was obvious from the second my backside touched the saddle. I'd raced on some wonderful jump horses, ridden a few very high-class flat runners in their work. I knew what class felt like. Kentish Town was something else again. It felt like sitting on a whiplash. Energy coursed through me and the colt wasn't even being particularly active. He was understandably fresh since he'd spent some time cooped up, but it wasn't anything pent-up that reverberated through the reins. Instead a raw, elemental power was condescending to being kept under control, waiting to be tapped. The sensation was electric. I was smiling as Sir Jocelyn grabbed the reins and led us onto the gallop that snaked and undulated for a mile into the distance.

This would be the real test of my fitness. Running miles was all very well, but being a jockey demanded a lot more from very different muscles. I gathered the reins, wriggled my big toes into the irons and prayed the horse wouldn't run away with me. He was pretty buzzed, looking around him at the unfamiliar ground and eager to be moving. The familiar first lunge forward felt like coming home. My infuriatingly long body coiled automatically into the shape in the saddle that fifteen years of competition had honed. My hands were feeling all that pent-up health and energy, while my mind desperately tried to tune into the half-ton mass of power underneath. I was playing mental handball in an attempt to get Kentish Town to acknowledge his physical superiority, but also to get the idea that it might be best if the man on his back decided when to relax and when to run.

It was like nothing else I'd ever experienced. We were doing a nice, easy canter, nothing too strenuous, and yet it might as well have been a trot for all the effort the horse put in. At one stage I glanced down just to make sure his feet were touching the wood-shavings. It felt like they weren't. We were floating. The big horse seemed to be skipping over the surface. I understood why some legendary horses were compared to dancers. It was balletic: sure, there was effort, but it wasn't evident underneath all the grace. Concentrate, I told myself, and tried to make myself as inconspicuous on his back as possible. After seven furlongs he thankfully obeyed my instructions to stop and he walked nonchalantly back down the gallop with his rider beaming an idiot smile.

"As good as that, huh?" De Beaufort said.

I just nodded.

"You really do ride well," he said. "It was obvious even from that piece of work. I don't know where you put yourself but it all looks real neat. And the horse was perfectly balanced the whole way."

It was nice of him to say so. The haughty aristocrat was nothing like the rather one-dimensional figure I'd dismissed him as being for so long. Instead he was exhibiting the very

216

best kind of English reserve, doing rather than talking, not making a song-and-dance. The man was getting easy to like, and who could have imagined that.

I was back in our isolated refuge before six. As far as I could tell, no one had seen us. I ran my hands, yet again, down the horse's legs and felt that familiar relief at finding nothing wrong. After hosing down his legs, and running the water lightly over his back and neck, Kentish Town got a rub-down and a big scoop of horse-nuts. Then, while he settled down for the day, familiarising himself with the new surroundings, I got back to the business of wasting.

There was no comfortable way of doing it: just sweating and starving. The not-eating part was relatively easy because there was a deadline to it. But sweating and drinking little or nothing to quench that terrible thirst was as underwhelming as I'd remembered.

By the following evening, almost thirty-six hours later, I was giving thanks that this was a short-term test. The resolution and determination of my youth was just a memory now. Only the routine of boxing up Kentish Town for his furtive trips to Sir Jocelyn's gallop interrupted the silent, self-punishing regime.

I left it a little late to drive there, just to make the evening ahead shorter. But there was more than enough daylight to allow us to do the short canter which was all Kentish Town needed. De Beaufort buzzed me in and was waiting at the edge of the yard again to follow the jeep on foot. He gave me a leg-up.

"I'll leave you to it," he said then.

"No problem."

Even at a jog there was a rush to being on Kentish Town that could lift any spirit. Now used to the surroundings, he was relaxed and loped through his paces without a care in the world while still leaving no doubt about all that power in reserve. We walked back slowly in the evening gloom after pulling up.

As we entered the yard, Sir Jocelyn hurried towards us and somehow I sensed something was amiss. Then another figure came from behind him. I started and Kentish Town shied a little.

"It's okay!" De Beaufort shouted at me, before turning around and addressing the woman who'd joined him, a tone of exasperation underlying his surface politeness. "I told you I was only leaving you for a minute, my dear."

I'd recognised Dani a split-second after she'd appeared. Her hair was tied up under a wide tweed cap I knew belonged to De Beaufort but the shape of her was unmistakable in a tight-fitting black office suit. She looked up at me and there was a moment before recognition of the rider under the bright-blue riding-helmet suddenly struck home.

"Hey, what are you doing here?" she yelled.

"Just riding out," I said. "How are you?"

"I'm great. Everything okay?"

"Yeah, everything's good. I'll just leave you to it."

The sight of her with De Beaufort threw me so much it took a little while for the significance of a reporter suddenly materialising out of nowhere in the circumstances to hit home. And not just any reporter: one who knew horses. Kentish Town was practically run up into the box such was my hurry to get out of there.

"I didn't expect to see you," Dani said.

She stood next to the driver's door, Sir Jocelyn hovering in the background looking sheepish, as I finished locking up the back. I walked up and smelled her perfume as I sat in behind the wheel.

"I didn't expect to see *you*," I replied. "I guess it's a small world."

"What are you doing here, riding out for Sir Jocelyn?"

"I'm here quite a bit. And I'm just keeping my eye in, riding this horse a foreign buyer wants to take off our hands. I want to see if we should let him go."

"Isn't that a bit odd? I mean . . ."

"It's an odd old world we live in, Dani. I'd better get this horse back to its box and settled in for the night. See you around."

"Yeah, okay," she said.

What she would make of my driving off into the night with Sir Jocelyn's supposed charge I didn't know. He'd have to deal with any questions. I looked in the side-mirror as he stood alongside her. He'd said nothing, obviously extremely uncomfortable with the situation. Nevertheless, as I steered around a corner, the last I saw was his arm snaking around her shoulders.

26

I came back from another quick jog in the woods to see there were five missed calls on my phone from De Beaufort. I dialled the messaging service first. There was one message. That familiar drawl came quickly to the point.

"Sorry about that. She was supposed to come tomorrow evening – I intended to warn you to stay away. No good crying over spilt milk – best option now is to tell her the truth rather than feed her dodgy lies. Had to tell her where you were – any fool could see there was something dubious going on and she's no fool. Good luck."

I hung up and turned around, just as the lights from Dani's car approached. Standing outside Kentish Town's box, I watched as she got out and walked quickly towards me.

"Your wife has done some job on you, pal," she said.

"What?"

"You certainly have a high opinion of women, don't you?" she continued, standing in front of me, staring intently with an anger she didn't bother to try and disguise. "How dare you!"

"Look, I don't know what's going on with you and De Beaufort but –"

"There's nothing going on with me and De Beaufort, you presumptuous, holier-than-thou prick! I'm here to do a piece about your Oaks filly. That's it. I'd arranged to come tomorrow evening – that's why Sir Jocelyn didn't tell you I'd be here tonight. How dare you assume there's something clandestine or sleazy going on!"

"I'm sorry."

"Actually, what the hell am I doing explaining myself to you? I don't owe you anything."

I kissed her. There was no decision about it, no moment of knowing. I just grabbed her shoulders and kissed her, felt her rigid surprise and didn't really care if it didn't change into acquiescence. There was nothing calculating about it. Seeing this woman thundering indignantly at me, sensing all that energy and passion and temper, made me reach out towards it, towards her. I wanted her so much that reason disappeared. And after that initial shock she kissed me back, hungrily, deeply. The feeling was intoxicating. So much so that the world around us might as well have melted away. There was nothing else but touch and taste and a desperate yearning to please: nothing else but the two of us. The concentration of emotion was intense and joyful and when I pleased her it felt like a gift from God.

Later I fell asleep and awoke with a start. Dani wasn't next to me on the rug I had thrown over our straw bed. My bearings were momentarily all over the place. And then she appeared at the door, her open shirt hanging loosely on her, barefoot, laughing as she picked out a piece of straw from her wonderful hair.

"I guess I'm the buxom farm girl now," she said.

"You look brilliant," I said in admiration.

"You're not too shabby yourself, cowboy," she grinned, and came back to me again.

Afterwards we clung to each other, saying nothing, simply concentrating on stars that flickered in our vision through the top of the stable door. I could have stayed like it forever.

"That's Kentish Town next door, isn't it?" she said.

"Yes," I said. "How did you guess?"

"It makes sense. Why else would you be here, in a place like this, three days before the Derby. Hardly flogging some nonentity to some make-believe buyer."

"I forgot you're a reporter."

"Mind me asking why?"

"Why I forgot?"

"No," she said, digging me in the ribs. "Why he's here!"

So, I told a reporter about how the Derby favourite had been stopped by a corrupt jockey in the pay of a criminal boss whose actions had forced one of the world's richest men into an attempted suicide. How I'd lost a finger. And how the horse just a few yards away from us was in hiding to avoid being 'nobbled' or worse before the world's most important race. Her face remained a blank as I spoke. But at the end Dani simply picked up my hand and kissed my injured finger. We dozed for a little longer, and then she got up again.

"We've got to keep your strength up, cowboy. When's

the last time you ate? Because I'm starving, and I have some stuff in the car I picked up earlier. Lucky you, huh?"

"Lucky me."

I followed her to the car and carried back to the kitchen a plastic grocery bag which she rooted around in.

"I'm afraid all I've got is chips, or crisps as you insist on calling them, and a couple of éclairs that are positively sinful."

She took them out, along with a bottle of red wine. There was also a thermos.

"Is that coffee," I asked.

"It sure is. Your wish is my command."

"I'll just have a coffee then."

"Nothing else?"

"I'm on a diet."

"What the hell for? You're skinny as a rake already."

"Well, there's another angle to this. I'm going to ride Kentish Town on Saturday," I said. "And I need to get quite a lot of meat off this rake."

I was getting used to the initial stunned expression on people's faces at the idea of me riding in the Derby. Dani rallied quickly though, concentrating on opening a packet of crisps while I uncorked the wine.

"Well?" I said.

"No well. Except that you are going to be a sitting duck for every critic if you don't win."

"I realise that. But this is what Jake Weinberger wants."

"He's a lucky man to have a friend like you," she said.

"We'll see about that after Saturday."

"And your family is lucky to have you too. Especially your wife. Does she realise it?"

"I don't know," I said after a long and uncomfortable pause.

"I think she must. Take it from me – your man riding to the rescue like that will do it."

"The knight-in-shining-armour bit."

"Hey, girls like fairytales. We want the knight, the castle and the horse."

"Well, I'm looking after a horse. The castle isn't much though," I said, looking around the bare walls. "And I'm no knight."

"The thing is, I'm no different to any other girl. I want the fairytale. Not a bit of one, or half of one. I want to be able to believe."

She picked at her crisps while I pretended to sip some black coffee.

"I'm bunking with the horse," I said eventually. "But my sleeping bag is pretty big. Will you stay with me?"

Dani peered around the bare concrete walls. There was a long silence before she looked back at me.

"I don't do regrets, Lorcan. And I certainly don't regret anything that we've done here tonight. It was too lovely. But it can't happen again, not like this. I don't know what it means to you, but this is not something I make a habit of. You've got a family, I don't. And I refuse to fill some clichéd role in someone else's domestic drama."

She stood up and said she was going to get a breath of fresh air. I watched her leave. I hadn't thought it was possible to traverse the limits of emotion so quickly or so deeply. She was remarkable, and right. But that didn't make her declaration any less devastating.

I went outside and heard her voice coming from Kentish Town's box. She was talking to the colt, who had placed his head on her shoulder and gave every sign of listening intently.

"And see that man outside that's listening to us," Dani said. "He's going to help you win the second most important race in the world in a few days' time."

"'Second most'?" I said, voice sounding a bit shaky.

"'*My old Kentucky home*!'" she sang.

The horse lifted his head and turned around to the water bucket, his interest in these strange humans already exhausted.

My sleeping bag had been laid out on the straw in a corner. The box was so big it didn't actually take up that much space.

"Are you going now?" I asked, knowing the answer.

"Yes. I think it's best, don't you?"

I could have gone down on my knees and pleaded with her to stay. I would have – if it'd had a chance of working. But it didn't. I already knew enough about Dani Simpson to know that.

"Yeah."

27

It was just before six when I got Kentish Town back to our hideaway after his early-morning exercise. With just two days to go to the Derby he felt magnificent. I hosed him down, brushed him and let him have a pick of grass. While he grazed, I rang Gerry. He answered on the first ring.

"Is everything alright?" he asked immediately.

"No problem. He's just done another canter and feels great," I said. "I presume we keep going as we are?"

"Yes, just canters. In fact, ease off on their speed just a tincture. I want him fresh. I also really should know where the hell the two of you are."

"You'll see him at Epsom. He's fine. You've done a great job."

"You haven't seen the front of the *Racing Post* then," he said.

"What does it say?"

"*Punter Unease about Kentish Town as Derby Favourite Drifts in the Betting*," Gerry read out. "I'll bet that's coming from this end. The lads in the yard are all wondering where the hell the horse is. I've told the head men he's been moved for security reasons but somehow that's got twisted into a rumour he's at a vet's and is bollixed and won't even run in the Derby. I actually overheard someone say that in Newbridge last night when I was walking down the street."

I'd answered a number of calls from reporters and reassured them everything was A1 with the horse. I didn't blame them for speculating though. Far too often in racing the steady-as-she-goes line dissolved into the reality of what the rumour mill had been suggesting all along. Not always though. Kentish Town looked in the pink as he continued his Wiltshire holiday.

"It's all just kite-flying. Turn your phone off. I'll deal with the media lads," I said. "He really does feel amazing."

"Good," Gerry said quickly. "How do you feel, and what do you weigh?"

"I feel great, thanks for asking. And as for weight, as soon as you hang up, I plan to step on the scales. Don't worry, I'll make ten stone."

"Jesus, ten stone," he muttered, and hung up.

I didn't blame him. It was such an unusual set of circumstances to have to cope with. But all the moving around hadn't affected the horse. He was eating well, drinking up, his coat gleamed and he was bright and alert. Kentish Town was the least of our worries. It was my weight that was the real concern. After closing the stable door, I couldn't put off the big moment any longer.

The scales came from De Beaufort's bathroom. I'd taken them earlier in the week after an hour-long bath where constantly topped-up hot water had boiled my already wrung carcass like a lobster. It was all I'd been able to do to drive back and relieve the trainer of guard duty.

"A long time since I've pulled sentry duty," he'd joked, taking in the scales, my pinched face and saying nothing more.

Stripping off and stepping on was like retracing the route walked to school. Once so familiar, it had been the biggest perk of all to stopping riding. The realisation that a burger for lunch wasn't ridiculous, or a couple of pints of beer wouldn't result in a painful purge the following morning, had been a delightful recurring surprise for quite some time after retiring. Now the routine was back.

I stepped on, closed my eyes briefly, and peered down – bang on ten stone.

Relief flooded through me. Thank Christ for that. In forty-eight hours, with a lot of effort, I could get another four or five pounds off. It might mean feeling ropey but it was just for one race. I got off feeling a lot more light-hearted.

I grinned, and looked at my watch. Final declarations for the Derby would be made at ten. A jockey would have to be declared by Gerry. I wondered what his face would look like, telling his secretary to key in L Donovan. The paperwork was all set. Being the public face of one of the biggest owners in Irish racing sometimes had perks: as in a lightning-fast processing of reapplication for a jockey's licence. The influence even extended to it all being kept strictly on the 'QT'. It was technically wrapped up and proper. But emotion was a different matter. I was under no illusions. Flak was going to be severe. The focus on this hopeless ex-steeplechase jock was going to be intense. I went for a walk around the woods, not to sweat, but to relish this last piece of calm in our little oasis.

At 10.04 the first call came. It was the BBC. They left

a message, demanding I ring back. I didn't. Then the phone seemed to come to life. I recognised some of the names and numbers that flashed up but there were many unfamiliar. There were plenty of messages. I didn't reply to any of them. The racing websites screamed out the news that the Derby favourite was going to be ridden by Lorcan Donovan. For once the shrieking shock-horror headlines really did have something to shout about. After half an hour of frenzied speculation on the web, I pressed 'send' on an email containing a brief statement from Jake. I'd spent hours on it earlier in the week and passed it with Judith. I could quote it verbatim.

"Due to parting of the ways with my retained jockey, Mike Clancy, I have decided to replace him on Kentish Town in the Derby with my racing manager, Lorcan Donovan. This is an unusual step, but it is my deepest belief that Lorcan is the best man for this particular job. He provides the horse with the best chance of winning. He is a former professional jockey with a proven big-race pedigree. His presence will mean Kentish Town will have to carry some overweight but Lorcan has undertaken to keep it to a minimum. With the usual racing luck, I believe my horse and jockey will be competitive in what is always a wonderful race."

A ravenous media, twisting itself into a frenzy like sharks getting the smell of blood, gobbled up the statement within minutes. It quickly appeared on every website, along with the first comment pieces questioning Jake's sanity and decrying what such a move meant to ordinary punters who couldn't in all conscience now back Kentish

Town. I logged off: morale would only suffer if I continued to read everything. I did make some calls, though, to Gerry, New York, Sir Jocelyn and last, but certainly not least, to Jimmy Walsh.

"Like to make a couple of grand for a couple of days' work, Jimmy?" I asked.

"You have my attention."

"I need you to lead up a horse for me."

"Sure. When and where?"

"Saturday – Epsom. I want you to lead up Kentish Town."

"Wo-ho!"

It was the first time I'd ever heard him surprised. In fact it was all I could do to imagine the big, bluff figure exhibiting any emotion other than quietly charming cynicism. The horse, man, race or event hadn't been invented that Jimmy Walsh of Waterford couldn't undercut with a carefully scathing line. That he remained a hugely popular figure amongst those who knew him said everything about the substance behind the scepticism.

We'd first met years before at a point-to-point meeting where the demands of keeping his weight at under 12 stone were already proving too much. Not that anyone would have known. He was the life and soul of the tent where we changed, trading insults and jokes with veterans twenty years older than him and figuring out which of the youngsters might be open to a little intimidation. I was one such novice and during a race the rather John Wayne-like riding-style of Mr Walsh helped carve me up at a bend. Only for the horse I was riding being nimble on his feet, we would have ended up head-butting a massive straw bale serving as a course marker. I could still remember him laughing as he galloped on, with me seething quietly at the injustice of it.

It took a month but I got him back: heading towards a gap in a ditch at another point-to-point, I moved across next to him, edging left all the while until he had nothing to run into except ditch. Typical Walsh, instead of slowing down, he kicked on, hoping his horse would jump it. The horse wasn't so stupid, jammed on the brakes and sent his brave pilot on a solo-flight over the ditch. A famous picture of the hefty jockey in bright-blue silks flying in mid-air was on the front of the following week's trade paper. By then Jimmy had decided I was okay. That was important. Despite being just a few years older than me, any pal of Jimmy Walsh, no matter how green, was never going to be blackguarded on the tough point-to-point fields. By the time he gave up the unequal battle against weight, I had established myself.

A succession of jobs within racing had taken Jimmy around the world. A remarkable natural horsemanship meant he was prized from Dubai to Durban to Dunedin. But he came back, met a Scottish girl, settled in Lambourn in Berkshire and was renowned as one of the great characters of English racing's second town. He worked mainly with jumpers whose activities eased off in the summer, which was lucky for me now.

"What's happening that you need me?" he asked.

"I'd like somebody I can trust to be with the horse when I can't be. And I'd still back you against most men when it comes to a scrap."

"Oh, you charmer, you! What's wrong with Gunning's people?"

"Nothing. But there's a chance somebody might try something with this horse so we're shuffling everything around," I said. "He's actually over here in England already. If you'd rather not, I'd understand."

"Bollocks to that, I'll do it. When else will I get the chance to lead up a Derby winner?"

"That's the other thing. I'm riding him."

"Yeah, right, and I'm on the Oaks favourite."

"I'm serious."

"Stop taking the piss."

"Are you anywhere near a computer?"

"Yeah."

"Then log onto any of the sports headlines."

I heard him tapping the keys, marvelling as much at the idea of Jimmy Walsh at a computer as what we had come to.

"Jesus H Christ," he said finally. "Are you for real? What the fuck have you got yourself into?"

"I'll tell you some other time. Will you lead this horse up for me?"

"I guess someone has to look after your Catholic ass."

I arranged to pick him up the following day at a place near Lambourn. He hung up laughing. I couldn't blame Jimmy. I was laughing myself at the incongruity of it all. And then I saw him.

It was just a flicker of movement, as much an impression as anything else. In a panorama of green and brown, there had been something black out there. I peered out, walking quickly towards the trees. When he broke cover and started running, I had a good hundred yards to make up. But I was fit now. And used to running here. He got to the edge of the trees and burst out onto a long meadow running downhill. I got to him within fifty yards and threw myself feet first at his back. He tried to scramble to his feet but I was quicker, catching him on the side of the head with a fist.

"Are you alone?" I screamed at him, desperately hoping a weapon wouldn't appear. "Are there any more of you?"

"It's me, just me!" he said, shielding his face, quite obviously terrified. His accent was rural English.

I sat up, but held on to his jacket, fist ready again. "Who are you?"

"Luke Deal. I work for Sir Jocelyn. Please don't hurt me."

"What were you doing?"

"I work here sometimes. And when I was cycling past yesterday I saw a horsebox coming out of the gates. I was just curious, that's all, Please believe me, please."

I did. I got off him, sat back on the grass, and Luke Deal took his opportunity. He staggered away.

"Sorry," I shouted. "I thought you might be someone else."

He didn't look back. I didn't blame him.

28

Derby Day began warm and with a heaviness in the air that promised even warmer. At Epsom's racecourse stableyard it was still too soon for the usual frenetic early-morning routine of looking after horses. The resounding echoes of stable doors being unlatched and boots scurrying around for feed, water and bedding was still a little bit away. As I peered through the grill on top of the box door, one of the security team lounged through the yard on one of his last patrols of the shift. The sun was well up and a haze hung over the famous racecourse. It looked like anticipation, and from the Kentish Town team's point of view, a little dread too.

The horse was his usual relaxed self, thrown down on the straw, breathing easily, eyes open, for all the world as if enjoying a lie-in on the morning of the race that hundreds of years of ancestry had been leading up to. He wasn't the one snoring. That was Jimmy. We'd swapped places in the sleeping bag every two hours during the night, one on guard, one supposedly asleep. One was considerably more successful. Jimmy's ability to sleep was legendary. No matter how manic the driving while tearing to the races, Walsh could always be relied upon to nod off peacefully in the back. But he was also capable of waking up in a split second on the back of any noise not being quite right. I looked at my old pal stretched next to the horse and also noticed the hammer nestling in the straw between them. There was no way I'd like to be first through the door if coming here for mischief.

Slipping outside, I went to the jeep and retrieved my running gear for one last jog. My legs ached from all the work they were being put through but after today it would all be over: easy then to focus on one last sweat. I ducked under the running rail on to the bright-green grass that was part of the long stretch after the post when we would be pulling up. Looking up the hill, it was easy to see the edge of the winning post, facing across to the massive stands that loomed over the course. I started running, away from the stands, under the rails and down the dusty roads towards the Derby start in the distance. It was getting harder and harder to sweat. There was nothing much left. Padding up on heavy clothes and belting out the miles wasn't nearly enough any more. In many ways it was a waste of time. But I ploughed on. It would be good to see what lay ahead in the afternoon.

Ducking under the rails again, I jogged downhill to the mile and a half start and turned around. The pull uphill really was remarkable. All the races I'd watched over the years on television didn't even come close to presenting the scale of the climb the Derby horses faced as soon as the gates opened. It got my legs working though. After half a mile I got to the highest point of the course. It was remarkable how much on the turn everything became. Going downhill, the drag to the left was constant. Ground conditions I noticed were perfect, a good fast surface for class three-year-olds. The descent to the famous Tattenham Corner and into the straight didn't hold any terrors. There were minor racetracks in Ireland with far steeper dips, and with surfaces only a fraction as forgiving.

It was the final half mile of the straight that worried me. The ground fell away dramatically from the rail to the right, cambering downwards to the inside rail. Clinging to that rail made everything straightforward but the inner was also where the most trouble in running awaited. Most of us would have to cope with the camber. At this stage the horses would start to face the pain barrier, galloping flat out, desperately delving into reserves, and at the same time coping with ground falling away from them. Even the most balanced would follow the camber downwards. Getting them to go straight would require skill, technique and maybe just brute strength. Did I have enough of everything required?

Finishing the run uphill to the finish line, I peered up at the stands. The Queen would be here watching, so too the racing establishments from everywhere around the globe. The world's media would also be scrambling for every angle possible. A story about a crazy ex-jockey, and an employer who many of the papers had decided to be non compos mentis after illness, was cat-nip. Millions more would be watching on TV. If my legs felt increasingly shaky, it wasn't just from running. There was a strong temptation to go right back down the straight to Tattenham station and get a train to anywhere else. But that was an escape option I was reserving for later if everything went pear-shaped.

The yard was in full swing when I got back. There were

a few curious glances as I walked through it towards where Kentish Town was quartered in comparative isolation at the very end. A couple of other Derby runners from Ireland had arrived the previous morning. There was also one from France. I'd decided to leave our arrival late, until after the Oaks' day meeting had finished and most of the crowds had gone. Jimmy had led the horse down, hammer stashed in an inside pocket, and we tried to leave things as low-key as possible. A few of the stable lads, keen to see Kentish Town, had wandered over and were told politely but firmly by Jimmy to get lost.

"Hi there, sweaty," the same Mr Walsh now greeted me cheerily.

He hadn't changed a bit over the years, except to expand a bit physically: still fun, still shrewd, still as strong as any horse. Jimmy had been brilliant the previous night. His presence alone was reassuring, and the catching-up process was lengthy, funny and fantastic at taking my mind off things for a merciful while. Even Marian Heights beating only one home in the Oaks was briefly forgotten. Even with me on his back, Kentish Town should be capable of better than that.

I brought the saddle and rest of the tack from the nearby jeep into the box, placing it in a corner for easy access later. Gerry Gunning would bring various other bits and pieces of cosmetic stuff, like the light rug with the initials 'GG' on it that would continue the illusion. My mind raced desperately trying to anticipate every possibility, no matter how remote. I felt tired, both physically and mentally.

"Right, you might have to sweat your life away, but I don't," Jimmy announced. "To you the glory later on – for me a bacon-and-egg bap right now."

He made for the stable lads' canteen and I concentrated

for the umpteenth time on the eleven rivals I would be racing later in the day. They were the best middle-distance three-year-olds in Europe. The horse that had won the Guineas was being kept to a mile but the runner-up was going to run and so were the winners of the main Derby trials in Britain, France and Ireland. I didn't fear the other Irish horses. But Zero Attitude, winner of the Dante, and Mont Tremblant, who'd twice won impressively in Paris during the spring, looked potentially top class. As always the Derby would decide on that potential. I was confident Kentish Town was the fastest horse in the race, but unlike the other two his stamina was not as assured. That presented a dilemma, to be either conservative or trust in his staying ability and be aggressive. But it wasn't the only problem.

Clancy's sudden availability had meant he had been snapped up to ride one of the outsiders by a trainer thrilled to have the great champion on his horse. Leafy Glen's chance of winning was minimal. He'd finished twenty lengths behind Zero Attitude at York. But a runner in the Derby was still a thrill for many owners and to have it ridden by Clancy would be even more so. I'd read a brief news report where the jockey had said he was delighted to be able to ride in the Derby. It was nagging away at the back of my mind how many others Clancy might have persuaded to be delighted.

"Mmnn," Jimmy said on his return, biting into a breakfast bap.

I could smell egg and butter. My tummy did a back-flip. To some it might have seemed insensitive of Jimmy to flaunt his breakfast in such a way but I had no problem with it. If I sensed he was hiding away, furtively eating to spare me, I'd have been mortified. He was the same when he was riding. Wasting was a strictly solo-exercise: empathy was futile. Better to be up-front and take the piss.

"No wonder you're a fat bastard," I grumbled half-heartedly.

"Not fat – stout. There is a difference," he grinned. "By the way, you're all over the papers."

He handed me the racing paper and a popular tabloid. My mug was on the front of both. The thrust of both headlines was the same. How could Kentish Town win with such a hack on his back? The trade rag reported how the best horse in the race was friendless among punters generally, but remarkably was still prominent in the betting. The tabloid also quoted an unnamed jockey saying he wouldn't let Donovan ride his lawnmower, never mind in the Derby. So much for professional solidarity. Although, as the articles kept emphasising, I hadn't ridden in years.

Even a conscious effort to stay away from the coverage couldn't prevent the impact of Jake's call to put me on his horse from making itself known. Snatches of radio when buying petrol, or a glance at a telly inveigled their way in. And there was no getting away from the constant newspaper attention. The more I ignored it, the more legs the coverage grew. But responding was not an option. Even afterwards, what would be the point? The more I thought about it, the more I reckoned that only winning could prevent this saturation.

"Do you remember Bobby McCarthy?" Jimmy suddenly asked. "That point-to-point lunatic from Tipperary?"

"Sure," I said. "I rode one for him one day and he hauled me off the horse afterwards and told me I wasn't a first cousin of a jockey."

"I remember. He did something of the same to me.

Everyone thought he was a fucking eejit because he used to do things differently to everyone else. He trained them different. Had them ridden different. And there was the fact that he was just plain different himself. He didn't give a fuck about what man or beast thought of him. And he'd tell you what he had to say up to your eyeballs. But here's the thing: he's still going. He's still winning points, picking out young horses, selling them on and making a damn good living. He's been doing it for damn near seventy years now."

"And your point is?" I asked.

"My point, my supposedly educated friend, is that different is not the same thing as wrong."

I nodded.

"You're a helluva horseman, Lorcan. Always were. Even in the days when I was trying to kill ya. You'll stand out from this crowd because you're taller and you won't have the same polish, won't be as neat. But that's just appearance. What matters is getting them to run. And without wishing to blow smoke up your ass, you're well able to do that."

He stuck a lead on Kentish Town's head-collar, leaned down for his trusty hammer and took the horse outside to the track to stretch his limbs. As he did so, I could see a man in a dark coat follow. I made to run after them but another two figures emerged too, asking Jimmy to pose for pictures with the horse – photographers. My heart was racing. I needed to calm down. Calm, though, was in short supply.

A few hours later, with the track starting to buzz as a hundred thousand people descended on it in helicopters, cars, by train and some on plain old foot, I wished Jimmy good luck. He gave me an awkward hug which only emphasised how different this day was. The big man had once told me how he didn't like hugging other men, on the basis you never knew when you'd meet the one who didn't want to let go. But here he was whispering "Be confident" into my ear. It was an unexpectedly touching moment that still didn't do much for any peace of mind.

There was a platoon of photographers waiting at the entrance to the weigh-room, accompanied by a platoon of reporters. Some of them I recognised, individuals I usually spoke to on the phone a couple of times a week, but any easy familiarity had disappeared in the rush not to be caught out by their competition. I understood, but that didn't make it less oppressive, having to inch my way along, with a couple of elderly gentlemen in uniform doing their best to secure a passage through.

The sanctuary of the weigh-room at least offered space, whatever about peace and quiet. I at least knew my way around. Other familiar faces, trainers and officials, made a point of wishing me good luck, shaking hands and then escaping, eager it seemed to not demand any time from the centre of attention. Any kind of diversion would have been welcome, but how were they supposed to know that?

I carried my bag down a short hall to the jockeys' room. Not many of the regular inhabitants had arrived yet but the valets were already hard at work, polishing boots and saddles, hanging up colours and generally getting ready for when their men would be rushing around later. A couple of them I recognised from my own riding days and they came over, shook hands and steered me to an out-of-the-way spot in a corner, away from the strict seating order of racing's inner sanctum. Quickly stripping down, I went through the old familiar routine of getting the gear on, pulling on boots that pinched just a little too much to be comfortable but which would have to do now, and putting a feather-light top on. There was no need to put on the back-protector yet. My mouth tasted terrible, tongue dry, throat parched. It was time to face the evidence of a week's deprivation.

Quite a lot of people went to quite a lot of effort not to appear interested in what the bright digital figures eventually settled at after I stood up on the scales. One hundred and thirty-six pounds: nine stone, ten. I was going to use the lightest saddle anyway, little more than a postage stamp. Even with the back protector, I would still come in at just under ten stone, maybe nine-twelve or nine-thirteen. It was only a tiny thing to everyone else but it felt like an early victory to me. Weight was always an intensely private battle. No one could do it for you. It was always a personal thing for me to make the weight I said I would, always had been. I'd managed it one more time. I resolved there and then never to try again.

Gerry Gunning puffed into the weigh-room just as I stepped off. He looked flushed, like he'd been running. He had.

"The horse looks okay, how about you?" he gasped.

"I should be able to do just under ten stone," I said.

He just nodded, said Jimmy looked big enough to lift Kentish Town around the parade ring if he had to, and cast a scornful glance outside at the groups of media still hoping for a glimpse of their quarry.

"Ridiculous attention-seeking," he muttered.

I said nothing. Everything must have seemed hopelessly out-of-kilter to Gerry. Having the horse of a lifetime was as stressful as it was thrilling anyway. Coping with a Derby run-in like this must have been nerve-shredding. We discussed what would happen afterwards. Kentish Town would head back to the Curragh under his trainer's care, back to the familiar routine, away from all these dramatics. He also stressed his desire to have a meeting with Jake as soon as possible. There was little doubt Gerry had given up on me as any sort of confidant. Everything he said sounded as if it had been washed through a legal tape beforehand: a pity.

"Any instructions?" I asked.

"What?"

"How do you think I should ride him?" I repeated.

Gerry's face betrayed his resignation to defeat. Kentish Town's winning chance had mentally already been consigned to the bin.

"Okay," he said, regathering. "You're on the fastest horse in the race so try to make your challenge last. Be the last to ask for everything. Even with Clancy on his back, that instruction would be the same. The fact he's going to have to give them almost a stone's start makes conserving energy even more important. So drop him in, get him settled, and hope he's as good as we think he is."

"Okay."

"But most important of all is once his chance is gone, don't beat him up. Just let him coast home in his own time."

In other words, I concluded, don't ruin him for when we can get a proper jockey back on him.

The traffic on Derby Day was always so bad that the jockeys' room filled up quickly well before the first race. I sat in my seat, next to the French rider who didn't speak much English and didn't show much inclination to speak to the curio anyway. There was a burst of laughter from the other side of the room. I looked up to see Clancy had just arrived and was grinning down at me.

"This is the fanciest hunt I've ever seen," he said to his appreciative audience. "We'd better have our wellies and Barbours ready today, lads."

I returned to looking at my paper, where an article indulged in much the same mocking tone. A television playing high up on the wall began its Derby Day coverage. They didn't waste any time proceeding to the Kentish Town story. Apparently me and Kentish Town were of central interest in story terms. There were pictures of me walking into the weigh-room. The implication of it all though was that finding the winner could safely be regarded as being a separate task.

Gerry's travelling head man arrived in with Kentish Town's colours. Normally a chatty, friendly guy, he barely said hello, merely hanging the silks up on the hook and making off again. I checked them. They looked awfully small. A quick try-out revealed they were too short, barely long enough to make the top of my breeches. This was all I needed. Me being the wrong shape had never been more obvious. I started sweating involuntarily.

"You alright, Lorcan?" one of the valets asked.

"These silks are too short," I whispered.

"Hold on."

He didn't come back for quite some time. But when he did he held up another set of Jake's colours. They were a bit faded and obviously older but identifiably Weinberger silks. And blessedly larger.

"Clancy gave out yards one day a while ago saying

Bartie's set of colours were good for a basketball player but not for him. He threw them away but for some reason one of the lads held on to them. Good job, huh?"

I could have kissed him. They fitted like a glove. On the telly the first race began and the rumble of the crowd's roars vibrated through the stands as the horses closed on the line. In our cavernous security it sounded like some great primal beast was outside, trying to find a way in. A note was handed to me by one of the doormen. It was from the BBC, requesting an interview before the big race. I looked at the elderly man in the smart suit and simply shook my head. A cameraman had been allowed into the usually exclusive jockeys' room to secure atmosphere shots and pictures of the more exhibitionist gurning at the world. But I deliberately stayed out of his way around the corner until it was time for me to weigh out.

"Need any lead?" some wise-ass shouted as I walked out with my saddle.

There was another camera waiting outside to glimpse what I would weigh out at. Whether it was stress or something else, fully kitted out I hit 138 pounds: nine stone, twelve pounds. Kentish Town would carry twelve pounds more than he should, about a five or six-length head-start. I went back to my corner and decided to hell with any rules forbidding the use of phones. I checked messages. There were too many to listen to. I phoned Judith.

"Hey there, Cool Hand," she said, her voice less than steady. "We're here in a room. Jake is out of the ICU and we've got Epsom up on a laptop. How are you feeling?"

"Okay. Tell Jake I'm doing nine stone twelve."

"Tell him yourself."

"Did I hear nine twelve?" the familiar voice asked. It

was a lot stronger. Not at full strength yet but better. "Well done, boy. That is a great effort."

"You sound good, boss."

"I feel good. About everything. Thanks, kid. Now go out there and give it your best shot."

"Yeah – let's see how good this horse of yours is."

29

In the parade before the race all I could think of was Bobby McCarthy and how Jimmy's old pal used to have a saying about a horse that was at the peak of physical well-being – like a salmon at the end of a line. That's what Kentish Town felt like, but not in a good way. He was behaving like one that could get away at any time.

Even Jimmy's bulk was not enough to stop him being carted along. I was useless to him. All I could do was take my feet out of the irons, let my legs hang and talk quietly to the horse, almost praying to him to calm down.

He'd been the same in the parade ring, prancing nervously, sweating on his neck and between his back legs.

"Jesus, he's never done anything like this before," Gerry swore as I stood, waiting to mount. "Why doesn't everybody get the hell away from him?"

Kentish Town was the focus of attention for every camera, flash phone and set of eyes at Epsom. There was a hum of anticipation everywhere he went. I could sympathise. Never a natural seeker of attention anyway, all this was more than a little uncomfortable and embarrassing for me. But at least I could front up to it. It was proving too much for the poor colt.

"Lorcan, I think you're going to have to just go. He's boiling up here," Jimmy shouted as another photographer ran in front of him.

To hell with rules about sticking out parades until the end: it was time to think of the horse.

"Let me go, Jim," I said as calmly as I could.

He let go of the reins and Kentish Town shot forward, lunging past the four others in front of him in the numerically ordered parade. There was a roar from the stands. I guessed it was for us but I was past caring.

It was all I could do to hang on to the colt all the way down the straight. Even the slightest change of grip on the reins would have seen him hit top speed in the blink of an eye. In a physical struggle he was clearly the winner: my only hope of maintaining control was to mentally persuade him to drop down through the gears. Turning right up the hill on the way to the start, a switch seemed to go off. Kentish Town dropped the bit and slowed down. It was his decision. I couldn't delude myself it was anything to do with me. My arms felt numb from the struggle and my injured hand ached. If he took off again, there wasn't going to be a whole pile I could do about it. But I determined to make the most of my chance. We cantered up the hill very slowly, the intense atmosphere thinning in correspondence to the numbers of people around.

At the very top of the track, the other runners started to join us. Everyone slowed to a walk and made single-file for under the trees that lined the outside rail down to the start. There wasn't a single horse that wasn't sweating. The sun was getting warmer and flies were buzzing everywhere, making the colts shake their heads irritably, but it was cooler under the trees. Kentish Town was still sweating but had relaxed immeasurably compared to just a few minutes previously. A hundred thousand people waited for us at the finish. The stands were half a mile away directly across from us. But it was remarkably quiet and calm as the stalls-handlers came to us and started to lead the runners around.

I jumped off and took a towel from one of the handlers to wipe some of the sweat off the horse. The other jockeys were swigging from bottles of water but I couldn't risk that. Even a drop could play hell with a system already badly out of whack. Zero Attitude plodded past as if out for a stroll, his black-and-yellow-silked jockey holding the reins casually as he walked the colt around. Mont Tremblant, I noticed, was more edgy but he was an excitable sort anyway from what I'd read and seen when studying the opposition. Once the gates opened he turned into a real professional.

Clancy was leaning casually on a rail behind the stalls, chatting to the starter, and looking as if he didn't have a care in the world. His colours were all yellow. They were seared into my brain as ones to stay away from.

"Okay, lads, let's get on with this!" the starter shouted.

Everyone got legged back up and made their way behind the gates. I felt better having stretched my legs. Kentish Town felt better too, but how much energy had he consumed already? The main priority now, the only priority, was to get him settled. If he took off on me again, his chances of lasting a mile and a half were nil. He had to relax.

We were drawn on the outside with all the others inside us. Leafy Glen I knew was going into stall two, thankfully a good bit away. Mont Tremblant was next to him and Zero Attitude in seven. The colours on every runner and the riding styles of their jockeys were committed to memory. At the speed we would be travelling, every decision on what to track or what to avoid would have to be instinctive. There would be no time for deliberation. I hung back, not wanting Kentish Town to be in the stalls for too long.

"Don't be an idiot," Clancy said.

I'd been concentrating so much I hadn't noticed him manoeuvre his horse next to mine.

"You've no chance, not given all that weight. But for your own sake, don't be an idiot."

Anyone looking at the pair of us wouldn't have guessed anything: just two riders having a last-minute chat about tactics, or girls, or the best place to go for a drink afterwards. It might even have looked like the big-hearted champion wishing a rival all the best. But the look Clancy flashed at me before pulling his goggles down and entering the stalls was malevolent. If he could get me in the race, he would.

"Last one!" the starter shouted.

That was us. I pulled the goggles down, tried not to notice the thick plaster on my hand and prayed Kentish Town would relax.

He didn't. As soon as the gates opened he took a fierce grip, desperate to run, wanting to go faster than the horses next to him. It was all I could do to hold him, but his head was tossing, infuriated at the impediment on his back. I prayed one of the others would rush up and cut out a fast pace that Kentish Town could settle off. But everybody seemed determined to take their time. Impulse would get me killed one day, I reckoned. Kentish Town resented being behind anything else. Clancy was among them, threatening God alone knew. Maybe the horse would stop trying to compete if he had nothing to compete against. I relaxed my grip and we went to the front.

The hill stretched in front of us as we took a brief right dog-leg and then made for the inside rail. Kentish Town was still too keen. I dropped my hands on to his withers, loosening the hold in the process. I could hear myself saying "Whoa!' and "Easy!" but the real communication was silent. I could hear that too – 'Please settle, please settle'. If he didn't we would be exhausted by the straight. Nothing could run this vigorously for a mile and a half, nothing. Please settle, I pleaded.

And just as suddenly as when he dropped the bit on the way to the start, he did the same now. He seemed to be confused, both at the unusual signals and having a wide open space ahead of him. His ears pricked, taking it all in, unsure and yet intrigued at the same time. But it all meant he stopped fighting me.

We got to the top of the hill. The hum of the crowd started to increase, giving just a hint of the cauldron of humanity we would soon be running into. It was even possible to hear snatches of the racecourse commentary. That wouldn't last for long. I concentrated on keeping Kentish Town on the correct lead leg for coming down the hill, letting him use his stride, encouraging him to enjoy it.

The others were right on our tail. I could see the wide chestnut face of one of the outsiders on our flank. A quick peep behind revealed Mont Tremblant's elegant black head sitting on our slipstream. I wasn't sure, but I reckoned there'd been a flash of yellow behind him. It made sense. Leafy Green had been drawn on the inside.

A blur of colour on either side blended in with a heaving noise level that continued to increase. And yet all I could see was the strip of green between Kentish Town's ears and all I sensed was the power he was generating. It was remarkable how strong he felt. Despite everything a reservoir of energy still felt available as he ran down the hill like he was on rails. The question for me was when to start reaching into it.

If there was one thing I felt happy to compare to my rivals it was judgement of pace. It might have been built up guiding young horses through bog-like ground in bumpers or nursing knackered steeplechasers over fences, but I knew tempo. This was of a faster variety but essentially the same. As we turned Tattenham Corner and faced down the straight, I knew there was more to come. I also knew Kentish Town had been galloping within himself. We'd basically been waiting in front. Now it was time to kick on.

I leaned into the colt, changing my grip on the reins. The response was instant. The camber didn't matter now. We were on the rail. I had my whip in my right hand. Kentish Town just had to run straight. I got even lower, praying my breathing held out. Riding low in the saddle placed such a strain on the body that it could sometimes feel like you were struggling for breath if not fit enough. All the running was paying off. It just had to hold out for another minute. In behind there was a brief sound of whips starting to strike that were soon drowned in an all-consuming wall of sound. It was like riding into a physical entity. I'd never experienced anything like it. God alone knew what the colt was making of it. But he was game. We started to race downhill. I remembered a great jockey of the past telling me once that the great mistake was to go for everything on that downhill stretch. It was vital to keep something for the final climb.

We were still in front. I could sense rather than see a horse getting closer. It was enough to make me automatically reach for the whip. But that had to remain a last resort. Instead I changed my hands again, tapped him down the shoulder a couple of times and tried to make myself as unobtrusive as possible. Mont Tremblant's black head ranged alongside us. His jockey's streamlined balance came into my vision. The noise around us suddenly disappeared. Instead it was two horses and two jockeys straining every sinew trying to get ahead. We might as well have been galloping up a deserted beach for all the input anyone else had. I waited until a hundred yards from the line and then used my whip. It was the final demand of Kentish Town's will-to-win. It hardly seemed credible but the more I asked the more he gave. My whip came down twice, hard. Mont Tremblant got to within a head of us but this final surge, combined with the struggle to deal with the camber proved to be too much for him. With fifty yards to go his head came up slightly, a silent but unmistakable signal of surrender. It was getting too much. I saw it and gave Kentish Town one final smack. He responded like a hero. We increased our lead to half a length. Three strides before the line it was all over. I sat up slightly, the colt pricked his ears again, and he went past the post like the champion he was.

He pulled himself up. Every ounce of strength I'd had seemed to evaporate. A couple of jockeys said "Well done!" once we'd come to a stop. The others wheeled around immediately and made their way back to unsaddle. Clancy was one of them. I didn't move. The winner was always the last to go back anyway but it suited me to hang back. It took everything I had in me to try and gather the emotions that were jumbling around inside. Mostly there was just relief. I hadn't been too much of an impediment. The horse had proved his exceptional talent. In spite of everything that had happened, Kentish Town was the Derby winner. We cantered back.

Jimmy was the first to meet us. The big man had tears in his eyes.

"You fucking beauty!" he roared, grabbing the reins, slapping me on the thigh and delivering a big thumbs-up to the camera that materialised in front of us. "Well done, Sweaty," he said, looking up at me, and shaking hands.

A TV reporter stuck a microphone under my nose and asked the perennial question about how I felt. I was too tired to do anything but thank Jake and Judith, praise Gerry and his team for a wonderful job, and give a special mention for the foul-mouthed character leading me up. After that I couldn't say much more because my tongue seemed to want to stick to the roof of my mouth.

The crowd were generous with their applause as we entered the most famous winner's circle in racing. Gerry was already standing there, looking stunned. I sketched a brief wave of acknowledgement, slid off the horse, hoped my legs would carry me, and slipped off the saddle.

"He stays alright," I said to Gerry. "Well done. He was trained to the minute. A great job."

"You too," he mumbled, and went to pat his colt's neck.

A steward grabbed my arm and led me through the mêlée of people. He didn't let go until we got to the scales. I thanked him. Everything was such a blur I could easily have committed the cardinal sin of not weighing in. Up came the 138 pounds again. The clerk of the scales said "Well done". So did a lot of others, including someone with headphones on who led me back out, through a tunnel of back-slaps and shaking hands, until we reached a presentation stand. Gerry was being interviewed and was busy thanking everyone connected with the horse. Even I got a mention. There was an incessant clicking of cameras as we accepted the winning trophies, including the big one on behalf of Jake. Then Gerry and I were led back to the weigh-room and the traditional press conference. Before we got there, we passed Sir Jocelyn standing in the hallway just outside. All he did was wink and slap me on the shoulder. It was getting very hard to keep disliking the guy.

The dark room was crammed and microphones were thrust in front of us even before we made the little stand at the top. I pressed forward to the table though and grabbed a couple of bottles of mineral water. Nothing had ever tasted better. I drained them and looked for more. It felt like a thirst that would never go away. But at least it freed my tongue up.

"Lorcan, the run-up to this Derby has been remarkable, even by the historical standards of this great race. Can you tell us what happened from your perspective?" one of the racing correspondents in the front row asked.

I wasn't sure if I made sense. My head was still spinning from what had happened out on the track. But I tried to steer as neutral a course as possible. Heaping praise on Gerry and Jake was no torture. There were plenty of queries about Clancy and why he had been taken off the horse. I resolutely followed a 'riding arrangements are the owner's prerogative' course. There were other questions about dieting and what it had taken to drop the weight. I fed them the line that I was looking forward to getting fat, a line I reckoned was sure to get prominence the following morning. The conference was a comparatively easy ride, so much so that it only reinforced what a struggle it would have been had Kentish Town not won. After half an hour, time was called and I could get back to the jockeys' room.

All eyes were on the next race being run but there were a few more handshakes and 'well dones'. Clancy was riding and came through in the closing stages to win. It barely registered. I quickly stripped off, started drinking another bottle of water and went straight to the showers. It felt great just to stand underneath the powerful stream. I emerged to don a towel and ask one of the doormen if he could organise a couple of cases of champagne for my erstwhile colleagues. He said it would be no problem and informed me he'd never seen any Derby like there'd just been, and he'd seen fifty of them.

"I don't know if that's a good thing, or a bad thing," I said.

"Oh, it's good," he replied quickly. "Very well done."

We shook hands and I went back to my sanctuary around the corner.

30

Gerry Gunning glanced sideways and his face paled. I followed his gaze. One of the guests was jokingly offering a sausage-roll to Kentish Town. The most valuable racehorse in the world briefly smelled the offering before declining. It was then that Gerry decided that the hundred-million-dollar-worth guest of honour might be better off at home. He put his glass of champagne down on a table and told the groom it was time to be off. They turned and made their way to the massive horsebox that had brought Kentish Town from the Curragh to Annagrove just for the occasion.

It was just a week since Epsom but the big horse hardly turned a hair as the party guests stood around and applauded him into the box. There were a hundred people, mostly hand-picked by Jake and Judith, friends and employees, everyone who had any input to the Derby success. Jimmy Walsh was there, charming a wealthy stockbroker's wife with ribald tales of horse life that she affected to be scandalised by but with increasingly raucous laughter. I noticed Niall Doherty standing slightly apart, drink in hand and smiling as he chatted to Cammie. Everyone had emerged from the large marquee to applaud Kentish Town. My dad applauded harder than most, laughing and whistling. Mum stood close to him, keeping him shepherded in boozy bonhomie and away from anything boorish.

"Down, down!" the little voice roared into my ear.

"Okay, but be careful," I said.

Max slid down from my arms and plonked himself on the grass, engrossed in playing with a plastic toy bought in St Aubin by Sebastian and which hadn't left his side since. I'd rung Manolo a few days previously, asking him and the big man to come to the celebration, all expenses paid. But apparently they were on a new assignment, in Sweden.

"There are always people who need us," Manolo explained.

I didn't doubt it, and thanked him for doing such a good job. He said it had been easy enough to make him feel almost guilty about taking the money. I told him the sight of my family arriving home the day after the Derby had been priceless. Max had run up to me and wished me *Bon chance*. Only then had the tension of the previous weeks dissolved. Burying my face in those sun-bleached curls, it took a lot not to blub embarrassingly.

Siobhán stood next to me and I gave her hand a squeeze, telling her she was brilliant and meaning it.

"Is everything back to relatively normal now?" she asked.

"I sure hope so."

"When will Kentish Town run again?"

"The Derby at the Curragh is in three weeks' time. He should be fully recovered well before that."

"Same jockey?" she grinned.

"No. Definitely not this time. We'll get somebody who knows what they're doing," I laughed.

A few minutes later the crowd gathered inside the marquee, facing a big screen that the girls in the office organised to allow Jake and Judith talk to everyone, from New York. My rather fundamental knowledge of technology got me off the hook of doing anything but suddenly the pair of them were on screen, waving and smiling, Jake in a hospital bed, thankfully free of any equipment hooked up to him. Judith held his hand as the applause in Annagrove travelled across the Atlantic.

"I hope everyone is enjoying themselves," Jake said, his voice strong and clear. "We're aiming to be at the Curragh for the Irish Derby – just as soon as I convince these doctors that I'm fine."

I'd have put a large bet on Jake watching his horse in person next time. Judith thanked a long list of people and Kentish Town, who she said had helped bring her husband back to her. Then both urged everyone to drink up.

"You have the air of a relieved man," a voice said behind me.

Niall Doherty was balancing an intricate-looking canapé while trying to hold on to his champagne glass. I took the flute off him to allow the food to be dispatched. He grinned as he took his drink back.

"Bloody good stuff. Is this how the élite eat every day?" he asked.

"I wouldn't know. This is hardly my scene usually," I said.

"Thanks for inviting me anyway. Normally polite society doesn't like me around."

"I'm very grateful for all your help."

"Sure. But you did say there might be a story in this for me."

"Did I?"

"You sure did," he said, reaching for another canapé on a tray carried by a waiter walking past.

"I hear our friend Mr Duggan was a big winner from you winning the Derby: in the sense that he has lost millions. I hear he bet hundreds of thousands of euro on your horse, trying to cover himself if you won. That's why your starting price was so comparatively short. Everyone thought Kentish Town's price would drift right out. But it didn't. Apparently Pinkie was shovelling money on you, wherever he could: bookies, exchanges, betting shops all over Ireland, you name it. Even doing that, he still ended up losing a fortune because he was so exposed. Apparently disgruntled Asian gamblers do more than break your thumbs if you don't pay up."

"The betting side of things isn't really my area," I said.

"Maybe, but standing up to ruthless gangsters is," he replied.

I said nothing, just took a sip of my own drink.

Doherty laughed. "You never said anything before so it's silly of me to expect anything different now, right?"

I smiled and asked if he'd tried the risotto.

"Okay. I get the message. There isn't a story and you've done me up like a kipper." He shrugged. "Whatever the truth of it is, fair play to you. There aren't many who've tweaked Pinkie Duggan's tail and come out the other side."

He raised his glass to me and turned around to smile at my wife who was leading Max by the hand.

"Back to more mundane matters, I'm afraid," Cammie

grinned. "Boys wouldn't be boys without the smell of wee-wee."

"Ain't that the truth," Doherty grinned. "Things weren't so mundane before?"

Cammie grinned, patted his arm and asked sweetly if he'd like more champers. I smiled despite myself.

"I see omertà runs in the family," the journalist sighed.

A few hours later the last of the guests left, leaving celebratory debris scattered behind them. Surveying the scene, I gave thanks for marquee services that included the clean-up. My parents were already calling it a night by the time I walked back to the cottage.

"Max's been asleep for a while," Mum smiled. "And your father won't be long after him."

Dad shook his head, kissed Cammie on the cheek, slapped me on the shoulder and dutifully did what he was told. Their room was closest to the living room and we could hear his base-rumble laughter teasing Mum before the pair of them started snoring.

"It's a good idea," Cammie said. "I'm bushed. See you in a minute?"

"Yeah, I'll just see to things first."

It didn't take long to make sure all the windows were closed, lights turned off and doors locked. What took longer was convincing myself not to go back and check everything one more time. The residue of all that fear and tension still remained. Despite everything, for the last week, I'd found myself looking behind me too much, checking the rear-view mirror while driving, almost jumping out of my skin when a reporter touched me on the shoulder at the races. A full night's sleep remained frustratingly elusive too, and it had nothing to do with Max's middle-of-the-night toiletry habits. It was time to snap out of it, I told myself. Normality had been hard earned; time then to enjoy it again.

Cammie was still awake as I slid into bed. She stared at me, her face browner than ever, expression unreadable.

"You okay?" I asked.

"I don't know. Are we okay?"

"I feel alright. You?"

"You know what I mean, Lorcan."

I did. I also knew I didn't relish the prospect of such a conversation. Everything had been so manic for so long it had been easy to forget about this stuff. Cammie had been brilliant, organising the party, dealing with everyone, back to her old self again. There were times when I'd looked at her and fiercely wanted to have her back to myself just as before, fiercely wished that things were the same as before.

"I don't know," I said simply.

"Well, I do," she said, grabbing my hand under the covers. "I want to go back to what we had. Everything that's happened, it only made me realise how wonderful our life was. And we can have that back now."

I didn't say anything, just lay there, staring at the ceiling and seeing nothing.

"Lorcan, I know I've hurt you. I wish the clock could be turned back. But we have too much to lose. I love you, and I love Max, and I want us to be together."

She slid across and moved her hand, teasing me gently. Her lips started kissing my neck. It was impossible not to respond. Her movements grew quicker.

"Stop, Cammie, just hold on," I said, leaning on an elbow and looking at her.

"What?" she said, her hand still working. "Please, I need you now."

"No."

She stared at me.

There was a lot I wanted to say, to ask, even to confess: fundamental stuff that kept nagging, refusing to go away. But she beat me to the punch.

"I have to make you trust me again. And I will, if you just give me the chance," Cammie said, taking my hand again.

I returned the squeeze. It felt good, lying next to this woman, the mother of my kid. And yet the nagging wouldn't stop, even when she kissed me lightly.

"Cammie, have you had anything to do with him since all this started?" I asked.

There was no doubting who the *him* was. She stopped kissing and looked at me straight.

"Of course I haven't," she said. "All that's just a bad dream now. All I want to do is forget."

So do I, I thought, as my wife started to kiss me again.

31

Marc-Pierre Dutroit carefully put down his fish fork and said he had a proposition for Jake.

"One of my more venerable owners, Madame Daladier, is having a disagreement with the tax authorities here," he announced quietly.

The restaurant was one of my favourites, a small place on the outskirts of Chantilly that didn't try too hard with the presentation, contenting itself with serving up fresh, beautifully cooked food. Marc-Pierre condemned my love for the place, said only an appreciation of life's sauces separated us from hyenas tearing on a carcass. He and Gerry Gunning were one of a kind in culinary terms. That he had volunteered to end the day here told me something had to be up.

"I'm sorry for Madame Daladier," I said.

"Don't be, she's a cheat who should have been having this trouble years ago," Marc-Pierre grinned conspiratorially. "But her financial woes mean she is considering selling off some of her assets, one of which just happens to be Festival Princess."

"Ah," I said.

"'Ah', is correct, my Irish friend," he replied. "The bitch is proposing sending the best horse in my stable to the sales next month. That would be a catastrophe!"

Festival Princess had won the French 1,000 Guineas and a couple of other Group-1 prizes the year before. Cheaply purchased by Marc-Pierre as a yearling, he had sold her on to the Frenchwoman who now could look to ease her financial pressures to the tune of at least a couple of million if Festival Princess went through the sales ring. The danger for the trainer, though, was that a new purchaser might also want a new trainer, or pack her straight off to the breeding farm.

"I've got her back, Lorcan," he said, leaning closer. "She has done nothing in her two starts this year but we discovered a muscle problem in her hind-quarters. She's working brilliantly again. I reckon we can get a couple of runs into her and then take her to America for the Breeders Cup. Jake would love that – if he bought her."

"And kept her with you."

"But of course," he grinned again. "It would be terrible to break up a winning combination."

"Time for dessert," I said.

While we scanned the menu, I did a quick tot in my head and reckoned the impoverished Madame Daladier might prefer to take her chances in the ring. Festival Princess was top-class on the track but her pedigree was comparatively low-key. That wouldn't appeal to Jake. The idea of the Breeders Cup would. It would require a financial balancing act that might not come down in favour of Marc-Pierre keeping his pride and joy. He was destined for disappointment on this, I reckoned.

But it felt great to be busy with horse matters again. Marc-Pierre might end up disappointed but he'd get over it, find his next star, aim for the next race. The next race was always the only one that counted. Already for most people Kentish Town's Derby was just another piece of form to help tease out the future: just as it should be.

I had flown over for a Group-1 race at Chantilly that morning and there was no great hardship in letting myself be persuaded into staying for an early dinner. Besides, Marc-Pierre was not the only one with something on his mind. I let him give me a few minutes more of his sales pitch and ended up convinced of at least one Frenchman's innate charm. It didn't make me budge from the figure in my head but I did promise to pitch Festival Princess to Jake. My host sat back satisfied.

"What do you make of young Pollet as a rider?" I asked about the most exciting new jockey in France.

"Julien? He's very young, just twenty. And he's quite tall so he's not the finished article in a finish yet. But he's going to be a champion jockey sooner rather than later."

"Has he ridden much for you?"

"Quite a bit on horses not owned by Jake. Great hands. I've put him up on horses I thought might run away with him and they've settled beautifully. You can't teach that. It's either there or not. Tactically he's good, he's cool, and he can communicate when he gets off them. I take it you're considering offering him Clancy's job?"

"Maybe. It might be too big a job for just one man, covering Britain, Ireland and France," I said. "But Jake likes to back young talent on the way up. You know all about that."

"It doesn't always work out," Marc-Pierre laughed. "But Pollet looks the real thing."

"He might cover the French side of things, at least initially," I ventured. "You'd have no problem with that?"

"None at all. I'd love to work with him. Though that Irishman that won the Derby might be the real answer!"

"Very funny," I smiled. "Believe me, that will never happen again."

"Are you ever going to say what happened? All of racing is consumed with interest. I've heard stories that would make your hair curl."

"Maybe some day. Right now, I'm trying to forget it."

"Why on earth would you want to forget winning the Derby?" he spluttered.

How to explain that it all could wait a while longer, a good while longer, when distance had poulticed the rawness of it all? I glanced at my hand and the finger which the doctor said could do without a bandage, advice I still couldn't bring myself to follow. Out of sight and out of mind could do for now. It was illogical but I reserved the right to be illogical when it came to the detritus of dealing with Pinkie Duggan.

We wound up our dinner and Marc-Pierre drove me to the airport. He gave me a big hug which I reckoned was only partly about Festival Princess. My offers to pay him back for St Aubin were flamboyantly rejected, as were my repeated expressions of thanks. I meant them too.

"Hey, I have to keep onside the man closest to my most important owner," he said. "If that requires me to be an ass-kisser, then so be it."

I would come up with something Marc-Pierre would really appreciate, I said to myself on the plane. It mightn't be Festival Princess, although at the right price it might be. But even so, I would get something personal. I'd ask Cammie; she was good at stuff like that.

It was the last flight back to Dublin. Most of the passengers seemed to be families heading home from Euro Disney, kids sleeping in seats strewn with toys and souvenirs, exhausted parents grabbing a nap too while they could. It wouldn't be long now before Max would enjoy such expeditions. The idea made me smile and momentarily ease the guilt at the speed with which I'd accepted Marc-Pierre's dinner invitation. I could have been home hours ago, if I'd wanted to. The question of whether or not I did want to was one that stubbornly refused to go away.

It was just after midnight by the time I left Arrivals and crossed the road to the short-term car-park. Despite the summer night-time warmth, there was a cold to the cavernous concrete building that made me grateful for the coat I always took racing. Enough rain-soaked summer days in Ireland had taught me never to go to the races without some kind of cover, no matter what the forecast. My shoes echoed off the concrete floor as I hurried to the car. There was no other sound except the beep-beep of the alarm switching off.

The feel of the cold gun-barrel under my ear was a complete shock.

"Do anything stupid and I'll blow your fucking head off," a bass voice said quietly. It was a foreign accent, Russian sounding.

Someone else grabbed both my hands and tied them tightly together behind my back. They were frighteningly efficient. Fear didn't encourage any resistance either.

I was half-lifted, half-frogmarched for less than a

hundred yards towards a large SUV. A car's headlights suddenly came towards us. Someone leaving, possibly one of the families who'd been on the Paris flight. All they would have seen was a group of large men walking closely together, almost completely blocking out any sight of the comparatively slight figure stumbling along in the middle of them.

After being expertly hoisted into the boot of the jeep, my legs were quickly tied up too and an evil-smelling bag placed over my head. The confined space meant curling up into a foetal position that couldn't stop a hard piece of metal pressing into my kidneys. That discomfort was nothing though to the vehemence with which I cursed my own stupidity. Sure part of me suspected it wouldn't be Duggan's style to skulk away defeated. But more of me reckoned the game was up. And logically it was. But what had logic to do with this?

I tried to concentrate on counting off minutes but quickly gave up. Despair washed over me. There was a matter-of-factness about what these men were doing that left little doubt about what was coming. But what little doubt there was I hung on to. There was nothing else.

We shuddered to a halt. I was dragged out and lifted, feet scrambling on the ground, inside a building. The restraints on my legs were taken off and I stumbled up stairs and then pushed onto what felt like a bed. A particularly rough set of hands sat me up and pulled the bag off my head.

It was a small box-room, the walls covered in pictures of pop and rap stars I didn't recognise. There were a few footballers as well that I did. Most importantly of all though, I recognised big Anto.

He wasn't dressed in all-black like the men who'd picked me up. And the lugubrious cynicism he exuded before was no more. Instead the big man was anxious, pacing around while listening on the phone.

"He's here," he said simply to the person on the other end.

I didn't need two goes to guess who.

I struggled to sit up, leaning against the wall, desperately trying to get my bearings. Anto listened some more on the phone, said nothing else and hung up. He walked over to the window, peeped out through a break in the curtains through which the reflection of a street-light shone. There was movement and noise downstairs but Anto resolutely stared out.

"Where am I?" I asked, my voice sounding desperately high and unnatural.

"Tallaght. Same house you were in before, remember?"

How could I forget?

"You're a stupid bastard," Anto continued. "All you had to do was do nothing."

He paced up and down in front of me. There didn't seem much to say. But Anto kept pacing, back and forth to the window, occasionally opening the door and looking out.

"Your boss is a lunatic," I said quietly. "If I die, he's going to jail. Simple as that."

"What do you mean?" Anto, said, stopping at the window and looking over his shoulder at me.

"I told him if me or mine was touched in any way, a file will first go to the papers, and then the police," I said.

The big man snorted, a smirk on his face. But he was considering this, I could see.

"I've put everything on record: dates, places, names, all that's happened to me. You're there too."

He stopped smirking at that. His boss might be consumed by hatred but Anto wasn't. I could almost hear his brain whirring, calculating the implications of what was being said, how likely they were to be true.

"He's out of control," I continued. "You say all I had to do was nothing. That's all he has to do now."

Anto resumed looking out the window. I needed desperately to keep his attention.

"You've done some terrible things for him: kidnapping my wife, putting my boss in a situation where he tried to kill himself –"

"That had nothing to do with me, asshole. If someone wants to top themselves, that's their business."

"That's not the way I've worded it."

Sweat wormed its way down my back. I knew the consequences of playing this wrong. This man in front of me had experienced horrors I probably couldn't even imagine, done things to people that would turn my stomach. A hard man, way too hard for me to even dream of tackling him physically. And not stupid either; that was obvious. He would sense a false note to what I was saying the second I said it.

"Duggan probably has the legal muscle to delay things for a while. Maybe even make a deal. But too many people know bits and pieces of what's happened now, and a whole lot more will know everything if I disappear."

The effort of not panicking, and forcing myself not to listen for Duggan's voice downstairs, made my voice sound even more unnatural. But the tone had to be right. If I was to have any chance, I had to convince this man.

"You know better than anyone who you're dealing with," I said. "And it's probably paid off for you over the years. But working for someone doesn't mean you sacrifice yourself for them. No money is worth that."

He turned and stared at something on the wall opposite, still saying nothing, looking as if he was barely listening.

"You know yourself, don't you?" I argued. "Getting rid of me isn't smart. It's not good business. It achieves nothing. In fact it's going to turn everything upside down. Think of it. Think of the beano the papers will have. It's only a week since the Derby. Getting rid of me will make headlines all over the place. And the cops will have to be seen to do something. It'll take a long time for it to become old news. And you'll be old news too by the time it happens."

Still he said nothing. There was a burst of laughter from downstairs and some raised voices. The language sounded Eastern European. Anto's lip curled slightly with distaste.

"How do I know you're not bullshitting me?" he eventually asked.

"You can't," I said, and bit my lip. The urge to keep talking had to be restrained now.

"Who's to say you won't shop me anyway?" he said.

"There's nothing," I replied. "But I won't. I just want to forget about all of this."

"Pinkie will never stop. He will track you down."

"Then he's an idiot," I said. "He can't win. Killing me will mean he's just spiting himself."

"That doesn't matter. He'll think of that when he has to."

"And that's not smart, is it?" I said. "Give me a chance. I won't forget it."

He looked at me. I couldn't read his expression.

"Don't be a mug," I almost whispered.

There was a moment's hesitation and then he pulled a small thin blade out of a trouser pocket. He approached, grabbed my hair and swung me to the side. Panicked, I jerked in a futile attempt to escape his clutches.

"Relax," he growled. "I'm going to the bog. It could be about a minute."

He left the room, shouted "I'm going to the jacks!" to someone and clattered noisily across the hall. It took a second to realise my hands were free, and another to comprehend that Anto had given me my chance. Swinging back the curtain, I opened a window, felt a cold blast of night air and looked outside. There was a long drop but to the left were a couple of bins. I squeezed out the window, crouched down and swung my legs off the sill. The concrete surface made it hard to get any kind of grip. I managed to haul myself along the sill for a couple of feet and then aimed for the bins. The noise they made on landing seemed horrific. I tucked and rolled just like a racing fall and ended up on a strip of grass in the back yard.

I had hauled myself over a neighbour's wall by the time Duggan's men emerged to check out the racket. There was a yell which could have meant anything but which I presumed meant I'd been seen. It was a correct presumption. A long alley between the backyards of two rows of houses led on to the main estate road. I recognised it from navigating my way to the hospital just a few weeks previously. This time I had no car, but I felt a lot better and a lot stronger. I ran like I'd never run before. Behind me there were more shouts and the sounds of car doors opening and engines being gunned into life.

Out-running them on the road was not on. Time, I

concluded, to start ducking through gardens. If it came to fitness, I would back myself. None of the men chasing me looked like prolonged running would suit them. But while considering where to duck, a car jerked backwards out of a driveway and veered towards me. I jumped to avoid getting hit, up on to the boot, and was bounced to the other side, landing on the road. The driver's door opened.

"What the fuck is going on?" shouted a young man, his indignation in proportion to the fear he had hurt somebody.

I was up in a moment, looked down the road for my pursuers and then grabbed the driver. There was no time for niceties. Surprise meant he fell out easily and I pushed him into a hedge. Thankfully he was small and light.

He was also angry. "Here, what are you doing? Get your hands off me!" he shouted. He was entitled to his anger.

I dove behind the wheel, slammed the gear lever into first and screeched away.

32

I turned left, heading away from the M50 and the city. A man crossing the road increased his pace only at the last second, when he realised the car approaching him was accelerating rather than slowing down. There was a brief snatch of swearing as I screeched past. I could see him in the rear-view mirror, waving his arms in fury. At the same time a couple of cars exploded out of the estate entrance and immediately turned left as well.

In less than a minute the street-lighting started to fade out as urban melted into rural. The main road headed towards west Wicklow. However a tiny signpost pointed left towards the mountains. It said: *Sally Gap – 30km*. I immediately turned.

The famous landmark on top of the Dublin-Wicklow mountains was familiar to me. One of the few ways to avoid having to go around the mountains that split County Wicklow, going over them meant bad roads and a twisting, winding view of a bare wilderness that barely seemed credible so close to a major city. During the winter with no tourists to get stuck behind, it sometimes meant getting from Annagrove to the Curragh quicker than if using the motorways. That is until bad weather made it impassable. There would be no snow now. Familiarity helped when driving up there. Maybe the chasing pack would be at a disadvantage.

I gunned my car into third gear and quickly began to climb. Dublin's glare was omnipresent in the mirror. But so were two sets of headlights that inexorably kept getting closer. I mercilessly put my car through the gears and the small engine whined in protest. It was a small vehicle designed for not wasting much petrol while stuck in traffic. As it struggled forwards into darkness there was no doubt it wasn't cut out for this kind of treatment.

No car appeared in front of us. If one had, the amount of time required to squeeze past and then build up a head of steam again would have resulted in those just a couple of hundred metres behind catching up in seconds. The road got even more twisty as we climbed but that was good. What my car lacked in speed, it could compensate for a little in terms of agility. I finished the climb, caught a last view of Dublin's lights, and plunged into the enveloping darkness.

Even the prospect of what would happen if caught couldn't shake my mind away from the job of concentrating on the road. Bumps jolted the light car all over the place as the road dipped and rose. At the speed we were travelling it needed only a slight miscalculation and my car would have left the road. I knew what lay for miles all around, a wilderness of bog and heath, a *Wuthering Heights* scene at almost fifteen hundred feet above sea-level. In essence little had changed since hundreds of years previously when the British put down a military road, designed to help catch those outside the law who employed the age-old tactic of heading for the hills. This current road followed the same course. There were some electricity poles now, the odd light from an isolated house, a few carefully tended picnic sites hewn out of the wild environment. But essentially the scene was the same, the hunters hunting, those on the run trying to get away.

The road got even worse, and so did the conditions. Squally rain fell intermittently but as I careered south for another twenty minutes what had been a light mist turned substantially thicker. Focusing on the road turned into focusing on the middle of it, hoping for some helpful white-lines every so often.

There were tantalising moments when after rounding a bend there would be no headlights and the hope would rise that the roads might have claimed more casualties. But they kept coming, a little further behind maybe, yet always there. I drove to the limits, fear sometimes taking me beyond. There was no shaking them. The mist got even thicker, involuntarily forcing me to squint over the steering wheel, my nose almost touching the windscreen. Despite that, I ploughed into the stag.

Deer were all over the mountains. During daytime they usually hid in the woods. At night they came out to feed, knowing only the lost, the reckless or the desperate would be about. The unfortunate creature jumped out of the gloom at the last second and landed on the road at just the wrong time. The impact stopped my little car in its tracks and shot me forward. My chest hit the steering wheel and my head bounced off the windscreen. But it was my knee that immediately started hurting. Whatever way it hit the bottom of the dashboard, the pain was intense.

Stumbling out, I limped a couple of paces and saw the young stag with his short antlers stretched on the tarmac, groaning with pain and blood coming out of its mouth. It didn't require veterinary knowledge to realise he was finished. A back leg was lying at a noticeably awkward angle. Even my standing over him couldn't encourage the beast to try and get up. He was finished. There was nothing to do but move.

I staggered to the side, felt the ground fall away and tried to keep my balance. Sharp heather and dense undergrowth came up to my waist and made it difficult to make progress in the pitch-black dark. As the cars pulled to a halt, I dropped to my hands and knees and moved as quietly as possible until I had put at least fifty yards between me and them.

The bang of a gunshot made turn around. The mist had cleared a little and in the light of the headlights I could see five men gathered around the deer. One of them had a gun, and I watched as he put a second bullet into the stricken creature. The driver of the second car remained behind the wheel. Everyone else had got out. They started to peer into the darkness on both sides of the road. Then a third car arrived and the familiar figure of Anto emerged. He took in the scene, talked to a couple of others and started shouting.

"What the fuck are you doing here?" he roared. "The bastard's out there somewhere. Get out there. Half of you left, the other half right. If you have flash-lights, use 'em. Come on, move yourselves!"

Just my luck, I reckoned. The hand that helped was now proving too damn smart for my own good. I turned around and forced self-pitying thoughts away. It was much more important to get my eyes used to this cold mix of black dark and thick swirling mist. But the sound of another car screeching to a halt made me start around again.

Pinkie emerged from the back with a speed I hadn't thought his bulk would allow. He marched to where Anto was standing over the carcass. The others were gingerly starting to advance into the jungle of ferns and heather. Four of them slowly crept into my side of the road. One would be directly on me in a minute if he kept straight. But I didn't move. My eyes never left the two men back on the road.

They were talking but I couldn't hear anything. And then Duggan put his hands to his mouth.

"When you find him, don't kill him!" he bellowed. *"He's mine. And if you don't find him, you'll all be mine!"*

He turned around to Anto and pulled something out of his pocket. It was too small to see, but then he shouted in temper and flung the object to the ground.

"What kind of fucking place is this that you can't get even get a fucking phone signal?" he roared in frustration.

Dublin city centre was less than twenty-five miles away but this was a telecommunications wilderness. I turned back into it, tried to ignore the throbbing in my knee and started crawling.

33

It wasn't possible to see more than a couple of feet in front. My pursuers had a single flashlight. I'd seen the beam a couple of times, stabbing erratically, but not coming anywhere close to picking me out. It was close to useless, but also close enough to keep me turning around every so often. There was an odd shout of anger and frustration behind me too but that was it. Otherwise it was eerily silent.

Frustration was understandable. The going was incredibly difficult. It was hard to go faster than a walk, something my knee was grateful for. I quickly gave up on my thin shoes. One was sucked off my foot in one of the clinging bog-holes that frequently held up progress even more. The other I threw away. Even the dry bits of ground were a rocky nightmare to shamble through. My feet were soon cut to ribbons. The mist quickly went through my suit which was covered in muck from all the times I'd fallen down. Teeth chattering with cold but with sweat flowing out of me with effort and fear, I stumbled on with no clue where I was going, just knowing it had to be away from those behind me.

Trees suddenly seemed to spring out of nowhere. The ground underneath got spongier and more level. I tried to increase the pace but quickly stopped as the knee protested even more vehemently. The idea of being able to move about more freely was so appealing. But I wouldn't be able to move fast enough. If they came this way and got a scent they would simply be able to move too fast for me.

I retraced my steps, ears and eyes straining for any sound. The trees suddenly stopped and the familiar combination of rock, heather, ferns and muck started again. The mist had thickened again and I couldn't see any kind of distance but I tried to veer off at what I felt might be an angle, in theory trying to circle these trees. They might have been a full forest, or just a small copse. But being in among them was not on.

There was no indication they were there. Not a sound, certainly no sight, not even a smell. I was shambling blindly and tripped over the first sheep who struggled to its feet, setting off the others who were huddled closely against the elements. After the silence it sounded incredibly loud as the animals scattered in the face of this unwelcome interloper. A few of them started baaing, making me mentally pray they'd quickly shut up.

I wasn't sure. It was impossible to be definite. But something had flickered to my right, I thought. If it was them they were no more than a hundred yards away and coming directly at me.

Panic threatened to take over. I dithered about which way to go. Looking above me, I prayed again for some ease in this mist, just something by which to get my bearings, somewhere to aim at. Blindly taking a few steps in one direction, the ground started to fall away a little. I kept going and the descent got steeper. It felt like a gully for rain water during the winter. It was desperately rocky and I suspected it was taking me towards Pinkie's men. But I stumbled on. After about fifty yards, I felt my feet in water. It was no more than a couple of inches. And then I sensed something overhead.

It was a massive concrete land-drainage pipe. Standing up straight inside it was not a problem. It was no more than five feet long but very wide and overhead was what seemed to be an old stone bridge. I was about to keep going when a beam of light suddenly snapped in front of me. Ducking back into the pipe, I cowered down, preparing to duck out either way. Noisy footsteps on the bridge stopped almost directly over me. Then the only thing I could hear was the sound of my heart hammering.

"I am so sick of this shit," a man whose voice I didn't recognise said. He had a Dublin accent. "Fucking falling all round this godforsaken shitehole. How the hell are we supposed to find this prick anyway? Half the time we can barely see each other."

"Why don't you tell Mr Duggan you want to go home?" another man said. His accent was foreign, Eastern European. "He understand."

"Yeah, he understand alright," the Irish voice replied scornfully. "And I understand keeping my mouth shut. I swear he's finally gone and lost it. The man's mad. Seriously mad. It's like this jockey fucker has flipped his mind. I've never seen him this rabid."

"He pissed off alright."

"I will be too if we can't find our way back to civilisation. Where the hell are we anyway?"

"I don't know. But we better keep going."

Their voices faded. I waited a minute before moving. The water in the gully didn't get deeper and the ground on either side kept getting higher, allowing me to straighten up and make some ground. If only I could find my way back to the cars. That was a huge long-shot but options were running out. It was too much to expect them to be unattended but there might be a chance of catching them off-guard and taking off, find a police station, even a house . . . although bringing this nightmare down on top of some poor unsuspecting family wasn't a runner. I knew the surprise bit wasn't on either but dissolving into despair was too real a prospect not to make me cling to whatever hope there might be.

The gully started to peter out after about half an hour. The ground started going uphill and the flow of water disappeared. I reckoned it must have hit some underground route. Cursing, I climbed a bank of rock and gorse that towered about four feet above my head. There had been nothing like this earlier in the night. My bearings were completely shot, even though the mist was starting to thin a little and the first stirrings of midsummer morning daylight were appearing. I climbed over the top of it, fell into a ditch on the other side, climbed out of it and stepped onto tarmac.

"Hold it right there, you bastard!"

Pinkie's voice cut through the silence like a blade. He was no more than twenty yards away, a heavy revolver in his hand and a snarling smile of satisfaction on his face. There was nothing recognisable around, no landmark or kink in the road. There was no sign of the cars or the dead animal. I groaned at the odds that saw my course coincide with Duggan again.

"Oh, I'm going to enjoy this," he said, approaching

carefully. There wasn't a quiver in his hand, not a deviation in the angle of the weapon. "Do you know how much you've cost me?"

There didn't seem much to say about that, or anything else.

"Get down on your knees," he ordered.

I dropped to my knees. He motioned for me to put my hands behind my head.

"You've no idea the trouble you've created for me," he said. "But you're going to pay now. Nobody sticks it to me like that. Nobody."

It was getting lighter. The effect was to make everything seem even colder. But that might have been just fear. I concentrated on one thing, the only thing I still had control over. No way was I going to break down in front of this man. It might be nothing, but he wouldn't get that satisfaction.

"A cool bastard, aren't you?" he said, standing over me, sneering down his nose. "But nobody sticks me."

Only because I was facing the way I was did I see the bull-barred SUV suddenly emerge from the gloom. There were no headlights. The driver and his pal admitted afterwards they were scouting for deer to shoot. They often drove without lights, not wanting to attract attention to activity that was strictly speaking illegal. There wasn't even a sound as the two men liked to glide their jeep downhill in case they spooked their quarry. They managed to reach 30 kilometres an hour on that stretch of road. Only the split second I got to propel myself sideways to the side of the road saved me. Pinkie never knew what hit him.

34

Kentish Town won the Irish Derby by an easy five lengths. Royal Armada was runner-up, completing a Weinberger one-two. Julien Pollet rode Kentish with a calm assurance that belied his youth and brought a style to the saddle that the dual-Derby winner's Epsom jockey couldn't have even dreamed of. The pair of them paraded in front of the stands afterwards, Julien waving shyly to the crowd and Kentish Town looking as if he could gallop around the Curragh again.

"They're made for each other," Jake said, standing next to me, applauding like everyone else. "It looks like you've found me another winner."

He was still a little thinner than before but, apart from that, Jake looked exactly the same, still exuding energy and charisma and a quiet pride in owning such a wonderful horse. Beside him, Judith was back to herself, gently teasing her husband while hanging on to his arm like it was a lifebelt, just as he'd done in the weeks before. I was a lucky man to work for such people.

Jake and Judith stood in next to Kentish Town as banks of photographers snapped the classic winner.

"Milk it, Julien, milk it!" Jake laughed and young Pollet blushed and gave a V for victory sign.

I laughed. Jake usually made his mind up quickly about people. Usually he was right too. And he looked to have warmed to Pollet.

"Any pangs of regret you're not on board this time too?" a voice said behind me.

It was one of the racing reporters, holding a phone up to record quotes. He was quickly joined by three or four others.

"Absolutely none. I think we can all see Julien is a much better fit," I said. "All Epsom did was show just how good this horse is."

"Any message for Mike Clancy?" a reporter I didn't recognise shouted from the sanctuary of the pack.

I smiled grimly, and said nothing. There were rumours flying around the industry about Clancy and the gangster Duggan who'd been killed a couple of weeks previously. My presence at the scene of Pinkie's death created an obvious link. But there was nothing concrete known. And there wasn't going to be any fuel added to the fire by me or Jake. For his part, Clancy's usual racecourse strut had apparently been replaced by a furtive determination to remain unobtrusive. Mike Clancy was going to say nothing.

My boss got some genuinely warm applause from the crowd as he accepted the trophy and we then negotiated the post-race press conference without incident. A flushed Gerry did most of the talking, describing Kentish Town as the best he'd ever trained. I chipped in that the colt was lucky to be trained by such a consummate professional.

Gerry bowed his head a little and hopefully the foundations for getting back to normal had been laid. As we stood up to leave, Jake winked at me.

Jake and I strode across the racecourse, heading back towards the Weinberger box in the stands, happily trying to come up with a future plan for the horse.

Suddenly Jake shouted "Hey!"

Cammie looked up, waved, put her hand back on top of her hat and resumed posing for a photographer. There were always a few of them roaming the crowd on Derby Day, looking for the pretty and famous to snap. My wife might not have been very famous but she undeniably looked great. A simple unadorned blue dress clung to her and the hat was similarly simple but striking. She looked spectacular.

"Wait for me!" she laughed, catching up. "Remind me to buy the papers tomorrow."

"You look great, honey," Judith said, linking her arm in Cammie's.

The box was the best the Curragh had to offer. Roomy and bright, it looked out over the finish line. With the sun for once shining down on Irish racing's headquarters, it was a conscious pleasure to take a soft drink from a creaking buffet table and sit outside. We had a runner in the last race but that was a handicap that didn't really feature on the Weinberger empire radar. With the big race won the pressure was off.

"I spoke to my mum. She says Max is having great fun speaking French to her," Cammie said, slipping into the seat next to me. "She offered to mind him again tonight. Give us the night to ourselves. Will I text her we'll see them in the morning?"

"Yeah. Max won't mind being spoiled for another while."

"I know. It's like a competition between your parents and mine about who can run after him more."

We sat looking out at the mass of people parading up and down in front of the stands. Jake and Judith would be leaving soon, heading to the airport and flying back to New York. They were inside entertaining friends and watching endless replays of the Derby. Niall Doherty was in the middle of them, shouting louder than most at the finish. The general sound of laughter and cheers made it impossible not to smile. I peered out over the Curragh and counted my blessings.

"What are you two doing out here?" Jake boomed. "Or should I leave you alone?"

He winked theatrically at Cammie who said chance would be a fine thing and my boss laughed out loud.

"I thought our boy here was trying to join me in the ICU when I saw him after that awfulness up in the mountains," he said more quietly. "But I think he should be up to performing his duty by now!"

"Don't worry," I replied. "I know my duty."

"Good to hear it," Jake continued. "Max should have a little brother or sister. Isn't that right, Cam?"

"Well, we'll have to discuss that," she smiled.

"To hell with discussion. Life is too short. You'll always find a reason not to do something if you give yourself enough time. Best to jump right in and start swimming," my boss proclaimed. "And if you're lucky enough to have someone precious, there's no excuse whatsoever."

"Oh, do shut up, you pompous old ass!" Judith said, saying they had to leave and thanking us for everything, especially the Derby.

"Thank Gerry and Julien. Nothing to do with me," I said.

"Right," Judith replied sarcastically, kissing us both.

Jake kissed Cam, slapped me on the shoulder and promised himself a margarita on the plane. "Don't forget what I said. Just jump, worry later. And text me if Messenger Boy wins the last."

Messenger Boy did indeed win the last under a ride of such finesse by young Pollet that praising the young Frenchman to the press boys afterwards was no chore. Cammie stood in for Judith in the prize-giving ceremony, charming the red-faced sponsor and provoking a few more camera snaps than usual.

As we walked out of the track towards the car-park, I shook hands with a number of people and contemplated the anaesthetising impact of a classic win on a painful knee. Cammie slipped her arm into mine. At the champagne bar, I invested in a small bottle to celebrate at home. As we sat into the car, she leaned across and kissed me lightly on the lips, keeping her hand on my thigh as we started the drive home.

Traffic onto the motorway was badly backed up. A young policeman shook his head when I asked how long the hold up might be.

"Where are you going?" he asked.

"Wicklow," I replied.

"Your best bet is to head across country and make for the Gap. Do you know it?"

I nodded, waved my thanks and veered out of the jam towards Kilcullen. From there it was a familiar twenty-minute run across bad roads towards Blessington. Ten minutes later we started to climb. It was a lot different in the evening sun, the sweep of the mountains majestic, the enormous expanse filled with vivid colour and a wind that was merely bracing rather than skinning. We slowly drove along the narrow road that snaked upwards from the western side of the mountains. Long lines of cars and buses carrying tourists meant no one was going anywhere in a hurry. It didn't matter.

"Jake seems keen for us to go again," Cammie said after a long silence.

"His authority stretches only so far," I told her.

"He could have a point. It might be just what we need," Cammie added. "How wonderful would it be to have another little Max – or Maxine. Actually the more I think about it, the better I feel about the whole idea."

The car in front pulled in to let us pass and a mercifully empty road allowed me to gun the car up the final climb towards the Sally Gap crossroads. Cyclists and walkers as well as the inevitable cars and buses crowded the top. Lots of cameras took lots of shots of the place I had dreamed of for a couple of uneasy nights. Mostly I'd dreamed of guns and hatred and the sound of metal crunching into flesh. But there'd been no dreams for almost a week now. That had to be a good sign, although when we got to the famous old crossroads I stared resolutely forwards, concentrating on the east and not glancing north to where Duggan died on the road just a couple of miles away.

"Don't leave me in suspense, Lorcan. What do you think of us having another child?" Cammie persisted, her hand slapping my leg.

There was a lay-by ahead and I pulled in. I kept looking east, the rays of the evening sun glinting in the rear-view mirror.

"Do you like me, Cam?"

"What sort of question is that?" she said. "I love you."

"No, Cam, you don't."

Despite all the vehicles around us, and people stopping to take in the views, we might as well have been up here alone in the middle of winter. It wasn't like I'd planned this. I could almost hear her face falling. There weren't many things I wouldn't have done instead of this. But there was no going back.

"How can you say that? That's a horrible thing to say," she said eventually.

"It's the truth. And it's also true to say that having another kid would be just about the worst thing we could do. A child isn't supposed to be a Band-aid. And no Band-aid is enough for this."

I looked at her, saw the tears starting to stream down her beautiful face.

"I don't trust you any more, Cam," I said. "I've tried, but we're only fooling ourselves."

"What about Max?" she blurted.

"Better for him to have parents who at least have a shot at happiness rather than living together for his sake, and ending up hating each other. No kid should have to carry that around with him."

"And that's it? You're going to give up everything we have, just like that."

"There's no just like that, Cam. It's just that for us to continue, I have to sink too much stuff down through me. I can't do it. And I shouldn't have to do it. I'm worth more than that – to me anyway."

We continued to sit there. A number of walkers strode past us, ski-poles rattling off the road, spirits high, completely unaware of the tumult unfolding in the car close to them. I wondered idly what it must look like to anyone looking in, to see people at their rawest and most vulnerable. But then, how raw could it be to have such thoughts at such a time?

"It would be better if we went straight to my mother's," she said eventually, drawing herself up in the seat and wiping away tears.

I agreed.

35

Finding the street was no trouble. The right house was more of a problem. A harassed-looking middle-aged man, a surly teenage boy and an elderly granny opened their door to a nervous caller clutching an outsize bouquet of flowers. It was the granny who directed me the right way.

"She's a lucky girl," she smiled after me.

"Let's wait a while before deciding," I said.

Dani opened the door in track-suit bottoms, a loose rugby shirt and runners. Her hair was in a pony-tail. She looked even better than I remembered.

"Oh yeah, what have we got here?" she grinned.

"Just me."

"Oh yeah?"

"Yeah," I said. "I don't suppose you've got a fairytale I could fit into at some stage?"

That got me a smile. It was all I needed.

If you enjoyed
Threaten to Win by Brian O'Connor
why not try
Bloodline also published by Poolbeg?
Here's a sneak preview of
Chapter's One and Two

Brian O'Connor
Bloodline

POOLBEG

1

I was trying so hard not to think of milk chocolate crumbling in my mouth that the skid was a shock. For the entire hour's drive from Dublin, the damn radio ad had played at every break and my husky-voiced tormentor had at last made my concentration slip. Just the slightest touch on the brake was enough. The wheels lost grip and no amount of leaning back in the seat stopped the car from careering towards the old railway bridge. Instinct took over: years of hitting the ground at thirty miles an hour had been a painful but useful education. I brought my arms up in front of my face and willed myself not to tense.

There was only ever going to be one winner in a battle of metal and stone and sure enough the ancient humpback bridge came off best. Automatically, I went through the checklist: twisted my neck around, moved every limb and wiggled toes in a voodoo ritual against dreaded paralysis. Everything was still intact and in much better shape than the car.

I got out, cursing stupidity and chocolate. Existing on minute portions of boiled chicken, large doses of vitamin pills and huge amounts of fresh air had long meant that my stomach no longer rumbled in protest at the starvation diet it had to exist on. But every so often my mouth would rebel and start to water at even the idea of something with sugar in it. On bad days it was almost unendurable. Dreams didn't consist of beautiful women or great horses or winning big races, but of being left alone with a burger, fries and a medium shake. Medium would do. I wasn't greedy.

But those dreams had been costly. The front of the car was caved in. There was no steam, no dramatics. A turn of the key didn't yield so much as a turn-over. It was almost like the engine didn't want to impinge on a deathly quiet night. The stars were startlingly bright in the black sky and a half-moon helped throw every shape on the flat Curragh plain into stark definition. Less than half a mile away, huge banks of the green, prickly gorse that thrived throughout the hundreds of acres of Irish horse-racing's headquarters were clearly visible in their new icy-white coat.

It was my own fault, driving in the early hours during a freeze-up. I'd given myself loads of time for the familiar trip from Dublin to the Curragh to ride out at Bailey McFarlane's stables. It wasn't particularly important, just a normal morning's exercise, but the cold weather had brought racing to a standstill for a while and boredom could provoke any amount of silly behaviour. Totalling the car was a heavy punishment though.

I was dressed to ride out so I pulled my jacket tight, retrieved a whip and a helmet from the boot and started to gingerly jog the mile or so to the yard. Road conditions weren't that bad: just my luck to have encountered a rogue piece of ice. The vast expanse of grass to the side of the road was white and crunchy-hard underfoot and I made good progress. Within minutes I was turning into the avenue leading to Bailey's yard. It was then I saw a figure in the distance, to the left of the avenue, walking quickly towards a huge clump of gorse.

What was anybody else doing around the Curragh in such weather before six in the morning? Nothing sinister crossed my mind. That would have been too incongruous on the peaceful night that was in it. And there was something familiar about the rolling gait as the man – it was clearly a man – disappeared behind the bushes. Upping the pace, I left the avenue and made for the clump of gorse, rounding it just as he was getting on a big tracker motorcycle.

"Everything alright?" I asked.

The figure started, then viciously kick-started the bike. He had the visor down on his helmet so I couldn't see his face. Even then I wasn't particularly alarmed. But he gunned the engine and came right at me. A hefty boot caught me on the side of the head as I tucked my body to roll on the hard ground. After a few tumbles, I jumped to my feet and watched the bike career southwards towards the lights of Kildare town.

Even then the most I suspected was that the guy had been trying to break into the tack room. There was a constant demand for cheap saddles and riding equipment and plenty were none too scrupulous about which lorry it might have fallen off the back of. It was a constant irritant but nothing serious.

Except now the cold darkness was suddenly interrupted by lights coming on in the yard, quickly followed by the sound of a man swearing. I recognised Rocky's voice and the unaccustomed panic in it. The stables' night-time security was a seventy-something ex-stable-lad whose habit of nodding off in the tack room was tolerated because of the general assumption that that would be the target for any intruder anyway. There was also a worldly shrewdness to the old man that made him far from a soft touch.

Running back to the main stables entrance, and vaulting the big iron gate into the yard, I made for Rocky's usual lair. All around me, the sixty horses of Bailey McFarlane's string were still cosily lurking behind stable-doors shut up against the cold. It was an old-fashioned yard, almost a hundred years old, rectangular, with boxes facing into a bare cobbled centre that was a nightmare to clean but which resonated with the history of past generations of thoroughbreds and people. I noticed as I ran that a light in Bailey's house next to the yard had also come on.

The tack room door was open but nobody was in there. I ran back out and only then saw Rocky's hunched form emerge from an alley that bisected the long row of boxes on one side. The old man was desperately trying to dial a number on his phone while cursing it at the same time.

"Rocky, what's going on?" I shouted.

"Oh Jesus, who is that?" he asked, backing away, his eyes struggling to focus in the harsh glare of the lights.

"It's Liam Dee, Rocky. Are you okay?"

"He's dead, Liam. He's dead. His head is caved in. Oh, Jesus!"

"What? Who's dead?"

He pointed a trembling finger down the alley that I knew was referred to by everybody as 'the dump'. It was long and dark and mostly full of empty drums and assorted bits of rubbish slyly discarded whenever those in charge weren't looking. A few yards down the alley to the left was a door into a box used for new horses. It had a low roof but it was roomy and was a more relaxed place for new arrivals to settle in because it didn't look directly on to the yard. Decades before, it had been a room where stable staff could stay and there was still an incongruous glass window facing out to the alley.

Rocky was pointing to its door. I would have given a lot not to have to walk down and look in. Rocky was no shrinking violet and he was badly shook-up.

The door was open and the floor was bare. Years of animals lying down on fresh straw had smoothed the surface so there was a slight sheen to it in the reflected light. Despite the weather it was surprisingly warm, which might have had something to do with the low timber-beamed roof.

He lay in a corner in a pool of dark blood. The slight body might have been asleep. I took a step closer, saw what remained of the back of his skull and struggled not to vomit.

I heard Rocky say something and then a new voice gave me an excuse to back up.

"What do you mean Liam is in there?"

I emerged to be met by the sight of my boss in an incongruous pink dressing-gown and Wellington boots. Her arm was around Rocky's shaking shoulders but her eyes were on me.

"Don't go in there," I said, scrambling in my jacket for a phone. "Rocky, did you ring the police?"

He shook his head. I noticed there were tears in his eyes.

"Okay. I'll do it."

"Would someone tell me what the hell is going on," Bailey thundered before pushing past me.

"Bailey, don't!"

I tried to grab her but it was too late. She turned around quickly, her hands on her face that was white with shock.

"Dear God, it's Anatoly."

2

The only sounds came from crows lazily gliding over the yard to examine flashing blue lights that still had enough power in the morning gloom to make you blink. But there wasn't a murmur where there should have been the snorting clatter of keyed-up horses emerging from their night's sleep and the shouts of frozen lads trying to keep them under control.

After the initial frenzied arrival of police cars and an ambulance, there was an eerily mundane hour where little seemed to happen. The crime scene was sealed off and so was the stable yard. But then things seemed to stand still in the wait for specialists to show up. Rocky, Bailey and myself told a couple of detectives what we'd seen. Rocky said he'd been in the tack room when he thought he heard someone running outside. He figured his ears were playing tricks on him at first but went out to have a look and saw the box door in the alley open. That was when he saw the body, turned on the lights and tried to call the guards. But

he'd heard an engine gunning outside the yard as well –
like a motorcycle, he said.

I told them how I'd encountered someone on a motor-
bike who'd tried to run me over.

"What did this person look like, sir?" the detective
asked.

"I'd guess he was about my height, but it's only a
guess. He was wearing a helmet so I couldn't see his
face. Apart from that, nothing really – jeans, a leather
jacket, boots. It was all so quick."

"What make of bike was it?"

"It was one of those trackers, like they use for racing
on mud."

He asked me what I was doing around the place so
early. I explained that I had just driven from Dublin. He
asked if anyone could verify what time I had left Dublin. I
told him there wasn't but I'd stopped for petrol soon after
leaving Sandyford and the people in the station knew me.

"And what were you doing here, sir?"

"I was coming down to ride work. I'm Mrs McFarlane's
jockey. My car skidded and hit the railway bridge so I
ran the rest of the way here."

"So you work here every day?"

"No. I usually just ride out one morning a week, or
come for schooling."

"Schooling?"

"Getting horses to practise their jumping."

The detective told me to stay around and I assured
him I wasn't going anywhere. It all felt completely
unreal. Such things didn't happen in the middle of the
Curragh. The bald, flat plain contained more horses than
people, and most of the villains had four legs. Anything

to do with horses could be dangerous and sometimes people were killed. But from a flailing leg or a bad fall: this was terribly different.

The staff arriving were met with the full tableau of a crime scene. Bewilderment reigned. I heard someone mention he'd seen Liam Dee's car crashed on the way to work which reminded me I should do something about it. I got permission to return and deal with it. After phoning the insurance company and a recovery vehicle, I retrieved a bag from the boot and walked back.

"Sorry, sir, you can't go any farther."

Even with the peaked cap pulled down over his eyes, the Garda on duty at the stables gates looked very young. Traces of acne peeped painfully over his tight shirt collar. It was true then, I thought. Noticing how young the cops are really is a sign of getting older. Not for the first time recently I wondered how someone else would see me.

It was just bad luck that I was too tall to be automatically nailed as a jockey. Riding over jumps meant the strict Lilliputian demands of the flat game didn't apply but, even so, being half an inch under six feet was simply the wrong shape for my job. The effort of keeping an infuriatingly lengthening body at a weight well below what it desired was hard work that never ended. Not that I deserved sympathy. It was my choice. In fact, it was no sort of choice. There wasn't a time when the idea of riding a racehorse didn't seem like the most exciting thing in the world to do. It still felt like that most of the time. More than enough reason to keep putting my thirty-four-year-old carcass through the wringer.

"My name is Liam Dee. I'm Mrs McFarlane's jockey."

As I spoke, a man dressed in a baggy white jump-suit emerged from the alley and pulled down a face mask. He leaned his head back and breathed out, releasing a long stream of cold, smoky carbon-dioxide towards the sky. He was followed by another similarly dressed man who walked to the back of the ambulance. As I watched, the radio strapped across the Guard's chest crackled to life and he gave my name. A few seconds later it crackled again.

"You can go into the house, sir."

Bailey McFarlane was sitting in the kitchen, back straight, shoulders wide, an untouched cup of tea in front of her. Even then, the depth of my affection at seeing that familiar figure surprised me. I had always been more outwardly friendly with other people in the yard. In fact, the venom of some of our past rows was still raked over with relish by both friends and rivals. It was hard to blame them. We were easy to cast in cartoon roles; we even did it ourselves.

I sometimes regarded Bailey as loud and uncompro-mising. She considered me too reserved all of the time. My natural inclination was to look inward. Bailey liked being looked at. The little differences had for a time become so magnified that there were a couple of years where we hadn't even spoken. I'd ridden other horses and Bailey employed other jockeys until one day at the races I received a smack on the shoulder and she leaned towards me to whisper: "What you need is a real woman!" That was typical: a big performance hiding all the subtlety underneath.

"Liam. Thank God. Come in," she said now.

The equally familiar figure of Eamon Dunne, the stables' head man, emerged into the kitchen from the big dining room. Through the open door I could hear the sound of people talking quietly. I put my hand on Bailey's arm. She grabbed it and squeezed tightly. Her skin was quite smooth considering how hard she worked in the open air, but the wrinkles still showed all the fifty-seven years she had so defiantly announced on her last birthday. The gesture, though, was enough for me look directly at her. Those vivid blue eyes that could twinkle with mischief and narrow into boiling rage now looked nothing but scared. Our larger-than-life boss was badly rattled.

"Just lying there in the box. Who could have done something like that to Anatoly?"

Anatoly. I didn't even know his surname. Stable staff changed all the time anyway, but the mix of nationalities made remembering names even harder. It was unusual for any sort of yard on the Curragh not to have at least one person in it from Eastern Europe or South America. Bailey liked dealing with an agency that supplied people from Ukraine; "real horse people" she called them approvingly. I calculated there must have been at least six of them working in the yard. Quiet, stoical workers who laughed among themselves in their own language and smiled shyly when dealing with anyone else.

"It's only a few days since he came and told me Bobbie had broken his leg – crying his eyes out, the poor devil."

Small, thin, blond hair. The only real reason his face stuck in my mind was the huge grin that looked faintly comical because of the big gap between his front teeth.

It made him look absurdly young. He couldn't have been more than nineteen or twenty anyway, looked fifteen, thousands of miles from home, living in a country he probably hadn't even heard of months before.

Among the four horses he looked after was Bobbie, or Another Rumble as he was known on the racecourse. That was way too much of a mouthful for everyday use, even for those with English as a first language, and 'Bobbie' tripped easily off any tongue. It was hard to affectionately tell a horse called 'Another Rumble' to move his arse while you mucked him out. Every horse has a pet name at home. Bobbie wasn't particularly good, but he tried hard and his willingness to work had resulted in a win at Galway the previous autumn. As we came back to the winner's enclosure, Anatoly had looked up at me with a smile that could have melted an ice-cap as he repeatedly patted the horse's sweating neck.

The tears he'd cried the previous week must have been bitter indeed. Bailey had phoned me for a chat about the horses in general and then, almost as an afterthought, mentioned that Bobbie had had to be put down after breaking a leg. The almost off-hand delivery only emphasised how much she must have felt the loss. But for Anatoly it would have been even worse. He looked after the horse every day, put up with his moods, cared enough to devote his own working life to keeping him happy. Apparently it was just a half-speed canter, the usual morning workout to keep muscles warm and the mind happy. But the kid would have felt the jarring sense of all that powerful rhythm underneath him suddenly turn to shattered bewilderment as Bobbie's leg snapped. There would have been no option but to end it quickly before the horse endured too much pain. Nothing else to do except hold the reins, speak gently to his stricken friend and try not to upset him by crying too much. From what Bailey said, the last part had been impossible.

A surge of unexpected bitterness made my mouth taste bad. Just a vague impression of a funny face and a story of tears at the death of a horse. It wasn't much, was it? That day in Galway had been only another race for me, but it must have been Anatoly's best day since getting off the plane. I found myself hoping desperately that he had made a much bigger impression on everyone else, that the others had taken the time to get to know him, shown more interest than their self-absorbed bloody jockey.

"Who's in the dining room?" I asked Eamon.

"The other Ukrainian lads," he said, sipping a cup of tea. "Poor bastards."

Eamon was a short, squat man with thinning hair and a ruddy face that frequently split into a wide grin. Jolly Eamon with his warm heart and kind eyes didn't usually do vehemence but there was a bitter twist to his mouth that spoke volumes for how the stables' head man had got to know poor Anatoly better than me.

"Right, let's do something constructive and try and help them," Bailey announced in her best no-nonsense tone. It was a long time since she had left public school in England, but her accent remained cut-glass clear, as did her desire to get on with things. She paused before going through the door and took a deep breath.

"Liam, can you come with me?" she asked.

I nodded and followed her into the wood-panelled

dining room that couldn't have changed much since her grandfather had first arrived on the Curragh from India and decided that this old house, with its forbidding stone and warm interior, was the perfect spot to train race-horses. The long table that dominated the room had also made the journey from the sub-continent. As always, there was a shine to it that reflected like a mirror, despite the nicks, scratches and blotches all over the top and the legs which only added to the feel of solidity that the table radiated. Bailey always joked that the damn thing was too big and one Halloween it was going to end up on the fire. I'd heard that first nearly fifteen years earlier but still the table remained. Bailey's respect for time and place meant that she would have thrown herself on any fire before that table was moved. Right now it was at the centre of a quiet desperation that was palpable as soon as we walked in.

Six figures stood up. One young lad, who couldn't have been more than twenty, was munching a mouthful of bacon sandwich as quickly as he could so as not to be eating in front of Bailey. They were standing almost to attention, six men ranging from just out of their teens to a hard-eyed thirty-something in the corner.

When Bailey spoke, I noticed a tremble to her voice I hadn't heard before.

"Are you all here?"

"Lara is visiting friends in Dublin," the older man replied. "She worked the last four weekends, so you gave her some days off. She will be back later."

Called Vaz by everyone in the yard, he spoke with a heavy accent, but his English was good and the others clearly deferred to him. He was too big to ride work and usually remained in the yard mucking out. But Eamon had told me his real value was in breaking in the young horses. He said the man was remarkable in how he could almost persuade the nervous youngsters by words alone to permit him on to their backs and to violate their tender mouths with bits of iron and leather. It was a fantastic gift and one that was invaluable to Bailey. A lot of talent in racing had been soured from day one because of a heavy hand.

Vaz spoke again. "We will go back to work now. Anatoly would not like horses to go hungry."

"There is no question of anyone going hungry," Bailey said. "The work will be done. But if anyone wants to go back to town and . . ."

"Thank you, but we will be okay."

They trooped out. Vaz nodded to me. Only after they had closed the kitchen door behind them did I ask Bailey where the local lads were.

"Must be out in the tack room or the feed room. Look, I'm sorry about this but I don't think I'm up to going out there. Eamon will be fine with the yard. Is there any chance you could carry on without me? Just canters. I spoke to one of the police. He understands the horses have to be taken out and fed and all the rest of it. They can't seal off the whole place."

"Yeah, that's no problem. You've had a terrible morning. Why don't you go back to bed for a while?"

"No, it's not that. I guess I'm just shaky about having to deal with all that's going to come now – the police and the papers and everything. God, it'll be terrible."

"It won't be great. But we'll get through it. Everyone will pitch in."

"He was such a lovely young lad, Liam. And some bastard does that to him!" She suddenly sobbed. Her shoulders heaved and grief took over. I put my arm around her.

"And you," she said. "You were lucky. He might have done the same to you. Dear God, what are we dealing with here? Did you get any look at him?"

"No. It's like I told the detective. It was all a bit of blur, just a helmet and a jacket and then a boot. But . . ."

"What?"

"Nothing. You go and lie down."

I gave her a hug. It was weird: we'd probably had more physical contact between us that morning than in all the years we'd known each other. I tried to come up with something appropriate to say but failed. Not that it mattered. What did anything matter with a young boy lying dead outside?

· ◆ ·

If you enjoyed these chapters from
Bloodline by Brian O'Connor,
why not order the full book online
@ www.poolbeg.com

· ◆ ·